RABID ATTACK

J.D. HUFF

RABID ATTACK

ISBN: *978-1-922861-87-0*

1

Anton stared at the reflection of the snow-capped mountain peak on the surface of the calm waters of the lake. Lazy white clouds loitering overhead joined in the panoramic view. It was almost too gorgeous to be real.

He had come here with his wife to celebrate their fifth anniversary. While enjoying a picnic by the shore, his still gorgeous bride had noticed movement in the green pastures spread out at the base of the mountain.

"Anton, look at that!" She pointed for emphasis.

Anton, reclining on a blanket beside his beloved, turned to follow her line of sight.

A large herd of cattle was moving down from the mountain towards the lake. They were a common sight on the slopes; brown dots against an emerald sea of grass, grazing peacefully upon a picturesque pasture. These particular animals weren't following that pattern, moving briskly in a tight formation. Anton didn't see any herders keeping them in check.

"It makes me wonder if they're all right," he said. "Could they be getting chased by something?"

As the couple watched, the herd turned left as one synchronized unit. Now skirting the shore of the lake, the cattle moved parallel to the water's edge. Their speed seemed to be increasing.

"If I didn't know better," Anton said, "I would swear they're coming purposely toward us."

Maja, his wife, responded in the strangely subdued tone of someone deep in thought. "How many animals do you think are in that herd?"

Anton ran a quick mental scan of his knowledge of cattle, searching for reasons to be concerned. He found none. They had been grazing on these open slopes for centuries without incident.

"Fifty or sixty, I suppose. But it's only cows. There's no need to panic. They're very gentle."

"Then why are they still running straight at us?"

He didn't have an answer.

The herd was quickly closing the distance—Anton could now hear their feet pounding the ground. As the animals came in to more detailed focus, he was surprised to see saliva dripping from their open mouths. *That's odd,* he thought. *Must be from exertion.*

Maja was in the midst of a position change, muscles coiled, poised to stand fully upright. "I think we should move."

Anton was still wrestling with the radical idea of being afraid of these benign creatures. But full-grown animals would weigh over a thousand pounds each. Safety relied entirely on them maintaining a passive demeanour, which was now in question.

"Maybe you're right. Let's give them room to pass by."

They both scrambled to their feet. "Head for the water's edge," Anton said. "Don't worry about the picnic. We'll clean up any mess after."

Maja couldn't hide the fear from her voice. "They're going to overrun us!"

It was obvious she was right. The animals that once presented as peaceful now looked dangerous and menacing. Anton grabbed her arm. Their time was about to expire.

"Run!" he urged.

She took one last glance. It was their eyes, inky-black and unworldly, that provided final confirmation of the danger.

"Come on!" Anton screamed as he yanked her into motion.

The herd was now in a full-out run—a slobbering, bellowing mob. The first one to overtake Maja butted her in the lower back as hard as it could. She screamed as her balance was lost. She tumbled over awkwardly and was immediately trampled by hooves nearly as hard as cement and animals heavy enough to break bone. The herd ran her into the ground.

"No!" Anton stopped to focus in horror on the woman who had shared his life. Watching her fall and be enveloped by the herd ruined any chances of his own escape. Multiple animals running at full speed plowed into him. He was knocked over and promptly trampled.

When it was over and the animals had moved on, the scene was a disgusting, bloody mess.

The herd hesitated for a moment, and then began to move towards a small, nearby town, accelerating back to jogging speed. No one there would be alarmed by their approach—it wouldn't be the first time that grazing animals had wandered onto the streets.

But unlike previous visits, the results would be catastrophic.

This was not the first time Captain Draco Hudak had been given unusual orders. But these might have been the strangest yet. There had been no time to enlighten his troops as they scrambled to deploy, so the briefing came while on route, fighting the noise of the chopper.

"Everybody huddle up." He had five soldiers with him, all that could fit in this configuration which was designed for quick deployments, not large ones. As the best trained squad he had ever commanded, he was certain they would be more than enough.

"What's up, Cap? This seems rather serious."

Of course, Lieutenant Kass Morina would be the first to speak up. Some found the only female in the squad annoyingly overbearing, perhaps compensating for her gender by being bold and aggressive. Hudak, however, had learned her true value in battle conditions. He was happy to have her.

"This is going to sound odd, so listen and don't interrupt. I probably won't have answers to your questions anyway. We've been deployed to an animal attack. Total casualties unknown at this time, but apparently there are some. The situation is currently unfolding in a town called Curragh, population nine hundred. There are as many as fifty animals currently prowling the streets. Our orders are simple—get in and secure Curragh as fast as possible. That means weapons hot as soon as we hit the ground. And don't leave any clips behind. You may need them all."

"What kind of animals are you talking about?" Specialist Kole Novak asked. He was the newest member of the squad and was still being analysed by the others as to what his value was going to be when under duress. He was envisioning bears or wolves.

"Before I answer that—yes, I'm serious." Hudak hesitated. "It's cattle."

Silence greeted his response, then smiles all around.

"And to think I was getting concerned," Corporal Dayan Kowalski said. "Why didn't you just tell us it was a training exercise?"

Hudak's expression was grim. "Listen to me. This is real and we'll be deploying in five. Wipe those fucking grins off your faces and get ready. If you find this amusing, you're in the wrong squad—something I can remedy when we get back."

The smiles vanished.

Touchdown hadn't actually occurred before the squad had boots on the ground. The chopper maintained full throttle while hovering and immediately lifted off again once they were deployed.

Hudak had studied a map on the way in and was fluent with the basic layout of the town. "Follow me!"

A minute of full-out sprinting put them in a sheltered position beside a concrete-walled building. Their breathing was steady and measured despite the exertion. At a quick glance, everything around them looked normal.

"Where is everybody?" Master Sergeant Ani Janovik, the longest serving member of the squad, asked.

"Taking shelter is my guess," Hudak said.

"If this is a cow invasion," Kowalski added, "I'm hoping somebody's decided to host the biggest barbeque in history. Anybody smell steak?"

Hudak rankled. "I can only hope, Corporal, that your sense of humor is still as exuberant once this mission's over." He waited for quiet. "We need to split up and find out what's happening. Bosch, Novak—you're with me. Morina, Kowalski, Janovik—you're the second group. If you look down this street to the west, you'll see a set of traffic lights. My group is going north from there. Morina, take your group south. Use the radio to stay in touch. Cover as much ground as possible until we can find some answers. Stay sharp and keep a lookout for civilians. No friendly fire casualties, got it?"

Everyone nodded.

"Good. Stay on your assigned street unless you have reason to deviate. Let's move out."

2

The second squad had been marching briskly for several minutes when Morina raised her right hand, elbow bent and locked beside her head, making a fist. Her group immediately froze into position. She looked back over her shoulder. "Either of you hear that?" Her voice was a whisper.

After a moment's hesitation, they both nodded.

Kowalski pointed. "Lieutenant…"

A cow came out from between two houses and wobbled onto the street, moving slowly towards them. Its head hung low, lolling pointlessly while its neck swung back and forth. Saliva dripped from its gaping mouth. Sounds of troubled breathing—gasping and wheezing—came from the large animal. It seemed to be in the advanced stages of some disease, condition or injury.

"Corporal," Morina said to Kowalski, "Put that animal down."

"Aye, Lieutenant." His sense of humor had disappeared. He raised his gun, took careful aim and fired one shot.

The cow didn't do anything spectacular. It simply fell over and lay still. The sound of the shot echoed through the town.

"Nicely done, Corporal. Let's give that thing a wide berth and see if there are more where it came from."

Kowalski gave it a critical look as they walked past, noticing the puddle of drool oozing from its mouth. "Barbeque suddenly doesn't seem so appealing."

"Focus!" Morina snapped. "Stay sharp."

They walked silently past the dead animal. Another intersection drew near.

"Let's see what we have here," Morina said.

They moved cautiously into a central position, establishing where they could view the streets in all directions.

Marina was first to react. "Oh shit!" She raised her weapon and assumed a firing position. The other two followed.

To their right all looked normal, but to their left, the street was strewn with numerous bodies. They had been crushed to a gory pulp. Blood splatter highlighted mangled parts. The bodies were so severely smashed on the surface of the asphalt that an exact count wasn't possible. From a short distance further down, a large herd was blundering listlessly towards them.

"What the fuck?" The carnage was worse than any battle scene Kowalski could have imagined.

"Focus! Hold your position." Morina pulled her radio out of its clip. "Captain, can you read me?"

The response wasn't immediate and that was a problem. The herd was now moving with structure and purpose. And they were picking up speed.

Finally, "Hudak here."

This was going to be very succinct. "We've made contact, on the left, second block past the lights. Multiple animals. We're under attack." She slid the radio back and lifted her semi-auto back into position. "Light 'em up!"

All three opened fire, drowning out the response from the Captain, if there was one. He would hear the gunfire and that would tell him all he needed to know.

Under the chaos of battle, perfect shots were not possible. These animals were large, and the ammo designed for human-sized targets was requiring multiple hits to neutralize them. That slowed the process significantly, and a herd this size, moving this fast, was soon going to overrun their position. Morina had made decisions under battlefield conditions before. She had learned that they didn't necessarily have to be perfect, they just had to be made quickly and in some way improve their situation. She stopped firing.

"Follow me!" She ran like an Olympic athlete towards a small church they previously walked by. It was probably locked, but it had a cement porch with a wrought iron railing around it at the front. At least her group would have their backs secured against the wall.

"Come on!" she encouraged as she flew up the three steps unto the porch. Kowalski and Janovik followed close behind.

She turned and saw they had a brief moment before the herd would reach them. "Defend our position! Choose your shots! Keep them from climbing the stairs and we should be able to hold out." She was worried about their ammo supply, but didn't have the time or inclination to share that bit of news.

Then, the herd was upon them. Most slammed into the rail and presented themselves as easy targets. One, however, went straight for the steps. Janovik had by chance assumed position there and was chagrined to discover that a head shot wasn't a sure kill. These animals must have very thick skulls, he concluded. Through a persistent barrage, he finally dropped the cow at the very top step. It slumped down and blocked the entire approach. The next cow that tried to climb up was thwarted by the bulky carcass. The dead cow made a perfect temporary blockade of the only access point. Sometimes it was better to be lucky than good.

Marina slammed in her last clip and tried to make an estimate of the remaining animals. Maybe two dozen left, but at the rate they were using up bullets, they were going to run out before the herd was gone. She didn't relish the idea of fighting a thousand pound animal with a knife but there wasn't time to dwell on it.

A sound from a different direction caught her attention.

"Look!" Kowalski yelled.

On the street, Hudak and his troops had appeared. Cross-fire was an issue, but they had positioned themselves to avoid that contingency as much as possible and were now attacking from the rear. The cattle seemed momentarily confused by the two-pronged barrage. Soon it didn't matter. Their number dropped into single digits and then the last few animals were finished off while trying to wander away.

A beautiful silence fell over the town.

"Everyone all right?" Hudak yelled over a sea of dead cattle.

"All present and accounted for," Marina replied.

"Can you get to the street without actually touching these animals? I'm not sure that direct contact is a good idea."

Marina analysed the pile of carcasses. "Permission to exit through the church, Captain?"

"Is it open?"

Janovik tried the knob. "It's locked!"

Scrambling over a mountain of diseased, dead cattle was the worst option. "Do whatever you have to, Lieutenant," Hudak said.

Marina knew Kowalski was the most likely to enjoy this task. "Break it down, Corporal."

A smile appeared. "Aye, Lieutenant."

3

It was an intimate meeting. Three people sat around the heavy oak table in a secluded corner of the bar. The owner of the facility knew that their privacy must be maintained, so nobody but their waitress would be allowed to go near.

One member of the group had decided to eat and was doing some damage to a roast beef on rye accompanied by a steaming mug of spicy vegetable soup. The other two ordered perfunctory cups of coffee which sat untouched while growing cold.

"I want to hear you say it again." The man who spoke looked across the table with piercing eyes. Zarja was director of an obscure government oversight body and gave the impression that he was thinking furiously all the time, pushing his mind like an athlete does their body while in a competition. Most people, while under his gaze, wouldn't attempt to keep up with him intellectually any more than they would jog alongside a professional runner during a marathon. It was exhausting and you were sure to fall behind.

Dmitry Kovaksz, manager of a research facility, continued to ignore his coffee. "As I've already made clear, we had nothing to do with this. All security protocols are in place and functioning perfectly. There has been no breach on our part."

"So evidence be damned, is that it? Apparently you are a believer in coincidence, Dmitry."

"I am a believer in procedure, review and oversight. Ours is unfailing, Zarja."

The dark eyes continued to remain locked on, looking at every movement and change of expression. "Has it not occurred to you that if we had faith in your precious security systems, this meeting wouldn't be necessary?"

The third man lowered his mug after slurping up some soup. "Let's not turn this into a childish fight. Return to facts, not innuendo or speculation. I have other things on my agenda today and I have no desire to let this drag out."

Zarja nodded. "As you wish, General."

The top ranking official in the Croatian army decided his meal could wait for a few brief moments. "As previously mentioned by you, Zarja, coincidence is not something I believe in either. While I know it can happen in rare cases, to rely on it as an explanation for a bad situation is the crutch of toadies and fools." He joined Zarja in staring at Dmitry. "Refresh my understanding of the work you are doing in your lab, Dmitry."

Dmitry was thankful for the opportunity to showcase their most impressive achievement, putting it in a more positive light than the one currently being cast. "Of course." He took a moment to choose his words. "Our research has made advances far beyond any ever achieved before. In your positions, you both have no doubt heard that we have successfully mutated one of the world's most dreaded viruses. It is now much more transferable while maintaining all the original deadly effects. This strain will provide weaponized support to our forces and provide powerful negotiation and deterrent tools to our political leaders. The mere mention of it tends to have a very frightening effect."

The General didn't mince words. "Rabies?"

Under these circumstances, Dmitry wished he could make the label seem more palatable. "Yes, that is correct."

"Please explain exactly what you mean by *much more transferable*."

"We have had success with aerosol, airborne transmission."

"It doesn't have to be through an actual bite?"

"That will also work, but no—it's no longer necessary with our variant."

"Anything else of note?"

"Current rabies vaccines, although widely available, will not work to protect against this strain."

The General took a moment to finish the last bite of his sandwich. "Do we have a workable vaccine for our own use?"

Dmitry allowed himself a smile. "Yes, General. In production and available."

"So once the virus is released and others have the chance to study it, vaccines will be created and distributed around the globe. It seems this wonderful deterrent will have a very short useful lifespan."

Dmitry shook his head. "The vaccine must be administered within twenty-four hours of exposure. Otherwise, the effects cannot be stopped. Only troops aware of its presence will be able to successfully vaccinate. Breathing it in isn't as demonstrative as being bitten. Most of those affected won't even know until it's too late. It is, as they are prone to say in the West, a game changer."

The General nodded. "Both impressive and frightening."

"The vaccine," Dmitry said, "can be administered orally. Taking it will provide protection for a two week period. Our troops can carry it with them at all times."

The General picked up his mug and finished his soup.

Zarja took the opportunity to rejoin the conversation. "So you weaponized a new variant of rabies, then less than two hundred kilometers from your lab, a herd of cattle, drooling from the mouth, runs amok and kills a number of people—an unprecedented event. Unless you've suddenly thought of another explanation, we're back to your unsubstantiated faith in coincidence."

"Can cattle get rabies?" the General asked.

"Any mammal can get it," Dmitry admitted.

"Do you not see our problem?" the General said.

"As I said, it couldn't have been our fault."

"It's obviously your fault!" the General yelled as he slammed his fist on the table. "It concerns me that you, of all people, are blind to the truth. Are you actually telling us that you're completely ignorant of what has happened in your lab? Frankly, a child should be able to discern where the blame lies. But you, in the critical position of overseeing this project, can't admit to what's right under your nose. I'm developing doubts that you are suited for this job."

Zarja said nothing, but smiled.

Dmitry was visibly shaken by the outburst. "But General, I have worked on the lab team for over a decade. My record is impeccable."

"Don't worry about that. I'm sure we can find you other work."

The secretive nature of this research was such that it wasn't possible to transfer out and walk away. In his current position, Dmitry was privy to top secret information. He would be too big of a liability to be allowed to simply leave.

The General stood. "I'll make the arrangements. Someone will let you know once they are complete. In the meantime, I want you to stop going to the lab altogether, starting immediately."

"Can I not work at the lab in another capacity?"

"Not unless you are a microbiologist. Zarja, take care of the bill."

"Yes, General. Of course." He had ample reason to be cooperative. The meeting was concluding exactly as he hoped it would.

"Now, I believe I'm going to visit the lab myself. I still have unanswered questions. I'll take the precaution of removing your security codes and all other means of access, Dmitry. No offense."

Dmitry made a feeble attempt to re-engage him in conversation, but the General simply walked away.

Zarja, looking supremely content with himself, smiled across the table at Dimitri. "That went well, don't you think?"

4

Douglas MacLellan, or Doug the Slug as his coworkers sometimes referred to him (his weight was a contributing factor), was sitting in his basement office, staring hard at his computer monitor. A coffee with too much creamer and a half-eaten donut sat on his desk, currently ignored.

His speciality was digging up secrets electronically. He had software which allowed him to access computers and servers all around the world, all supposedly secure and private. He also had a blanket order signed by a district judge that allowed him to use this ability without restriction in the interest of national security. The order would probably not survive extensive scrutiny in open court, but it really didn't matter. Only a handful of people knew about what he did in the bowels of the FBI building. If a tree falls in the forest and no one is there to hear it, does it make a sound? If a man spies on someone and doesn't get caught, has he really committed a crime? Doug didn't carry any excessive guilt.

"Doug!"

It was no secret that Doug, working alone in this isolated space, was jumpy when interrupted. It was a running gag. His only counter was to completely ignore it. He did, however, flinch noticeably when his name was yelled. "I thought something smelled bad," he responded, unable to stop himself.

"Probably what you just dropped in your pants."

Doug swivelled in his chair. "Hello, Len. Still haven't reached the point in your career where somebody cares that you're not actually working?"

Len nodded in appreciation. "Good one. You do know I keep score and always retaliate?"

"And that sums up what's important in your life. It's sad, really."

Len smiled. Hidden by their good-natured antagonism was a friendship that had endured for many years. "Speaking of what's important, you seem to be in a work-trance. Dig up something good?"

"It's well above your pay grade. Ask me again ten years from now when it no longer matters."

"You're getting too good at this verbal jousting. I'm clearly rubbing off on you."

Doug subconsciously twirled his handlebar moustache, a feature unique among all staff in the building. "Close the door and grab a chair."

Len was glad to oblige. Sometimes the stuff Doug discovered was fascinating and it was very cool to be among the first to know about it.

Doug gave him a warning look. "For your eyes and ears only."

Len slid a chair close to the desk. "Understood."

Doug changed his screen as he backtracked to the origin of his discovery. "This is a Facebook account. The owner is a twenty-eight year old male from Slovenia."

Len nodded. "I thought things were relatively quiet in Central Europe these days."

"Generally speaking, they are. But I've stumbled onto something very weird and therefore intriguing. I want your take on this."

"Why?"

"I don't know if I should run this up the ladder or ignore it as unsubstantiated nonsense. Your opinion might help."

"As long as I don't accrue any responsibility."

Doug reached for his cold coffee and took a sip. "You were never here."

"In that case, please proceed."

"The actual name of this fellow contains way too many consonants and far too few vowels. I'm going to refer to him as Joe."

Len was looking over the home page now on the screen. "What did Joe do to warrant this intrusive attention?"

Doug set his mug down. "He really didn't do anything except put up an interesting post that disappeared after only twenty minutes. It looks like it was removed, and not by Joe. That also raises my interest."

"How did you find a post from Joe in Slovenia if it was only up for twenty minutes?"

"I'm constantly scanning. Certain words and phrases are tagged by the software and when they come up, I can do a quick perusal. Most of them turn out to be harmless. But occasionally, the computer scores something that's genuinely concerning. And that's what this turned out to be. Or at least that's what I think."

"So what is Joe involved in which he should have kept hush-hush?"

"That's where it gets murky. He claims that the town of Curragh is now blocked off by the military and no one can get in or out without permission."

"I've never heard of Curragh," Len said.

"It's in south-central Slovenia, population nine hundred. No real claim to fame, except that they get some tourism due to the scenic views afforded by the Southern Alps."

"So why close it off? Nuclear generator meltdown? Local uprising? Ebola outbreak?"

"Not even close. He heard through a third party that some sort of attack happened there. Claims were made that multiple victims were involved, including some fatalities."

Len pondered. "What was the source of the attacks? Terrorism?"

"It's vague at this point. I searched and found other postings confirming that the town is closed off. There's conflicting speculation about why."

"That's thin," Len said.

"There are different reports about the source of the trouble, but get this— several list it as an animal attack."

Len sat back, assuming a more upright position. "Why would the government close off a town for that?"

Doug shook his head. "They wouldn't. But something major, something out of the ordinary, clearly happened."

"I'm not sure how I can help you, buddy," Len said.

"I don't know what my next step should be. My gut tells me it's important, but I really don't have anything substantial to back it up."

Len was also a spy—making his living by getting information and knowing how to use it. It could be gathered from many places, including inside their own office. "Call Peterson and ask him for a favor. Get him to take some pictures next time the satellite swings over. Rumor is that he just started dating again and can't keep the grin off his face. You'll never catch him in a better mood."

Doug, who knew that Len's assessments were always dead-on, was already reaching for the phone. "I'll make the call. Thanks, bud."

Len stood and opened the door. "Let me know if you find out anything more."

Doug had no intention of doing that. Friends were friends, but he had no idea what this could turn into. "You betcha. Oh, and close the door on your way out."

5

"Welcome, General." Everyone at the lab knew who he was and the authority he wielded. Luka was no exception. "It's always an honor to have you grace us with your presence."

The General's expression didn't change in response to the cordial greeting. "This isn't a bullshit day, Luka. Find us a private place to talk."

Luka Karmic, assistant general manager of the Trans Euro Laboratory and Research Station, gave a partial bow. He had no way of knowing that he was about to get an unexpected promotion. "Of course, General. We have such a place. Please follow me."

The room was small, but filled the requirement of being secluded. The door was shut and they sat on adjacent chairs in close proximity. This arrangement was uncomfortable for Luka, but he would not show it. He would have surrendered a day's pay to have a desk as a buffer between them, however.

"May I offer you a snack or beverage, General?"

"No, I just ate lunch. I wish to have a conversation— that's all."

Luka nodded in agreement. "Of course. I am here to assist in any way."

"I just relieved Dmitry of his position. I'm offering it to you."

Luka was taken by surprise. He tried to look comfortable with the news. "I…would be honored, General. I hope all is well with Dmitry."

"It isn't. Have you heard about the incident in Curragh?" The General knew that an honest answer always flowed out quickly, no manipulation necessary. Luka hesitated, obviously formulating his response. The General was not having it. "Do you recall me saying that this is not a bullshit day? Answer all my questions with complete honesty, or you will be of no value to me, just like Dmitry."

Luka nodded enthusiastically. "Of course." He swallowed to clear his throat. "I have heard of this incident."

"What are your conclusions?"

More hesitation. To be fair, it was an obscure question and the General knew it.

"Do you think your research here is in any way involved?"

"Well…"

"The truth!" the General roared, making Luka jump. "Tell me the truth or I'll assume the worst about you and this lab."

"When certain details became available, we concluded that there could be a possible connection."

"Are you aware I was never contacted about this? How did you respond?"

"Our investigation is in the early stages, still not complete—that's why we didn't call. We have reviewed all security measures. We did an inventory of samples. Everything was accounted for. All inventories balanced correctly. We're currently checking security camera footage as well as the inventory of test subjects. So far nothing has been found that could have led to a breach."

"But the virus spreads easily. Could it not have walked out the door through an infected employee?"

Luka shook his head. "No. That is something we monitor constantly. Everyone here knows how essential it is to maintain a sterile, safe environment at all times. It's more than our job—our very lives depend on it."

"What about waste? Could the virus transfer out on some trash?"

"In theory, it could. But we have a rigorous procedure to ensure this cannot happen. Biohazardous waste is handled with extreme care. All trash, of every sort, is sterilized here on-site, and then picked up by a licensed company which sends employees in full hazmat suits. It's taken to an industrial furnace and incinerated at extremely high temperatures. This kills any virus in the waste."

The General rubbed his chin. "I suppose if an employee was exposed, you would soon know it."

"Every time someone calls in sick, they must give a detailed summary of their symptoms. In truth, our absenteeism rates are very low. And we, for a certainty, know that no one has ever been exposed."

The General sighed. "Something happened. And we're all in peril because of it. You're in charge now, and I need you to find out definitively whether this lab is in any way connected to the incident. Time is of the essence."

"May I ask a question?"

The General looked over in mild surprise. "Of course. Speak freely."

"Have the animals involved in the incident been tested for disease?"

"No results so far. As it happened across the border, certain difficulties arise in getting timely information."

"General," Luka said, leaning in closer.

"What is it?"

"I hope that our work here is not in any way involved. However…"

"What are you thinking?"

"If in fact these animals were carrying it, there's nothing to stop the virus from spreading beyond them."

"To people, you mean?"

"Yes. Or any other mammals."

"How long before they would show signs if this happened?"

"Our strain will typically show symptoms in three to five days after exposure. Unfortunately, at that point it's already too late to administer the vaccine."

"When would they be contagious?"

"It coincides with the early symptoms."

"So we have perhaps as little as one day from now before that point is reached?"

"If anyone was exposed, yes."

"Damn. I'm going to make some calls. I have friends in the Slovenian government. Tell me, Luka, what should be done with the people who were potentially exposed?"

"Get them all in isolation immediately. Keep them sedated and as comfortable as possible. Feed and hydrate through IV. After three weeks, if there is no sign of the disease, they may be pronounced healthy and released."

"And what is the likely rate of infection under these conditions?"

That caused Luka to hesitate. "To achieve a significant airborne likelihood of being contracted, the virus has to be spread by a man-made process. If you're talking about infection by animals breathing out the virus, then the rate is low but proximity matters. Any who were close to the animals when they were alive and breathing will be at the highest risk. Those within fifty feet of the animals will have a very slight chance of contracting it. Everyone beyond this distance would have only a miniscule chance of acquiring the disease. Remember that it was engineered to spread easily, but only when weaponized. In natural settings, it can be passed by breathing it in but only in very close contact. People together inside an enclosed space would be at much greater risk. In an outdoor exposure, like this one, the risk drops significantly."

The General looked grim. "I want you to continue looking into this on all fronts. I'll give you a number to call the moment you find anything definitive. Do the rest of the staff know about the possible outside exposure?"

"Only a select few who are participating in the investigation."

"Keep it that way. We've got enough problems." The General stood, signaling an end to the meeting. "Now I have to decide whether or not to inform the authorities in Slovenia about what we might have done."

6

"What am I looking at?" Deputy Secretary of Defense Gerald Vanderveen was not happy about being called in for an unplanned briefing on a day when his schedule was already full.

"That is a large pile of dead cattle." Chuck Peterson, mid-west Regional Director of the FBI, was hosting this meeting in his Washington office. "Our satellite picked up these images about an hour ago."

"Tell me something, Chuck. In my position, why would I care? Shouldn't somebody from agriculture be looking at this? And how does a pile of dead cattle justify the use of a billion-dollar piece of equipment anyway? Now that I think about it, did you randomly stumble onto this, or are you actually looking for deceased livestock intentionally? Is this a new initiative for the Bureau?"

Peterson moved the picture, readjusting the focus. "No. We were tipped off about this. Our concern is what's off to the side of the pile."

Vanderveen looked as the picture zoomed in and refocused. "What the hell am I looking at?"

Peterson pointed with his finger. "These are people in full hazmat suits. There appears to be at least a dozen of them. You can also see a variety of emergency response vehicles parked nearby."

"So they're cleaning up the dead cows? Again, how does that fall under my sphere of influence?"

"They're not cleaning up the cattle. They're cleaning up this." Peterson made another adjustment and an open stretch of street came into view. The pavement was covered with what looked like some sort of garbage. Once it focused, he pointed at a specific spot. "This is definitely a human arm. You can just barely make out the fingers on the hand."

Vanderveen squinted. "Then where's the rest of the body?"

"I think it's all there." His tone was sombre.

"It looks like jam spread on a giant cracker."

"Now you know why I called you."

"Where did you say this was?"

"It's a small town in Slovenia."

Vanderveen looked up from the screen. "Is this the result of some kind of military operation?"

Peterson shook his head. "I can't say with absolute certainty, but I don't think so. Besides, why would the military do something like that to its own people? And there haven't been any encroachments in the area that we're aware of."

"What could possibly do this kind of damage? Have the bodies been liquefied by some kind of chemical?"

Peterson hesitated. "Keep in mind this info is very new. I only know what I can interpret from the same images you're seeing. But I can tell you one thing."

"Please do."

"The staff member who tipped me off discovered that the locals were talking about this online. They were referring to it as an animal attack."

Vanderveen blinked rapidly several times, a sign of displeasure. "Some animal killed a bunch of cows and piled them in town, then attacked and liquefied some of the residents? You're not your usual convincing self today, Chuck. Is this the work of aliens, in your now questionable opinion?"

Peterson mulled over his response. "As far as seeming legitimate, I'm afraid it may get worse." He drummed his fingers, dreading what he had to say next. It was not likely to be well-received. "One online report was that the cattle themselves were responsible for the attack."

Vanderveen pulled back. "Oh bull-shit…no pun intended. Have you lost your mind? Cows don't attack towns and kill all the people they find. And then what—they all somehow committed mass suicide in a big pile?"

"The posts from which we gleaned this information are being pulled down as fast as the government finds them. What does that tell you?"

"That they don't want to be a laughing stock? What else could it be?"

"This looks and smells like a cover up. The town is blockaded and the communications cut off. There must be something rotten that the government is worried about from a political point of view."

Vanderveen looked towards the door without realizing it. A quick exit was on his mind. "Look, I don't like to think that I'm intellectually deficient, but I'm lost in all this. You called me in…why? What's wrong here and how does it impact our military? If you can't explain that, then I chalk this up to speculation and tell you to kiss my ass as I head off to greener pastures, this time pun intended."

"I asked you to come in hoping you could answer one question."

"Ask away, Chuck, and make it quick. Your time has expired."

"I wanted you to take a broad, open-minded look at this. Can you think of any potential military explanation? Any kind of potential covert involvement?"

"Wait a minute. You already told me this wasn't a military operation."

"It's definitely not a *planned* operation. But what if something unintended happened? Is that possible under these circumstances?"

"A pile of dead cows and a street full of liquefied bodies? Are you nuts? You want to hear what I'm worried about in all of this, besides your sanity?"

Peterson shrugged. "I do, actually."

Vanderveen stood, his intent to leave. "I'm worried some bovine disease that started in the middle of nowhere is going to drive up food prices to the point we'll have to pay seventy bucks for a mediocre steak. I suggest you talk to agriculture about this."

Peterson smiled, but not in a happy way. "Thanks for coming in, Gerald."

Vanderveen's smile, in contrast, did seem happy. "Kiss my ass, Chuck."

It was hours later, at the end of the day, when Peterson got an unexpected call.

"Gerald Vanderveen on line two for you, sir."

Peterson raised an eyebrow. "Thanks, Sandra. I'll take in here."

"Very well. Have a good night, sir."

Peterson braced himself for more abuse. "Gerald… hello. Didn't expect to hear from you again anytime soon."

"Listen—it occurs to me that I might have been out of line with the *kiss my ass* comment."

An apology of any sort was the last thing Peterson expected. "Don't worry, I took it as a joke. I appreciate you making time for me."

"It wasn't a joke. And one more thing, Chuck."

"What's that?"

"Tell your people to keep monitoring communications in that region. If anything intriguing comes up, let me know."

"You're still taking my calls?"

"Not a chance. Have your people call my people."

Peterson chuckled. "I will. Thanks, Gerald."

He hung up the phone, happy but wondering why the Deputy Secretary had such a change of heart.

7

"Hello up there! What's the problem?"

Cutting down trees was so much easier when done outside of town—it always put Filip in a good frame of mind. Fewer worries about dropping a branch on a house, or car, or pedestrian were great, but that didn't mean he wanted the job to take all day. Time was money. His hired man, Jakob, was half-way up the large maple, belted to the trunk for safety. A chainsaw was in one hand, the other hanging loose.

"Did you fall asleep?"

"There's a squirrel up here."

Filip couldn't believe it. Of all the stupid, stereotypical things to get distracted over. "We see squirrels every day. If it's not playing a guitar and singing folk songs, get back to work."

"I think it's sick." The squirrel was way too close. It had been climbing slowly down the trunk since Jakob first noticed it. It was having trouble holding on, nearly losing its grip on the bark several times. Its eyes were filled with black, like its pupils had dilated way beyond normal. And most disconcerting, there was foam dripping from the black fur at the base of its jaw. "Can squirrels get rabies?"

That got Filip's attention. He squinted to improve his focus but it didn't help much from this distance. "Why are you asking?"

The squirrel was a mere three feet away now, its unnatural, glistening eyes locked on Jakob. He feared it was lining him up before taking a leap at his face. In his position, even a small animal would have him at a serious disadvantage. It was too late to disconnect and climb down. He certainly didn't want to drop the saw in a spontaneous moment of panic. Jakob reached slowly for the leather glove in his rear pants pocket with his free hand.

"Can you hear me?" Filip yelled when there was no immediate reply. He was getting concerned.

Jakob feared if he responded while this close to the squirrel, his voice might trigger an attack. He pulled the glove out and wondered how to slip it on without making any significant movement. At least it would afford some protection for his free hand. Then, in a nightmare moment, the squirrel hissed and released its grip on the bark. As it fell towards him, Jakob swatted at it with the glove. It was pure reflex, but the glove hit the falling squirrel in the side of its face and diverted its course enough that it missed Jakob's arm. The animal fell, tumbling and hissing, until it landed in the grass below.

Jakob's heart was racing. That had been way too close.

Filip saw the animal fall. It was now lying on its back, tail twitching but no other movement apparent. "You didn't have to knock it out of the tree," he called up.

"Stay away from it!"

But Filip was an animal lover and had a soft heart. He walked over and stood over the small creature. It looked like it was in its final death throes, experiencing the last few spastic moves before leaving this world forever. He reached down slowly, and got no reaction from the squirrel.

"Don't touch it!" Jakob yelled with urgency in his voice.

"I'm just checking on it. I want to see if there's anything I can do." The words were barely out of his mouth when the squirrel rolled over and latched onto his hand. The long, sharp incisors easily penetrated deeply into the soft flesh at the base of his thumb. Filip screamed in pain and surprise, the squirrel still holding on as he raised his hand and tried to flick the animal loose. Not knowing what to do, and afraid if he pulled it off by force his hand would get shredded in the process, he continued to scream and hold his arm straight out away from his body.

Jakob abandoned his work and started to climb down. By the time he reached the ground, the squirrel had somehow released its grip. Filip, in a bizarre, rage-induced reversal of personality, screamed like a wild animal and stomped the squirrel under his work boots. He repeated the process until Jakob reached him and put a hand on his shoulder.

"Easy now."

Filip stopped. His hand was bleeding profusely, red dripping down off his fingers in a steady flow. "Shit." He was gasping.

"We need to go to town and get that looked at," Jakob said.

Filip looked back towards their truck. "I have a first aid kit. Let me clean this up and put on some gauze to stop the bleeding."

"Filip, I think the squirrel was sick. It was foaming at the mouth."

"Shit," he repeated for the second time. "All right. But I need to stop the bleeding first."

"I'll drive," Jakob volunteered. "Just get a rag and wrap it tightly around it. They'll clean and disinfect it at the hospital. I'm sure they'll look at you straight away in your condition."

"Jakob?"

"What is it?"

It was a difficult request. "I think we should bring the squirrel, you know, for testing."

Jakob looked with distaste towards the crushed, bloody body. "You think so?"

"We shouldn't leave it here. The family dog might try to eat it."

"I suppose." Jakob sighed. "All right. I'll wrap it in a rag or something."

"Just throw the equipment in the back of the truck. We'll straighten this all out after I get taken care of."

Staff at the hospital—after hearing the details of the incident—were convinced a rabies vaccine was required. The animal would be tested first, but they immediately made an appointment for Filip to return in a couple of days and get the shot. If the animal test was negative, the shot could be cancelled. The circumstances, however, were highly suspect.

Leaving the hospital, Filip's thoughts were refocused on work. His hand was sore, but functional. The nurse did a good job of wrapping it up. They would change the dressing when he came in to get the vaccine, but other than that, he was good to go.

In reality, he was a dead man but didn't know it. In less than a week, symptoms would appear. They would worsen steadily, taking him down a path of pain and physical decay. He would be a foaming beast before it was over. The best modern medicine could do was to ease his passing.

Jakob, despite his close call, would suffer nothing more than the inconvenience of finding a new job. Of course, losing a friend was far worse.

He would vow to never again allow a squirrel to get anywhere near him.

8

Antonio's attention was being pulled in two different directions. The lovely Aurora, especially with the exquisite (and revealing) dress she was wearing, had initially mesmerized him. Now, the Festa Benedetta was the one taking his breath away.

Located in central Rome, already a romantic place by most accounts, this restaurant was setting a whole new standard.

He had chosen to make a reservation in the outdoor garden level, a decision he now felt self-congratulatory about. The two of them sat at a small, round table draped by soft, lemon-colored cloth, enchanted by their surroundings. The sun had nearly set, but lights had been set up to provide an appropriate ambience. Their table, chairs and even their own feet were settled on a carpet of natural, soft grass. An actual olive tree grew beside them, overhanging branches providing cover. The lower trunk was so gnarly, it looked like a prop in a fantasy movie, ready to sprout legs and walk away while talking to itself. Insects chirped and buzzed softly overhead, accompanied by soft music flowing from hidden speakers. A murmur of conversation emanated from the other tables, which Antonio found easy to ignore. As far as he was concerned, they were the only two there.

"This place is amazing," Aurora said once the waiter departed after pouring them some red wine.

"And almost as gorgeous as you," he responded, taking advantage of the unintended setup she had just provided. He raised his glass. "Salute."

She followed his example, taking a small sip.

Antonio allowed his eyes to enjoy the display of her flawless attributes. "You look like a goddess on steroids."

"Flattery might get you somewhere," she whispered.

"Don't tell me that. I won't be able to concentrate on my meal."

"I don't think that will be a problem," she countered. "They say this is the best food in Rome."

Antonio lowered his voice. "If you were on the menu, I know what everyone would be ordering."

It was a little racy and contrived, but she smiled and blushed regardless. "Try to control yourself. If you take me here on the table, they'll never let us come back."

"A price worth paying, in my estimation."

Another couple, sitting several tables away, raised their voices noticeably and stood up so suddenly, one of their chairs got tipped over. It momentarily intruded on the tranquil atmosphere.

"What's that all about?" Aurora asked discreetly.

"I've no idea."

The affected couple was staring at the hedge which surrounded the garden portion of the restaurant. They were also backing away from it.

"Perhaps a lover's spat?" Aurora said.

Another sound could now be heard. It hadn't come from the couple. In fact, it didn't sound human at all. More people were abandoning their tables.

"Antonio, what's going on?"

He was staring, looking for some indication. "I don't know."

"Should we move?"

He shook his head. "No, we'll be fine. I'm sure the waiter will take care of it, whatever it is."

Someone screamed.

A large animal, covered with coarse greyish-brown hair, walked through the shrubbery and made a full appearance.

Antonio and the lovely Aurora both stood abruptly.

"What is that?" she asked in panic. It was hard to hear now. Screams filled the air.

"It's a wild boar! Let's get out of here."

They melded into the exodus of crazed diners. As Antonio glanced back, two more hogs came into view.

The throng bumbled its way into the lobby. Only once the glass door swung shut behind them, did any degree of calm return. Antonio, emboldened by the now safe environment they were in, walked over to the glass and had a look at what was transpiring outside.

"Be careful," Aurora ironically said as she approached to see for herself.

"We're all right," he replied. "They don't know how to use a door."

She scrunched up her pretty face. "Is there something wrong with them? They don't look healthy."

The animals were wandering with no apparent purpose, bumping into chairs and table legs. Their movements were clumsy and unfocused. Rather than holding their heads in an upright and alert position, they hung pointlessly, limp and listless.

"Here's the Capo Cameriere," Aurora whispered.

A distinguished man dressed in some sort of tuxedo variant was winding through the throng of unhappy customers, all pestering him with a mishmash of overlapping questions and complaints. He made his way to the door and actually forced himself between Antonio and his date.

"What is happening out there?"

"You've been overrun by wild boars," Antonio said.

"Good heavens!" He turned and gestured insistently. Two waiters worked their way through the crowd.

"Grab some brooms and chase those things away! Then get that mess cleaned up."

The two young men looked at each other for a moment before returning to grab their weapons of choice.

The Capo Cameriere faced the crowd and held up his hands, trying to restore some semblance of order. He was not easily deterred from his self-appointed task and the crowd eventually quieted down. "Ladies and gentlemen, please accept my sincere apologies for this interruption. We will soon have the situation under control, and you will be able to continue with your meals. I will visit all of you at your tables, and we can discuss how the Festa Benedetta can make this right."

"Free booze?" someone yelled, motivating the crowd to laugh. At least they seemed happier now.

"A complimentary drink is not out of the question," he replied. "Now, please make way for my staff."

The waiters were returning, brooms in hand.

"Get rid of those disgusting creatures," he hissed.

Antonio and Aurora stepped aside to allow access to the door. The two men moved with some degree of caution into the garden. The door swung shut behind them.

"May I say," the man in charge said to Aurora in an attempt to distract her from the show which was about to unfold, "you look absolutely enchanting."

She continued to keep her focus on the two men as they approached the animals, brooms held out in front like they were some formidable weapon. The boars hadn't shown any sign of acknowledgement yet. "Is it safe for them to do that?"

"Oh yes," he answered without hesitation. And then, "Are you two visiting from out of town?"

Antonio fielded that question. "As a matter of fact, we are. Is it that obvious?"

"No, no, nothing like that." He smiled in an often used artificial manner. "It's just that you seem unaware of our problem." He lowered his voice. "Rome has over twenty thousand wild hogs living in it. It is common to see them, even in busy parts of the city. Our elected officials haven't yet found a solution, so… (he looked at the waiters with their brooms), we do the best we can. They will run away when challenged."

All three boars now stood motionless, staring at the approaching men.

"Why are they just standing there?" Aurora asked.

It was apparent that the men were preparing to poke them with the brooms. "Don't worry. They won't be here much longer. Watch this."

The waiter to the left of their view lunged out, poking one of the hogs in the ribs. The animal showed no reaction. It simply stared, its black vacant eyes now locked on the man.

A feeling of impending peril washed over Aurora, so real that the hairs stood up on her arms. "I don't like this," she said. "Get them back inside."

An ear-piercing squeal broke the silence. All three boars, as if by preconceived agreement, rushed the closest waiter, knocking him to the ground. While the other waiter stood in shock, they climbed on top of him, pinning him. These boars were mature enough to have more than teeth as weapons. They started ripping at him with sharp, hooked tusks. Clothing didn't offer much protection, and soon it was his flesh that was being torn.

The lobby erupted in screams as the crowd suffered a clear view of a man being gored. The other waiter screamed hysterically as well and started hitting the boars with the broom. It had no effect, and he eventually dropped it and ran back inside. He continued to run mindlessly all the way through the mob and out the other side of the lobby until he disappeared entirely.

"They're killing him!" Aurora shrieked.

The Capo Cameriere faced the crowd in desperation. "Someone call the police!"

9

Doug the Slug was surprised to see this particular figure in the doorway to his office. "Director Peterson. What an unexpected surprise."

Peterson walked in and sat in the unoccupied chair. "It's an impromptu decision on my part. I felt like I needed to get out of my office."

"Can I help you with anything?"

"Let's have a short conversation." Peterson reached out from his seated position until his hand could touch the door, and then swung it shut.

Doug, unsure of what this was about, waited patiently.

"You sent me a message yesterday. Due to scheduling issues, I didn't open it until this morning."

Doug responded with a nod. "The restaurant incident?"

"That's the one. I'm wondering if there could be any connection between the Slovenian cattle massacre, or whatever you want to call it, and this restaurant thing."

"That's why I sent it to you."

"Because you think there is?"

"I think it's a possibility."

Peterson grunted, his position apparently not entirely comfortable. "I can see the similarities, but not a definitive connection. I feel like I need more information."

"Me too."

"You think we're justified digging into this?"

Doug shrugged. "Depends on how important this turns out to be."

Peterson thought about his response. "If this incident is a coincidence, then it's probably of no importance at all. But if it's another manifestation of some new strain of disease, it's definitely important."

"I agree," Doug said.

"What's the worst-case scenario? What could this, in our darkest nightmares, turn out to be that would justify an active interest from our office?"

"For me, it's the military component in Slovenia that got my attention."

Peterson squirmed, still looking for the perfect seating position. "Continue."

"They responded very quickly. If it was a run-of-the-mill animal attack, I can't see any reason for that. If they knew some sort of naturally occurring disease was involved…maybe. It would depend on the scope and potential impact on people or farm animals and by extension, the economic effects. I would still call into question the speed of the response, though. Somebody, somewhere, must have suspected something unusual was unfolding."

"And what about the restaurant? No mention of military involvement there."

"No, but think about it. The first incident happened in Slovenia. This one happened in Italy. Whatever this latest attack was, if there's a connection, it originated in another country. Italian officials probably didn't know anything about that. To them, it would seem like a fluke...a one-off that would never be repeated."

"Speaking of that," Peterson said, "Why didn't the Italian media run with this? Or for that matter, the international media. A man gets gored to death in front of a crowd of on-lookers? Come on, that's got *headliner* written all over it."

"I think it's because there's no apparent end-of-the-world, apocalyptic scenario here. It's not easily connected to a bigger problem. That makes it regionalized and unable to create the reaction the media is looking for on a broader scope."

"How do you explain the spread of this—assuming these incidents are related?"

"Slovenia and Italy are neighbors. They share a stretch of border. It's not implausible based on the distance."

"Then lay it out for me. I realize we're in the realm of speculation and I know how dangerous that can be. We have to be careful, but I need to flesh this out. What's the worst thing that could happen if these are related?"

"First," Doug said, "the animal attack explanation for what happened in Slovenia hasn't been displaced with a more plausible story. It's going to fade into urban legend over time, and it's not being openly publicized, but an animal attack is the only explanation still being put forward."

"By animals, you mean cattle?"

"I do. And that's another one of the things that makes this interesting. It's unprecedented. I mean, yes, cattle have stampeded before and hurt people, but that was always an unintended side-effect, a result of something else. Something spooks the cattle and causes the initial stampede. Five minutes after it's over, the animals are back to their normal, peaceful selves. And yes, bulls can be irritable and have attacked people in rare cases. But that's not what this was. So, what's the answer to the question of worst-case-scenario? I'm thinking a mutated virus or something similar."

"Mutated how? Naturally?"

"It happens. Constantly, as a matter of fact. But when the result is this dramatic and unprecedented, I can't help but suspect man's interference."

Peterson was grim. "I still have doubts and a ton of questions. But frankly, you just scared the daylights out of me. And this line of thinking would explain the fast military response. We need further investigation and some tangible information."

Doug wasn't sure what he was supposed to say at this point. An idea occurred to him. "Don't you have an agent who specializes in this sort of unusual thing?"

Peterson thought it over before responding. "Yes. Maybe that's not such a bad idea."

"Just a thought," Doug said.

"Can I use your phone?"

Doug spun it so the digits faced the director. "Absolutely."

"This won't take long." He punched in his extension. "Sandra, can you find Special Agent Specht and have him meet me at the sub-level office? Thank you."

"Do you want some privacy?" Doug asked.

"Quite the contrary. Please stay. You might be able to help with any questions he may have."

That meant lunch would be late, but what could he do? "Glad to help."

10

"Still up to your neck in paperwork?" Special Agent Robert Specht had appeared out of nowhere and was now leaning casually against the open door frame.

"You could offer to help instead of asking questions," his partner replied. Jan Collins had no love of office work and he knew it.

"You don't want that. I'd lower your standards."

"It's a risk I'm willing to take." She was glad for the distraction despite her grousing. "Tell me you're here because you have good news."

"Does flying to Rome sound like good news to you?"

The paperwork was now forgotten. "This better not be a joke."

"How long before you can be ready?" he asked.

"Immediately, if not sooner."

He smiled. "Your grasp of the English language is questionable but I'll overlook it. The boss said we may need several changes of clothes."

"I've got some here, just in case of emergency," the tall blond replied.

"Then close this operation down and follow me. We've got a flight to catch."

Collins took a swig of cold water straight from the bottle and then refocused on her partner. He sat across from her, arms resting on the small table. The agency's jet was now cruising smoothly at altitude.

"So what is it that requires our presence in Rome?"

"An animal attack."

She frowned. "How am I supposed to know when you're being serious if you keep saying ridiculous things?"

"I'm always serious."

"That's hard to accept when half of everything that comes out of your mouth is utterly preposterous."

"You already know Peterson is trying to make me quit by assigning the weirdest cases to me. There's the precedent…it confirms my explanation."

"Assigning the weirdest cases to *us*, you mean—which is really the heart of the problem."

"I think you should hear me out before jumping to conclusions."

She frowned in response. "I know your past reputation. If the word *werewolf* comes out of your mouth even once during this explanation, I'm making David turn the plane around."

"He's too much a company man for that."

"Even at gunpoint?"

Specht allowed himself to chuckle. "Just listen, okay?"

"Fine." She leaned back and tried to find a more comfortable position.

"A man was killed two nights ago at a restaurant in central Rome. The circumstances are somewhat odd."

"How could an animal attack at a restaurant *not* be odd?" Collins retorted. "And how did a bear manage to get a reservation during peak tourist season anyway?"

"This particular restaurant has three separate seating areas. One of them is an outdoor space they refer to as *The Garden*. Apparently, it is very popular. That's where the attack occurred."

"But it's located in the heart of one of the largest cities in the world, not Yosemite."

"An employee was attacked while trying to scare away three wild boars. They gored him and he died from his injuries. It was quite gruesome and unfortunately happened in front of a group of diners."

"How did three wild boars get into a restaurant garden in downtown Rome?"

"I did some research," Specht said. "Apparently Italy, and Rome itself, are being overrun with these things. It is estimated that there are twenty thousand living in Rome alone."

"You're kidding. How is that possible?"

"They're adapting to civilization, like coyotes and raccoons in North America. People throw away vast amounts of food waste every day, which is concentrated more in high population areas. These animals have learned that they can eat well by rooting through garbage. Now they're seen on the streets everywhere. The garden was only protected by a hedge."

She pursed her lips while thinking. "Okay. But there are still at least two questions I can think of immediately."

"Let's have them."

"Have these animals ever attacked people before?"

"Attacked? Rarely and with minor injuries. And usually only when cornered or surprised. Killed? No."

"As my second question, why did we get called in to investigate?"

"Roman police shot and killed the pigs. They were tested and came back positive for rabies."

"Yuck. But that only reinforces my question. If Italian authorities are all over this, then why are we going?"

"Because there's more to this than what's apparent on the surface, or at least that's what Peterson is thinking. Incidentally, we weren't requested and the Italians don't know we're coming."

"Further enlighten me, please."

"Around a week ago, another animal attack happened, this time in the neighboring country of Slovenia. This one was stranger yet."

"You're not going to ruin my appetite with this story, are you?" Collins asked. "Because there's a tuna on whole-wheat in the mini fridge with my name on it."

"It's a distinct possibility."

"Thanks for the warning. I'll brace myself."

Specht refocused. "The government seems intent on covering this story up. They closed off the town where it happened, and blocked communications so no details could be spread."

"Why?"

"That's the big question—the one we've been sent to answer."

"Okay. I'll try to stop interrupting now. Please continue."

"This is recently discovered information that we dug up ourselves. A herd of cattle, grazing in a pasture, suddenly stampeded into a small town. They proceeded to trample multiple people to death before the military could get there and neutralize them. The carcasses were tested and came back positive for rabies."

Collins ran her fingers through her short, blond hair as she processed this revelation. "You're not going to like this, but I now have a bunch of new questions."

"Not a problem," Specht replied. "Ask away."

"Cows can get rabies?"

"Any mammal can, as long as they're bitten by a carrier."

"But an entire herd all at the same time?"

"It's never happened before, if that's what you're asking."

"Has any cow ever attacked and killed a person?"

"Just isolated fluke stuff," Specht said. "Mostly from stampedes."

Collins pondered. "Is the agency thinking that there's a connection between the restaurant attack and this one?"

"Information is vague, but there were some anomalies found in the virus when rabies testing was done on the hogs. Nobody yet seems certain what that means, but it ramps up our concern. And that's why we're going to Rome."

"How many people were killed in this first attack?"

"We're not certain of the exact number," Specht said. "We're thinking it was more than ten, but that's a guesstimate at this time."

"Again, yuck. So how and why would rabies get involved in two unprecedented attacks?"

Specht took a sip of coffee. "We have absolutely no evidence to support this, but there's some concern that a mutated strain of the virus could be responsible. And the other concern is that the mutation didn't happen naturally."

"Oh shit."

"Indeed. And that's the real reason we're going for a European vacation."

"Robert, if a foreign government is mucking around in something this dangerous and illegal, they're in no way going to be happy about us poking our noses in it."

"Discretion is the key, Collins. You know that."

"And to think I was excited to see Rome."

11

"Can I go look out over the water now?" Denise asked. As a typical teenager, impatience was a major component of her personality.

Her father, Terrance, was still eating his meal. He was barely able to stop himself from putting another piece of the delicious fish in his mouth before he replied. "Be careful. Don't lean over the railing."

"I won't." He was protective to the point of smothering the freedom completely out of her. But she'd been chipping away at him since the vacation started and had made some progress. She intended to keep pushing forward with her efforts once the trip was over. The more immediate plan, however, was to find the cute boy who smiled at her on the deck earlier.

They had left the harbor located in the city of Bulja nearly two hours ago. The ship was now slowly sailing in the calm waters of the Adriatic Sea, an altogether enjoyable experience even before the excellent meal had been served. But this excursion was the *Sunset Dolphin Tour*, and these creatures, the stars of the show, were said to make an appearance just prior to the sun going down. Based on how low it was on the horizon, that would be soon.

Denise found an open spot and settled up against the rail. She could see Bulja across the bay, lights from the city now reflecting off the water. She looked around for the boy she had seen earlier but there was no indication of where he was. So, she focused on the water, hoping to be among the first to see a dolphin.

"Hello…"

She spun around, caught by surprise. The cutie was standing right there, looking shyly at her. Where did he appear from? she wondered before deciding it didn't matter. "Hi."

"Can I stand beside you? I mean, is there room?"

"Sure."

He sidled in cautiously, like he was carrying a box loaded with glassware.

"I'm Denise."

"Jordan. Nice to meet you."

He was polite, that was good. His nervousness was somehow endearing as well.

"Have you been on this cruise before?" she asked.

He shook his head. "First time. You?"

"Same."

Jordan looked out over the water, settling in. "On vacation?"

"With my dad. We're bonding or something."

That got a smile in response. "Sounds fun. Lucky you."

"Kind of, I guess." She had friends' parents to compare her dad to. She knew he was a good one, even if a little bothersome at times.

"Just a warning…my little brother could show up anytime. He's in some sort of clingy stage. I can't get rid of him."

Denise giggled. "Sounds like my dad."

"This railing might get crowded," Jordan said.

Some sort of commotion now drew their attention. A man was pointing out over the water.

"I bet he saw a dolphin," Jordan concluded.

A moment later, one jumped clear of the surface. It arched gracefully and made a perfectly clean entrance back into the bay.

"That's the prettiest fish I've ever seen," Denise said.

"It's not a fish," Jordan corrected. "It's a mammal, just like us."

"It's not just like us," she defended. "It lives in the water and looks exactly like a fish."

"Except it has lungs, breathes air and is warm-blooded."

Denise, unintentionally, gave him a hard look.

Jordan shrugged. "Not that it's important."

"I hope it comes in closer," Denise replied, refocusing on the dolphin.

"They usually travel in groups. Maybe we'll get to see a bunch of them."

"It's not called a group. It's a pod." She had been paying attention at the briefing before they left the dock. She smiled at his uncertain expression. "Now we're even."

He returned the smile. "Okay, I get it. Sorry."

Denise looked straight down and was startled by what she saw. "Look!" She pointed to it for clarification.

A dolphin was swimming directly beside the hull. It was easily visible while it moved just under the surface. But something wasn't right. It was sluggish, and having trouble staying perfectly upright. It started to tip over, then caught itself and overcorrected.

"Do you think there's something wrong with it?" Denise asked.

"Hey, there's one right over here," somebody announced. Bodies began to crowd around them on both sides.

"I've never seen one this close," a female voice said, delivered in a loud, know-it-all tone. A stout, middle aged woman pushed her way to a clear vantage point. The marine biologist want-to-be waved a breadstick. "Here…come and get it." She turned to someone behind her. "Watch this."

Denise knew they weren't to feed these animals; it was part of the earlier presentation. She wanted to say something, but anticipated the overbearing woman would have none of it, especially coming from a kid.

The woman was leaning perilously far over the rail, several partially displaced people giving her a dirty look but saying nothing. "Come on, you lazy fish; it's right here. I can't get any closer. Jump for it."

The dolphin disappeared as it went deeper under the water.

"Can you believe that?" the woman complained. "And after I did all that work. Where are you, stupid fish?"

The dolphin launched out of the water, easily reaching the woman. Rather than taking a bite of the extended breadstick, it latched on to the front of her shirt. The woman was no lightweight, but the adult dolphin weighed close to three hundred pounds. Arms flailing wildly, the woman pivoted over the rail and tumbled into the water. She made a significant splash, but popped up again quickly. Her face showed surprise and indignation. Whoever was in charge of the random things that happened in the universe owed her an explanation, as did the owners and crew of this boat.

"Help me!" she roared, more a demand than a request.

A crew member had been attracted by the commotion. "Hang on!" he yelled and then ran towards the emergency gear. He returned quickly, lifejacket in hand. "Here, put this on while we turn around to pick you up." He tossed it well, and it landed only a couple feet from her. She made no effort to grab it.

"You'll do no such thing! You pick me up right now, do you hear? I will not wait."

That she had no choice in the matter apparently hadn't occurred to her. The boat was moving away and couldn't be stopped in time even if they tried. Maybe she wasn't as smart as a marine biologist after all.

The crew member hesitated, unable to think of what he should say. Her lack of cooperation stunned him. This wasn't part of the training when they rehearsed this procedure.

"Oh my God," Denise exclaimed. The dolphin was back, swimming towards the woman. It was moving fast.

Reading the faces of the people at the rail, the woman turned, saw it, and screamed as another new reality check was forced upon her. The dolphin struck her hard in the face.

"She needs help!" Denise yelled. The woman looked to be unconscious. Blood was pouring from a wound on her cheek.

The Captain ran over and looked for himself. "Grab the rescue pole!" he yelled to a crew member beside him. "And tell Joe to call the harbor patrol!"

The dolphin reappeared. This time it bumped into the lady from behind. It grasped her by the collar of her shirt and with a power swipe of its tail, swam under with her in its grasp.

"No!" Denise screamed, horrified. She wished she had stayed at the table with her dad and never seen any of this.

The Captain stared, unbelieving. He had never heard of anything like what he had just seen. He wondered how long until she would come back to the surface. The thought made his skin crawl.

12

"Special Agent Specht, Agent Collins…please come in."

The room was small, but then again, so was the entire setup. As a field office, that came as no surprise.

"Please take a seat." The person in charge was Feldman, a middle-aged, portly man with thinning grey hair and piercing eyes that missed nothing. He noticed Collins looking out the window behind him. "Rome is a beautiful city. Is this your first visit, Agent Collins?"

"It is."

"I hope you enjoy it. Now, how can I be of service?"

"We were hoping you already knew the answer to that," Specht said.

Feldman nodded. "I read the preliminary report, which is what you would already have. I'm afraid there's not much more I can add."

Specht knew his type. It wasn't that he couldn't or wouldn't be helpful. If he and Collins couldn't be bothered to work for it, Feldman wouldn't offer it.

"That's disappointing. Nothing at all?"

"The report covers it."

"Have there been any other attacks?"

"None have been reported." It was a carefully calculated choice of words.

"Seems strange," Specht said. "Three animals together in the centre of the city had the disease, and they were the only ones out of the thousands that live here in Rome to contract it."

"Again, there haven't been any attacks. There have, however, been reports of animals acting strangely. A number of other hogs have been dispatched and sent for testing."

"Do you know the results of the tests?"

"They're not all back yet."

"But some are?"

For the first time, Feldman seemed slightly uncomfortable. "They're coming back positive for rabies."

Specht frowned. "How many so far?"

"I'm not privy to an exact number."

"Roughly?"

"Dozens."

"Why isn't the city in an uproar?" Collins asked. And then, "Is it even safe to be on the streets?"

Feldman gave her a look that wasn't exactly welcoming. "As I said, there haven't been any more attacks."

"But this one resulted in a fatality, and that was a full-grown man."

Feldman didn't reply for so long, Collins started to feel uncomfortable. It was done intentionally. "Let me bore you with some economic statistics, Agent

Collins. Rome has a population of three million people, significantly larger than Paris. Amazingly, it draws in over ten million tourists annually. That pumps four and a half billion dollars into the pockets of the citizens and businesses here. That's with a "B", Agent Collins. Can you imagine the impact of a full-blown panic over some sick pigs?"

"So you've been able to put a price on people's safety. Good for you."

Specht didn't want this to go any further. Once Collins got started, she could be very confrontational. It could only hurt their efforts. "We're not here to debate economic impacts of government oversight. Instead, I would like to know this. Have there been any indications of the virus in other species here in Rome—dogs, cats, other wild animals?"

"No indications yet," Feldman said.

"What about in the countryside? Any signs of the virus outside of the city?"

"I'm reluctant to share any information I can't confirm."

"We can take that into account when doing our analysis," Specht said. "Anything you can give us would be helpful."

"There are some reports of farm animals being affected. Sheep and cattle primarily."

Specht was stunned. "Obviously you know about the incident in Slovenia."

"There's something troublesome happening, Agent Specht, no doubt. We would all appreciate you getting to the bottom of this before it gets any worse."

"That's our intent. It feels a little like we have a very tall mountain to climb before we get to the solution, unfortunately."

Feldman picked up and then extended a manila envelope in Collins' direction. She took it after a moment of hesitation. "Speaking of mountains, I believe congratulations are in order. You two will be getting a scenic view of the Alps while vacationing in Slovenia for your anniversary, or honeymoon, or whatever this is supposed to represent."

Collins gave Specht a look. That kind of smile could only mean she was about to say something inappropriate. "You lecherous old perv!"

Specht shook his head. "More likely a dolt about to lose everything over a trophy wife."

Collins perked up. "You think I could be a trophy wife?"

"I think we can end this conversation right now." He extended a hand to Feldman. "Thank you for your help."

"If anything of substantial value comes up, I'll pass it on."

"Thank you." He turned his gaze back to Collins. "Come on, and bring that envelope. Apparently we've got some reading to do."

13

"This is gorgeous!" Collins repeated.

Specht had lost track of exactly how many times she had made the same observation.

"Why have I never heard of Slovenia before?" she asked.

The road wound along the base of gently sloping, pine covered hills. Beyond them were larger mountains rising towards the sky, some high enough to be adorned with snow-capped peaks. An occasional buffer of flat pasture reached out to the edge of the highway. On them, homes resembling ski chalets had been built. Herds of sheep and cattle grazed without concern.

"It feels like we're driving through a giant screen saver."

In the distance, a lake was gradually coming into view on their right. The road was going to run directly along the shore.

"If you like this," Specht said, "you're going to love what's next."

She saw it now. "I can't think of a better place to spend our anniversary."

Specht winced. "I think we've already established your feelings about that. Have you been paying any attention to the herds? Do the animals look all right?"

"As far as I can tell. But this really is the last place you'd expect something horrible to appear."

Specht was keeping busy with small steering adjustments to accommodate the winding road. "If you can fit it into your busy schedule, check the GPS. Find out how much longer until we get to Curragh."

"Just did. Hour and a half. I sure hope it looks exactly like this when we get there."

"As a matter of fact, you don't care what it looks like, since we're only here to do a job."

"That's what I meant to say."

"Any progress on your research?" Specht asked.

"I didn't know you were going to be this demanding when I agreed to marry you."

Specht sighed.

"All right, enough is enough."

"Have you formed any idea why livestock seems to be the primary species being affected by this strain?

"No. That part is really strange. The most common animals back home to get infected are bats, coyotes, foxes, raccoons and skunks. I assume that list would be similar here."

"No herbivores at all."

"No. Carnivores and omnivores only. But again, it can infect any mammal."

"But why the dramatic shift? What has changed? Why are they so susceptible to this new variant, if in fact, that's what this is?"

"I don't know. Can we brainstorm while you drive?"

Specht had committed to focus his primary attention on the curvy road. Above and beyond that, perhaps a little mental capacity was left over. "Why not."

"What if it has to do with speed? Cattle and sheep are rather sluggish, right? They stand around most of the day grazing. They're not in training for the animal Olympics, that's for sure."

"So what? Something sneaks up and bites every animal in the whole herd?"

"Maybe something small, like a mouse or a rat. They might not even feel it."

Specht frowned. "If Rome was overrun with rabid rodents, why would they just bite wild hogs? Why not cats, or dogs, or even people?"

"Okay, good point. Strike one."

"I also don't understand how the virus appears to be moving so rapidly. It's like it's jumped a hundred miles or more in a few days. How's that possible?"

"What moves that fast?" Collins asked.

"None of the animals we've been talking about."

"What about trains or trucks? Do any of these creatures hitch rides?"

"I don't know," Specht said. And then, "Don't get me wrong, I'm pretty sure that does happen, but I don't know what species or under what circumstances. Nor do I know how common it would be. And it definitely wouldn't be a large farm animal doing it."

"I won't rule it out yet," Collins decided. "Clearly more research is required."

"Let's look at this from another perspective. If this is the worst-case scenario and man's interference has caused this, then what mutations could have been intentionally added that would explain these things?"

Collins looked out over the lake as they overtook it, now only partially focused on its scenic value. "Great question. What would explain a spread over long distances in a short amount of time? That's a tricky one."

"It really is." Specht drifted off into thought.

"You okay, partner? You want me to drive?"

He risked a quick glance at her. "What if…the entire purpose of the mutation was to make it easier to spread? For example, what if a bite wasn't required?"

Collins considered it. "If you were a sick enough son-of-a-bitch to want that, I suppose."

"But how? What way do other viruses pass that's quicker and easier than a bite?"

"Oh God." Her face grew pale. "That's easy."

"Say it out loud."

"Through the air. A sneeze, a cough or even normal breathing. And that probably brings touching into play. Airborne virus lands on a door handle, somebody touches it and then rubs their eyes. Before you know it, it spreads around the whole world. Sound familiar?"

"Too much so. But wait, before we panic or buy into this completely—that still doesn't explain why it's primarily happening to livestock." Specht stopped talking as he steered around a sharp turn.

"You're right. What would go around biting or breathing only on herds of farm animals?"

"I feel like we're on the right track. But something is still eluding us. It still doesn't make sense."

"I just thought of something else," Collins added. "Are there any research facilities in this region that could be doing this sort of work? I mean, our foundation of understanding is built on the premise that this originated here, in Slovenia. That could prove to be untrue. But if it's correct, then it had to come from somewhere nearby, wouldn't you think?"

"You won't find that info in the yellow pages," Specht said. "If you're working on biological weapons, it doesn't get advertised."

"Peterson could help. He'll put Doug the Slug on it."

"Send him a request."

She raised her phone. "Give me thirty seconds."

"And not to encourage your so-called sense of humor in any way, but as food for thought—the honeymoon suite undoubtedly has only one bed."

She smiled as she typed. "A man of your stature should easily fit on the couch."

No surprise there. "I'm getting too old for this," Specht said.

"I also expect flowers every morning and champagne every night."

Specht decided that to further engage would not be in his best interests.

14

Helen had never been happier. Their Austrian vacation was turning into everything she hoped it would. That Kevin would quickly grow bored of looking at scenic views and want to go hang gliding or some other death-defying activity had been a concern. But he was standing beside her, smiling and mesmerized, just as intrigued as she was.

"I told you," she said, unable to fight off the urge to gloat. "Isn't this gorgeous?"

They were on the far side of the lake, looking back across the water towards the towering building that the tour guide referred to as Grundenburg Castle. The sun reflecting off of its white walls created a magnificent reflection on the mirror flat surface.

"Not bad," he conceded.

Three large swans swam towards them, adding another nice effect to the view.

"I wish I could pet them," Helen said.

"One is probably an offspring. I'm sure they'd get defensive if they saw you as a threat."

"Then let's start back. I can't wait to eat lunch in a castle."

Kevin smiled. He was starving.

Out on the lake, the three swans hissed loudly, lowered their heads and started to move towards them with speed.

"What's their problem?" Kevin asked.

They were lifting off the water, picking up speed and trying to get fully airborne.

"They're coming right at us!" Helen screamed. She turned and started to jog back along the path.

Kevin didn't follow. A basic physics calculation told him the act was useless. The swans were already upon them.

"Shit!" he yelled without thought. Two of the birds struck him, one high in the face, the other in his chest. They were big and heavy, and their momentum knocked him over onto his back. They fluttered and squawked, hovering awkwardly as they pecked ferociously at him.

"Stop it!" he screamed in a tone of voice he'd never used before, trying to protect himself with his hands.

Helen fared no better. The remaining swan smacked her from behind and she lost her balance, toppling over as a result. She lay face down, yelling hysterically as the large bird pecked and swatted her in the back and shoulders. It managed to get her ear in its beak and did a fine job of trying to pull it off. Her screams got louder.

Others from the same excursion heard the commotion and ran to help. But the swans were not easily deterred. Finally, after a concerted effort by the rescuers, the birds turned their aggression on the newcomers. This resulted in more screaming, pecking and flailing.

The victims were soon exhausted to the point of losing the ability to defend themselves. The birds showed no signs of stopping or growing tired. Finally, one man surprised and horrified himself when, with minimal thought, he picked up a rock out of sheer desperation and brought it down hard on the nearest swan. It must have done some injury to it, as the bird flopped over and couldn't seem to right itself. A second hit finished it off—it lay twitching, wings flapping spastically. Problem was—the other two kept attacking.

The nearby victims, bolstered by his success, eventually finished off the other two swans with a ruthless pummelling.

Horrified, the seven tourists stood in disbelief—gasping for air and looking at the bloodied bodies of the swans.

Helen touched her ear. It hurt, and when she pulled her hand away, there was a good amount of blood on it.

"What did you two do to those swans to set them off like that?" one of the rescuers asked.

Kevin rankled. "We didn't do anything! We were walking away when this all started."

A woman standing with them pointed across the lake. "My God! Look!"

A group of five swans was flying low over the water in a close formation. They were flying straight towards them.

"Run!" someone screamed, and they all scattered.

But this wasn't over.

Collins was pleasantly surprised by the hotel. As she and Specht stood at the reception counter, she couldn't help but look around in all directions while he dealt with the check-in procedure.

"You can see the lake from the dining room," she said, pointing.

"It's a beautiful place," he agreed. He wasn't sure how critical it was to maintain the illusion of being a married couple, but that was the arrangement made by his boss. He would play along.

"You did good, sweetheart," Collins gushed. "What a perfect place for our anniversary."

Cornered, Specht managed a smile. "I'm so glad you like it, honey."

The young lady checking them in looked up from the computer screen. "If there's any way we can help to make your stay special, please don't hesitate to ask."

"We appreciate that," Specht said as he leaned over to sign the paperwork she had offered. "Oh, that reminds me. We heard there's a scenic place to have a picnic, just outside of Curragh. Could you give us directions?"

She reacted at the name of the town, but in a subtle manner. Specht only noticed because he had been trained to.

"Of course. When were you planning to go?"

Why do you need to know that? Specht wondered. "It's getting too late to do it now. Probably tomorrow for lunch."

That seemed to be an acceptable answer. "Very good. Here, I'll write out directions that you can take with you. It's easy to find from here. By the way, are you planning to actually go into the town itself?"

"Yes, we thought it would be nice to see since we were so close anyway. Why do you ask?" He was curious to hear the answer.

"There have been some renovations in the town. Some streets and businesses may be closed."

"We appreciate you passing that on."

"How long of a drive is it?" Collins asked.

"Not long," she responded. "Thirty minutes and you're there. Here you go." Specht accepted the keys. "Thank you."

"Your room is ready. Supper is at six. Enjoy your stay."

"Oh, we will," Collins said in an exaggerated voice, knowing it would annoy her partner. She also made it clear by her unencumbered exit that he was to carry both their bags to the room.

Once in the elevator, Specht gave her a sideways look. "You don't have to play the role with this much enthusiasm."

"Don't discourage me. It's my job."

"Our job is to find out what's going on with the animal attacks."

"Which I'm hoping, at least for tonight, means drinking champagne on the terrace and looking out over the lake."

"You're a piece of work, Collins."

"I'll take that as a compliment." The elevator door opened. "You okay with those bags?" Then, she flashed a quick smile and walked out into the hallway.

"Apparently." Specht struggled to keep up.

"This is ours," she said as she stopped in front of a door. "And it's on the lake side of the building." She seemed genuinely excited.

"Beats office work, I guess." He set down the bags, unlocked it and swung it wide open.

Collins nearly ran inside.

"I've got these. Don't worry." Specht followed behind.

"Look at the view through these windows!"

Specht set the bags down, and then strolled into the main part of the room. "Very nice. And the room's bigger than I expected."

"Too bad the couch is so small." Again, the insincere smile made an appearance.

"I'll survive."

Collins opened the drapes as far as possible and drank in the view. "Good. You've got a lot of work to do. Sorry, I meant *we*."

"Then let's plan out our agenda for tomorrow. It'll keep us busy until supper time."

There was a knock on the door which Specht answered. An employee stood with a vase full of roses.

"Compliments of the hotel, sir."
"Thank you so much." He took them and shut the door.
Collins grinned. "Now you're talking."

15

When the General arrived, Luka immediately ushered him into a private room. This was promising to be the worst encounter of his life and he wanted to get it over with.

The General had already read his expression and the tone of his voice. "This is something important, yes?"

Luka looked grim. "Most certainly."

"But not good news?"

"I wish it was, but no. It's bad. The worst, really."

"Tell me. Don't omit anything, don't mince words, and don't you dare misrepresent yourself in any way."

Luka felt ill. Perhaps he could do this quickly and then visit the washroom. Due to the extreme nerves which were messing with his metabolism, he felt like he needed to expel from both top and bottom. But he nodded in agreement. The question now was how to start this conversation. Bluntly, he decided.

"One of our employees has rabies."

The General, expecting the worst, still managed to look and feel shocked. "How?"

Luka paused for a sigh. It was often the smallest things that brought down the mighty. "At one point, we had some caged birds here in the lab area. They're especially susceptible to any contaminates in the air, so we used them as a sort of biological alarm system to give us advanced warning of any chemical that might have found its way into the atmosphere. We also have modern alarm systems, of course—but the birds weren't a big expense for the lab, and the employees liked having them around. It was a morale booster, as they say."

"What is the connection?"

"It was eventually decided that the birds should be removed. Several employees took them home to be pets rather than see them put down. This happened very recently. The man who has contracted the disease took one of them."

"I don't understand. What does the bird have to do with this?"

"After the bird had been at this man's home for several days, it began to exhibit strange behavior. It was clumsy in its movements, stopped eating and eventually began to act aggressively towards the man and his daughter who was the primary caretaker of the bird. Both of them were pecked by it hard enough to draw a little blood."

The General sat back. "Wait a minute. These are symptoms of rabies. And the bird had these symptoms?"

"Yes. The bird eventually and accidentally escaped from the cage due to its aggressive behavior and managed to fly out of the front door, never to be seen again."

"What exactly are you telling me?"

"When the man couldn't report to work, we were immediately concerned about his symptoms. Tests were quickly done and the results came back positive."

"But surely he couldn't have gotten it from a bird. This disease is exclusive to mammals."

"The bird was gone, so we couldn't test it. We brought in all the other birds that were still in employees' possession and tested them. They all tested negative."

"There, you see?"

Luka wished this was going to transfer to good news. It wasn't. "We brought other birds into the lab, new ones, and exposed them to airborne virus particles. We felt an additional test was warranted."

"And what happened?" the General asked.

"They all tested positive."

"What! That can't be."

"Although it was never in the original parameters of the virus mutation, it appears certain that it now has an avian component."

"Birds can get it?"

Luka nodded solemnly. "They can get it. And they can spread it."

"Good Lord!"

"This man and his daughter both have it."

"The daughter as well?" This caught the General further off guard. "What can be done for them?"

Luka had already tortured himself over the answer to that question. "Nothing. It is too late. They will both succumb."

The General still had a look of shock. "And you said this bird escaped?"

He nodded.

"Could it have spread the virus once outside?"

Luka resisted the urge to shrug. "We have many questions that need to be answered. We simply haven't had time to do sufficient testing."

The General replied with an edge to his voice. "Then when will this testing happen?"

"It is happening now, even as we speak. But the virus has time constraints. We have to let it proceed through the various stages before we can get definitive answers."

"So it will be days before we know?"

"It could be weeks, at least with some of the questions."

The General leaned back until he was looking at the ceiling. "Do you know what this means?"

"I honestly don't think I have an answer for that."

"This could be the end. For you. For the lab. For me. For all of us." He collected his thoughts. "So the escaped bird that started all of this could also have spread the virus to wild creatures, which are in turn spreading it right now."

"We just don't know the answer to that."

"If birds can spread it, it'll move quickly over large areas. Over borders, over rivers and lakes…potentially going anywhere and everywhere. Who will be safe?"

"Again, I don't have an answer."

"Tell me we haven't just started an apocalyptic event that will affect all life on Earth!"

Luka really needed to visit the washroom.

The General stood and slowly paced. "I don't know what to do. Who do I tell? How do I advise them?" The more he envisioned the path this was likely to take, the worse it got. His eyes looked haunted. "How can we stop this now? It's already out of control."

"I suspect that the birds won't be very good at transmitting it," Luka offered. "These people were pecked when they grabbed at it in the cage, but in the wild, that may never happen."

The General didn't find any comfort in the speculation. "You don't know that. You don't have a clue how this is going to unfold. Their ability to spread it would explain the attacks we're already aware of, would it not?"

Luka didn't respond.

The General wondered if he could survive this fiasco. All of the power and influence of his position now transformed into something very different. Responsibility. He looked at Luka and saw a broken man perhaps about to get ill. "What do I do now?"

Luka was having trouble thinking at all. "Well, we will keep testing, getting answers to all the important questions."

"Yes. Do that. And let me know immediately every time you learn anything new, whether good or bad."

"Of course, General."

The leader of the military walked to the door and opened it. "This is not going to be a good day," he said before disappearing out into the hall. *Will any of us ever have another good day?* he wondered as he walked out.

16

There was a checkpoint at the entrance to Curragh. Specht gave the attending officer his story in an awkward process of over-emphasised words and hand signs—anniversary trip, staying at the local hotel, looking for a nice place for lunch. This finally seemed acceptable and he let them pass.

"Nicely done, partner," Collins said. "Who needs to speak Slovenian?"

"Thanks. He probably thought we were selling vacuum cleaners. How's a coffee and pastry sound?"

"Think we could find an espresso in this town?"

"One way to find out. We'll cruise the main street—you keep a sharp eye out for anything promising."

"I like this new priority. I was expecting a rigid *the job comes first* agenda."

Specht was alternating from looking at the road to checking out approaching signs that he couldn't read anyway. "That's exactly what this is. We need an English-speaking local who likes to spread gossip."

Collins nodded. "And where better to find one than at the coffee shop?"

"Now we're on the same page. I think it's our best shot."

"Slow down, if you can. I have to look in through the windows to figure out what's what."

"At least they use Euros as currency here. I think I've got that pretty much figured out."

Collins pointed. "Hey, this might work. I can see people sitting around tables in there."

"And look at this…a parking spot right out front." Specht activated the turn signal.

"Perfect. Take your time. I just got a message from Peterson."

Specht parked cautiously, not interested in getting into even a minor fender-bender in a foreign country.

"Get this," Collins said, reading from her phone. "There's a lab across the border in Croatia that's suspected of doing some military research. It's only a hundred miles or so from here."

"Everybody is so close to each other here in Europe. That's not always a good thing."

"If something unnatural is going on, they could be involved."

Specht agreed. "Their proximity is suggestive. For now, let's see if anybody in here speaks our language."

"And if there isn't?"

Specht stepped out onto the sidewalk. "As long as I can figure out how to get a coffee, it won't be a wasted trip."

It was a small restaurant set up café style. Specht knew the moment they entered that coffee was brewing by the pleasant aroma.

He sat at the counter to place their order while Collins found an open table. The waitress approached and asked him something in Slovenian. It was almost certainly along the lines of *how can I help you*, but Specht couldn't understand a word.

"I don't suppose you speak English?" he asked without much hope.

"English?" she responded.

That was encouraging. "Yes, English."

She shook her head. "Ne."

The meaning was obvious enough. "Does anyone working here speak English?"

This time she shrugged and looked confused.

Ordering was going to be tricky, and getting information about any incidents that happened in town impossible. Specht wondered if there was another spot where they might have better luck.

"Excuse me."

He turned to see a middle-aged woman with salt and pepper hair done up in a bun addressing him.

"I heard you talking. I speak both English and Slovenian. Can I be of any service?"

What a relief this was. "Yes! And thank you so much. Could you help me place my order?"

The woman happily agreed. Specht convinced her to allow him to buy her a tea, and to join them at their table.

Collins figured she might as well make the best of this unexpected situation. "Darling, I leave you alone for five minutes and you return with another woman."

"May I introduce you to Ana, our benefactor for the moment. Ana, this is my wife, Jan."

She sat across the table and extended a hand. "Pleasure to meet you, Jan." She showed no reaction, subtle or overt, to the difference in their age.

Specht settled in. "Ana, as you have no doubt already noticed, speaks fluent English. In a very real sense, you should thank her for your drink and snack."

Collins smiled a genuine smile. "You saved my life."

"My pleasure."

"So Ana," Specht said, "How is it you are so fluent in our home tongue? Are you not from around here?"

"Oh yes. I was born and raised in this very town. But I left some years ago to teach abroad. I was in Samoa, Japan and the Philippines before returning. I came back full of memories and foreign language skills."

Collins stepped in while Specht tasted his coffee. "This is our first time in Slovenia. I can't believe how gorgeous it is. Your scenery is breathtaking!"

"How long have you been here?"

"Arrived yesterday. We started in Rome, and then decided to get more adventurous. Am I ever glad we did." Collins kept her answers as truthful and genuine as possible.

"On behalf of the people of Slovenia, thank you for your kind words."

Specht's coffee seemed to have passed the taste test based on his reaction. "Ana, what would you recommend for a couple with no agenda for the afternoon? Is there anything in or around town that's worth seeing?"

"The lake is really the highlight. If you drive around the western side, there's a small area where you can pull over and go for a nice stroll. It's peaceful and full of great views. Bring a camera of some sort if you go."

"Could we have a picnic there?" Specht asked.

"I don't see why not," Ana said. "There are no tables that I am aware of, but if you don't mind sitting on the grass, it should work out nicely."

"Perfect!"

Collins decided to interject with carefully chosen words. "Ana, this is our first time here. Do you mind if I ask you something? Is it normal to go through a security checkpoint to get into town?"

She shook her head. "Not at all. I've heard that the barricade is coming down any day now. We had an incident which took some time to clean up. But things are back to normal."

Collins smiled and nodded. She desperately wanted more information, but didn't want to raise any suspicions with too many questions.

"I thought that sort of thing only happened in America," Specht said offhandedly, a subtle attempt to encourage more conversation.

"Apparently not," was her only reply.

The rest of their visit was small talk about unimportant things. Specht and Collins eventually excused themselves, thanked Ana again for her assistance, and strolled back out to the car.

"Should we kidnap her and torture her for more information?" Collins asked.

"She knew more than she told us, that's for sure. But she wasn't comfortable talking about it. It's too soon for us to blow our cover by being unusually nosey."

"Now what?"

Specht pulled out carefully and waved as they passed by the window in case Ana was watching. "I think we should return to the hotel. Finding Ana was a miracle—I doubt we'd ever find another English-speaking soul out here in the boonies. Lots of people speak English at the hotel. Let's just hang out like typical tourists do, and keep our ears open. Maybe we can stumble across a conversation without doing a lot of prying. If the incident was anything like we suspect, it should still be on people's minds."

"The bar in the lounge might be a good place to start. Tongues always loosen up in the presence of booze."

"That's actually not a bad idea," Specht said. "We can start out together, like a loving couple would, then split up and wander independently. We can meet up again perhaps mid-afternoon and compare notes."

"Think there are any clothing stores in this town? I need a new dress to wear around the hotel."

Specht frowned. "Seriously?"

Her expression said it all.

"I guess we can look, then."

17

It was the regularly scheduled meeting of the top elected Croatian officials, all major cabinet ministers, and the President and Prime Minister in attendance. It was heavy on formalities and procedure, dragging out late into the afternoon as the sputtering economy dominated the conversation.

Having accomplished nothing that was likely to make things improve, the meeting nonetheless concluded and important people with other places to be started to disperse. The President signalled the Prime Minister and the Minister of Defense.

"We need to talk. Let's use my office." His tone was serious.

This was a disappointing turn of events, but not uncommon for those near the top of the political chain of command. They entered and the door was shut behind them. They were the only three in the room at that point.

"This just came in. No one outside this room can be made aware of anything we are about to discuss."

There was a perfunctory nodding of heads—this restriction was always assumed.

"Let's do this sitting down. I don't need anyone falling over."

They all did, their seats predetermined many meetings ago.

"This won't be easy or pleasant. General Horvat committed suicide at his home a little over an hour ago."

The two Ministers were stunned.

"What! Are you certain?" the Minister of Defense said.

"Yes. I'm sorry to convey this terrible news."

"But…he wasn't that kind of man. What could have driven him to this? Was he ill?"

"What else do we know about this incident?" the Prime Minister added.

"He left a note. It was more for us than his family."

"What did it say?" the Prime Minister said.

"It was cryptic. In it, he alludes to some sort of failure that he felt would have far-reaching traumatic effects. Defense Minister, do you have any idea what this refers to?"

The man was visibly upset. "He called me a short time ago," he said in a now subdued voice. "We were in the middle of our meeting, so I ignored it." He withdrew his phone. "It seems he left a message."

"Have you listened to it yet?" the President asked.

"No. Could you indulge me for a minute while I retrieve it?"

The President contemplated. "Why don't you put it on speaker?"

The Defense Minister hesitated. "I have no idea what he's going to say."

"That's all right. We all need to hear it."

"Very well." He pushed several buttons. He set the phone on the edge of the table between them.

At first, soft static background noise was all that could be heard. And then, "Hello Andri."

Silence again, and then a sigh.

"I'm sorry for this call. But you need to know what has happened. I've been remiss in my oversight, and now a terrible price must be paid. I don't even know how far-reaching the effects will be. I do, however, fear the worst.

"There's been an incident with our biological defense research. The lab has had a breach. The virus has been leaked.

"All the traits that made the disease seem so viable, so potentially intimidating to our enemies, now only make it unstoppable. It's loose, Andri. An employee has it. And it has possibly crossed the border into Slovenia. It can spread more easily than we thought. There's an avian aspect to this…birds can catch it. They can spread it.

"Do you know of the animal attack that involved cattle in Slovenia? Also related, or that's what I fear.

"Andri, I don't know how to fix this. I don't even know if it can be fixed. It's out there and who knows what it will do. We're all at risk. And to think I watched this happen. I was so smitten by the rate of its success. And now, we've created something worse than nuclear war. It's untethered and acting on its own accord. It's possibly the end of life as we know it and I was there! I could have stopped it! I let the opportunity pass by, and now…

"I cannot look at myself in the mirror—so how can I stand the scrutiny of others? How will I be remembered, if there is anyone left to remember?

"I am a coward, Andri. I cannot find the strength to face what is to come. I pray that there will be a resolution. I pray that you find it. And I pray that a loving God will somehow find a way to forgive me. Goodbye, my friend."

The phone clicked and went dead.

Three very white faces stared horror-stricken at each other.

"What was he talking about?" the President said, looking at the Defense Minister.

He removed his glasses and wiped his eyes. "I was never informed of these problems."

"Informed of what problems?" the Prime Minister shouted. "Surely you must know exactly what this is."

The Defense Minister left his glasses off. Maybe he didn't want to see the world in perfect focus at this moment. "We contracted a private lab to do research and development on a new biological weapon. The last report was very encouraging."

"Not so much like *this* phone call, eh?" the Prime Minister snipped.

The President signalled for calm. "Talk to us, Andri. Tell us everything you know. It's the only way we can work this out."

He collected himself. "The research centered around a pre-existing virus. It's a frightening thing, but difficult to get, and easy to remedy with a vaccine. The plan was to make it much more transferrable, so that it could be altered into a form that could be weaponized. The mutation would also render current vaccines useless, adding to its level of intimidation."

"Good Lord," the President exclaimed. "What is this virus? Would we know it?"

He hesitated before answering. "It's rabies."

"Rabies!" the Prime Minister roared. "Are you insane?"

"We already have a vaccine for the new strain. This was to be used as a deterrent, nothing more. Outside of military use, it would still be easy to control."

"Can you please give us more details?" the President asked, somehow maintaining his composure.

"It was to be designed so that it could spread through the air, not just by a bite from an infected animal. But unless dispersed manually in an aerosol form, it still could not spread easily. It wouldn't run wild like a cold or the flu."

The Prime Minister was visibly upset. "The General said birds can get it. How would that be possible?"

The Defense Minister was in a corner from which he didn't have a way to escape. "I don't know. Like I said, I was never notified of any of these issues."

"What was the chain of command for this research?" the President asked.

"The General was the top overseer. He was to keep me informed of any noteworthy events."

"Such as a breach?" the Prime Minister said.

"A military report was sent to both of you some time ago that briefly mentioned the research in general terms. Perhaps you overlooked it."

The President stood and paced slowly around the room. "We need information. As much as possible; as accurate as possible. We need it now. Andri, can you contact the lab and find out exactly what has happened? They must be aware, or the General wouldn't have known about it."

"Of course."

"I strongly suggest the three of us stay here until you're able to report on your findings."

The other two, with no visible enthusiasm, nodded in agreement.

18

Specht and Collins met in the dining room. She was wearing the new dress she had bought earlier, sporting an eye-catching slit up the side. Coupled with a pair of stiletto heels, she was putting on a noticeable display.

"I'm not sure I approve of my wife's choice of attire," Specht said as he held the chair out for her to get seated.

"Men are so easily predictable and manipulated," she said as she sat. "You wouldn't believe how many offers I had to buy me a drink after you left."

Specht assumed his position across the table. He picked up the menu, although he already knew what he wanted. "Were you able to get engaged in any meaningful conversations?"

"Not until a few minutes before I came back here to meet you."

"I'm intrigued. May we discuss this here?"

"Not in detail. I can share one tidbit perhaps."

"Please do," Specht said as he set his menu back down. There was enough background conversation to offer some degree of privacy.

"A news flash just came across the television mounted over the bar before I left. Seems Croatia has closed its borders."

Specht kept his outward reaction in check. "Just with Slovenia?"

"No. The whole country is closed off."

"Do you know why?"

"Not at all. Of course, they offered up some vague and inane drivel about a prison break and an escaped drug lord. Neither I nor my new friends, who were drinking at the bar, put any credence into that."

"I'll take their opinions into account when formulating my own," Specht said.

"There's more, but I think we should save that for a more private setting."

Specht signalled for a waiter. "On that note, I do believe I'm ready to order."

Later, Specht and Collins sat on their private balcony, a small table between them with two glasses of red wine poured.

"What is it?" Collins asked. "You seem…I don't know—out of sorts."

Specht squirmed. "Listen. You're my first female partner. And you're a good one, no doubt. Maybe the best I've had. You're intuitive, brave, committed to the job…"

"But…"

He sighed. "Every time you cross your legs with that damn dress on, I feel like I should be stuffing small bills into a G-string."

She laughed out loud. "I concede. You're right. Give me two minutes to slip into something less revealing."

"Thank you," he replied sincerely.

"Keep an eye on that lake. Don't let it go anywhere."

"Hurry up before Peterson calls for an update."

"On it!" she called from somewhere inside the room.

Two sips later, Specht watched her return in sweat pants and a hooded seater with a team logo on the front.

"From one extreme to the other," Specht observed, things now back to normal.

"I'd be satisfied with this, if I was you. You don't want to know what comes next."

He set his glass down. "Fair enough. Now, tell me about this interesting conversation you were involved in."

"More like *overheard* than involved in."

"Either way."

"Immediately after the announcement about the borders, the bartender and some random guy at the end of the bar got into a brief but informative talk. It wasn't deep in details, but it did confirm one thing."

Specht was all ears at this point. "Tell me!"

"There *was* an animal attack in Curragh. A herd of cattle stampeded into town and trampled some people to death. And apparently another couple was also victimized before the animals even made it to the town itself."

Specht looked away, out over the beautiful lake without even seeing it. "Even after knowing this was a possibility, it stuns me to hear that it really happened."

She nodded in agreement. "Exactly. We now have verbal confirmation. We also saw the checkpoint at the edge of town. Put the two together…"

"Sounds like evidence to me," Specht said.

"And now the border closure."

Specht decided another sip of wine was in order. "And that happened shortly after we found out that there's a lab located there."

"We're still in the realm of coincidence on that end, I think."

"One foot in and one foot out, perhaps," Specht added.

Collins emptied her glass and took inventory of what was remaining in the bottle. "Where do we go from here?"

"Good question. We have to remember that we're on foreign soil, uninvited, with no official acknowledgement from our government. We have to be discreet."

"Discreet is my middle name," Collins said.

"I'm not sure your friends at the bar would agree."

"You're right. Maybe I should get it legally changed to *Legs*. Has a nice ring to it, don't you think? And by the way, may I finish the bottle?"

Specht smiled. "Of course. I've had enough."

"I suppose visiting Croatia is out of the question," she said as she poured the bottle dry.

"With the borders closed? Definitely."

"So what's left for us to do?"

Specht looked away, engaged in thought. "You said there was another couple killed?"

"According to my partially inebriated sources."

"And an unknown number of victims in town?"

"Yes."

"I think," Specht said, "that there's an angle of exploration we haven't even considered."

Collins dug through her thoughts and realized she had nothing. "Tell me, partner."

"You've got a good read of the layout of the hotel. Have you noticed any newspapers in English lying around?"

She smiled. "No, but I know what else will work."

Specht held his hands open in a gesture to indicate emptiness. "And what would that be?"

"The Slovenia Times is available online in English."

"How do you know that?" he asked.

"I checked it out while you were driving on the way here."

He smiled. "I'm impressed."

"So what do you want to look at? Headlines?"

"Not at all."

"I can't help if you don't tell me."

"Obituaries from last week."

She raised her eyebrows in surprise. His idea began to come into focus. "Let me see what I can do."

19

"It's all true." For the first time, the Defense Minister regretted his career choice. "All of it. Every allegation the General made."

"Birds can get rabies?" the President asked.

"They can now."

The Prime Minister looked exhausted. "Can we focus on what's of utmost importance?"

"Meaning what?" the Defense Minister replied.

"How can this be controlled?"

"What did the laboratory people tell you about any possible resolution?" the President added.

"The avian component was a completely unplanned surprise. As such, there was never a contingency for it. Right now, they have no answers."

"But they have a vaccine, right?" the Prime Minister said.

The Defense Minister wasn't upbeat about it. "Yes. Tests have suggested that it's very effective. Another bright spot is that it can be taken orally rather than through an injection."

"Wait," the Prime Minister said. "That's great news! At least people can be protected. We can resolve the rest over time, but that's the main priority. Right?"

"There are issues. Timeliness is the main problem. It must be taken within hours of exposure. And with airborne exposure now possible, people may not even realize they were contaminated."

Silence fell.

"It can still work," the Prime Minister said. "We'll have to make it available to everyone in the country, but that's very doable."

"It might work, although much is still unknown and the logistics will be daunting. But you must understand what has to happen first. Have you not thought this through?"

Prime Minister Nowak wasn't a happy man. "Just say it! No games."

"We have to tell everyone, literally the entire world, what we've done."

The room was silent once again.

"You can't distribute the vaccine and expect it to work if people haven't been told what it's for and why they might need it."

The President put his head down on his desk. When he raised it again, he somehow looked older. "They're going to eventually figure it out as it spreads anyway. Surely you wouldn't propose that we cover this up and deny accountability while it kills who knows how many people, both in Croatia and beyond?"

"No," the Defense Minister said quietly. "I'm not suggesting that. But the three of us need to be fully aware of what's about to happen."

"Spell it out for us," the Prime Minister said. "I'm too tired to think."

"We're all liable, even if only in the public's eye. Best case scenario is that we all lose our jobs. Worst case is we end up in prison, or executed."

A new reality settled over them. No one voiced an argument. It was now deathly silent.

"None of us will ever see this office again once this meeting is over. Whatever decisions we make now will be our last. We and our families will live in fear and shame from this time forward. The entire world will see us as monsters. We've lost everything, no matter what happens now."

The Prime Minister was nearly in tears. "But I didn't even know about this!"

"That's not plausible. The three of us are the top political leaders in the country. If we didn't know about it, we should have. If you make that argument, it will not avail you. No one will believe you. If anything, it will probably make you look even worse. Not only are you a monster, but you're also a liar. You see?"

"But the military is your portfolio, not mine!"

"You outrank me. You can't escape responsibility."

"You're right," the President said quietly. "From the first moment this virus escaped the lab, our fate was sealed." He looked at the other two men. "What do we do now?"

"Call the Vice-President," the Defense Minister said. "Have him come in immediately. We'll make sure he has no direct accountability with this mess. At least that way there'll be a smooth and immediate transition of power. He can be sworn in tonight. He'll have a big say in what happens to us, at least in an initial sense. We can talk that through as well. And we can help him put together some sort of government response. Also, our country and the world will have to be made aware. It might as well come from us, and it might as well happen while we still have some semblance of control."

The Prime Minister was sniffling. "But this could mean hanging or a firing squad for us."

The Defense Minister already knew that. He was determined to be as stoic as possible. "Everybody dies of something. Be thankful it's not rabies."

Dr. Hanna Petrova pivoted her chair away from the computer screen and lined it up with the office phone on her desk before reaching for it. "Yes?"

"Dr. Petrova, can I see you in the lab?"

"Your timing is perfect, Dimas," she said. "I needed to get off this chair anyway."

"See you."

She hung up and stood, stretching as she did so. The walk to the lab was short, just a few steps down the hall. After the reason for the call got resolved, she decided to do a couple of laps around the parking lot. It was at least fresh air and exercise.

The door to the lab was heavy and she strained to push it open.

"Over here," said a young man as he greeted her with a wave. Like her, he was also a doctor of veterinary science.

"What exciting thing has happened in your lab today?" she asked in jest.

Dimas picked up a single sheet of paper and waved it. "These are the results of the autopsy from that dolphin."

"And something unusual has been reported?"

"Very much so. It had rabies."

Dr. Petrova was momentarily speechless. "What? Are you certain?"

He nodded. Dolphins were on a watch list for protected species, so a detailed test for toxins and diseases had been carried out when the body had been found.

"I know it's possible, but I've never heard of such a thing. Had it been bitten? Were there wounds on the animal?"

Dimas had done the autopsy himself. "No. At least not typical bite marks. There were some small abrasions on its back, but they were definitely not bites."

"But there would have to be in order for the disease to spread to it. Are you sure?"

"Yes. I took photos if you want to see them."

"Are they handy? Do you have them here?"

He was already reaching for a folder. "Yes. See for yourself."

She leaned over. Her first thought was about the detail and quality of the images. "Nicely done."

He nodded in acknowledgement.

"It looks like it was poked by something. Certainly not a major injury, but enough to break the skin. But as you said, it's not a typical bite."

"Looks more like it was pecked by a bird," Dimas observed.

"But how could that even happen? Dolphins only surface for brief moments to breathe and possibly chase after prey. And that can't account for the transfer of the disease."

"I don't know. Just chasing after an answer."

"Well, good work anyway. It's certainly an interesting case."

"Should I file it now?"

"Yes. Keep it in mind, though. Let's hope it's an anomaly, but if any other dolphins come in, let me know immediately."

"Thank you, Doctor." He turned back to his work.

"Dimas?" she asked.

"Yes?"

"You didn't get exposed to any body fluids from this animal during the autopsy, correct?"

He was a little slighted, but didn't show it. "All protocols were followed to the letter. There was no exposure. And everything was properly sterilized afterwards."

"I knew that would be the answer. Thanks for making me feel better."

"Of course."

"I'm going for a short walk," she announced as she disappeared out the door.

20

Specht was finishing his normal morning routine—showering, shaving and dressing. The door swung open as he did up the last button on his shirt. Collins poked her head inside the bathroom.

"Get out here! You need to see this."

Based on the urgency in her tone, he didn't question her. The television was on, turned to a European version of CNN. The picture was of an official looking man making an announcement of some sort. It was obviously now being rerun, as all sorts of comments and analysis were cycling across the bottom of the screen.

"What's this?" he asked, hoping to cut through the clutter.

"Croatia admitted to leaking some new virus."

That was truly a shock. "Good heavens! Things must be worse than we thought. Owning up to something like that is a worst-case scenario for any government."

"That guy is the Vice-President. Or was. He's the top man now. Apparently some of the former officials have been arrested."

"How long have you been watching?"

"Maybe a minute before I came to get you."

That meant she hadn't had time to absorb all the details. "I'll put on a pot of coffee. We need to hear this."

Both of their phones pinged simultaneously.

"Peterson," Specht said.

"Bet I know what he wants."

"Same message for both, no doubt. You read; I'll brew. Keep the TV going."

She sat, phone in hand. "I'll save you a front row seat."

After watching the story cycle through twice, and tolerating some 'expert' analysis (which was blatant speculation and nothing more), Specht finally reached for the remote and turned down the volume.

"This could be the biggest news story of our lifetime. Any comments?"

Collins drummed her fingers on the arm of her chair while putting her thoughts together. "It was shocking. But details were really lacking. Either there's a lot they don't know, or they're not ready to say."

"Did it answer any of the questions from our investigation?"

"I think one revelation did. It was the most shocking thing of all, as far as I was concerned—birds contracting and passing on rabies! That would explain how the virus jumped over large distances to reach the centre of a major city."

"It explains the distance, but not the choice of victim. Why pigs and cattle?"

Collins shook her head. "I don't know."

Specht stood. "I'm going out on the balcony for a few minutes. I need to clear my head."

Collins stood as well. "I'll join you, if you don't mind."

"Not at all. We have some major questions to answer." Specht opened the door and stepped out.

"Such as what comes next for us?"

"Exactly."

She swung her chair so it faced the lake. "It doesn't look like the end of the world out there."

Specht took a sip from his steaming mug. "Let's hope it doesn't come down to that."

"What if Slovenia decides to implement travel restrictions as well?"

"Tell you what," Specht answered, "Let's create a mental file called 'Peripheral Issues' and stuff that in there. I think we need to keep our immediate focus on a fairly narrow field. Namely, what needs to be done right now, and how can we do it."

"Won't Peterson give us our marching orders?"

"Two potential problems with that. First, he may hesitate. He doesn't like to make mistakes. He's been known to waffle, waiting to see what momentum an issue naturally takes before deciding on how to deal with it. And that's even more likely with something this unprecedented. Second, even after hesitating, he may make the wrong decision. He has one eye on his future with the agency every time he chooses a direction. He'd rather pass up a high risk opportunity to resolve an issue and stay the conservative route that's less likely to get him fired or demoted."

"So what needs to be done?"

That answer wasn't as obvious as Specht would have preferred. "Can you see any way we can help to resolve this?"

"We came to confirm if anything unusual had actually happened," Collins replied. "The whole world knows the answer to that question now. Second to that was, how did it happen? In general terms, we know the answer to that as well."

"If there was a new focus, what do you think it would be?"

She turned to face her partner. "How do we stop it?"

"Exactly. The new Croatian President said they already have a vaccine. That sounds like a good start."

"If that's true and not just propaganda to save face, then what are the remaining problems? Why are we still concerned…or should we be?"

Specht came to a conclusion. "I think we're going to run around in circles here, largely because we either don't trust the information we have, or the information is incomplete."

"Meaning what as far as you and I are concerned?" Collins asked.

"I think clear, timely and accurate information still has a high value in all of this. We need to keep digging. What are the remaining questions that are still unanswered? You start."

Collins seemed a little off balance. "Questions as of yet unanswered? Well, why are cattle and pigs being affected so much?"

"Very good. Also, how long since the first breach occurred? Knowing that date exactly would easily translate into an accurate rate of how fast it's spreading."

"Has the disease been transmitted to any people as a result of the cattle attack?" she asked.

"Excellent! Have there been any bird attacks on people?"

Collins listened to chirping sounds coming from the shrubs below them. "Thanks for that."

"Sorry. I'll tell you what…let's write a two columned list. One side will be questions Doug the Slug can dig up, the other will be questions we can work on ourselves. What do you think?"

"It's so crazy, it just might work. By the way, I have lousy secretarial skills."

Specht knew to pick his battles. "I'll make the list."

"Before or after we go down for breakfast?"

"Before," he said without hesitation. "That gives us motivation to get it done."

Collins rolled her eyes. "My fault. I should have known better than to ask."

21

The New World EcoDome had been a typical government subsidized project from the beginning, at least in terms of budget and oversight. Construction cost overruns had been substantial. Delays in the building schedule became demoralizing even for the staunchest supporters. Once the framework appeared on the horizon and proceeded to extend at a snail's pace while visible from the nearby expressway, the lack of progress went from discouraging to outright annoying.

But now, the jewel of the largest zoo in Hungary was finally finished. The grand opening had been a tremendous success, both in attendance and feedback. Previous issues were quickly fading away. The original planners and designers were now lauded as visionaries and even geniuses.

The name was somewhat deceiving. It wasn't a dome in the strictest sense, but in fact was a sprawling structure, roughly shaped like a capital letter 'E' tipped on its side. The construction consisted of a series of intersecting partial domes, each wide open to the next. This arching design gave support to the roof, but kept the interior both open and spacious.

Tropical trees and plants were thriving in the controlled environment. Raised walkways had been incorporated to allow easy, unencumbered movement while minimizing interference to the animal's behavior. Non-invasive, interactive displays made additional information available to visitors as they did the tour.

A busload of elementary students from Budapest had arrived early on this day. It turned out to be drizzly and dark outside, but in the EcoDome everything was dry and comfortable. Birds and animals were putting on a good show and the kids were piling up memories and experiences to relay to their parents when they arrived back home.

Hans Muller was the director of the zoo. He tried to split his time between his executive duties and actually getting out and interacting with the animals. It was easy to justify spending time in the EcoDome as it was their newest and biggest attraction. It represented the future of this zoo, and perhaps would even be a trend that would eventually transform zoos around the world. Many dignitaries were lining up for escorted tours. The publicity would be great, but Hans still preferred the company of creatures over people.

Today Hans was watching the elephants being fed. There were currently five of them in the EcoDome—two calves, two cows and a bull named Hercules. The big guy got a lot of the attention from visitors simply because of his massive size. Hans reached through the heavy fence, trying to touch the animals as they munched on the feed in the trough. He had limited success due to his short arms, but still had a blast just being there.

He touched an employee on the shoulder to get their attention. "Helena, what's up with Hercules?"

He hadn't come in to eat, but stood at a distance, head hanging down. It swung listlessly from side to side.

"I don't know. He's been off his feed for two days now. The vet is going to check him out later this afternoon."

"Good. Can you ask him to tell me what his conclusions are?"

"Certainly."

Hans turned his attention back to Hercules. "What is it, my friend? What ails you?"

The big head lowered even more. Now Hercules was looking at the feeding area through the upper extent of his eyes, a decidedly creepy appearance.

Hans saw something previously undetected. Hercules was drooling. Foaming at the mouth, actually.

Hans felt his blood turn to ice. Like everyone else on the planet, he had heard about the rabies variant that was loose in Europe. He was to meet with his staff at the end of this very day to discuss possible implications. But here, in the EcoDome? And this fast? It couldn't be.

"Helena," he said, "did you notice him doing *that* before?"

She looked out at the massive animal. "On my God! No, never."

"I think we should separate him from the other animals. Can he be safely moved?"

"I think so. He went into the sleeping quarters last night with no issues."

"Good. Get a couple of other hands to help you. And lend me your radio, please. I'll try to get the vet to look at him immediately."

"Of course." She handed it to him and walked briskly away.

Hans wasted no time. "Dr. Lamont, this is Hans Muller. Can you read me?"

A deafening sound that was more like a roar than a trumpet call shocked everyone in the building. Muller looked over to see Hercules charging full bore towards the trough.

"Stop!" he yelled, although there was no chance of it having any effect.

Hercules crashed into Matilda, one of the cows, and jammed her into the trough, her face striking the fence beyond while she bellowed in pain and surprise.

"Don't do that!" Muller yelled again.

Hercules rammed Matilda a second time, now toppling her over on top of a calf that had been feeding beside her. They both cried out loudly.

Directly above, the students had all had their attention drawn to the elephant pen.

"What are they doing?" one of them asked the nearest chaperone.

"I have no idea," she replied.

They all began to crowd around the railing, mesmerized.

Meanwhile, the huge bull reared up, and then stomped down hard on the trough. It broke away from the fence and toppled over, spilling feed all over the ground. Hercules then pushed it with his tusks, growling like a bear as he did so.

Once shoved aside, the fence was all that remained between the massive elephant and the director. That was when he charged.

The impact was substantial, but the fence was designed to safely hold very large animals. The problem was that this portion wasn't exactly fence, it was a gate. It was strong, yes—but the latch and the hinges were the weak link and they were not capable of withstanding Hercules as he inflicted a raging attack. The next impact heralded the sound of the latch ripping loose from the frame. The gate now hung partially ajar.

Hans knew what the next impact would do. He turned and ran.

Hercules smashed into the gate again. This time the latching mechanism failed completely. The gate pivoted, teetered, then fell onto the ground.

The elephant roared, running out of the pen and onto the walkway used by staff members. Muller was the closest, and was moving enough to catch the beast's attention. Hercules charged.

A full grown bull elephant can reach up to forty miles per hour on a dead run. He caught Muller in a few brief moments, knocked him over and started to trample him into the cement floor. The energy of the impacts of his feet created thousands of pounds of pressure. Muller's body was crushed to a pulp.

Screams could be heard echoing throughout the EcoDome. The children's were amongst them.

"Get them back! Get away from the railing!" a teacher yelled. The children looked stunned, and one was throwing up.

Hercules, meanwhile, had turned around and was stumbling towards the pen he had just escaped from. He would continue his rampage by turning his attention back to the other elephants. The only way to stop him now was to dispatch him with a rifle shot, in front of all the visitors.

The children would bring many memories home this day.

22

The world-wide media was in full frenzy mode. The revelation of the release of the virus was quickly joined and bolstered by the zoo attack story. Ratings would no doubt be sky high. Every reporter on the planet began to scour for potential evidence of rabies in their particular region. Things were about to get jumbled and disjointed in the 'news'.

Specht had taken a call from Peterson, his boss. Fearing they were going to get recalled home, he was pleased to find out the exact opposite was true. When he returned to the supper table in the dining hall, Collins was straining to read the expression on his face.

"You're positively glowing. Don't tell me you have good news?"

He sat, and leaned towards her. "Don't mind me if I keep my voice down."

"No problem. This is our anniversary, remember? People will think you're whispering sweet nothings in my ear."

"I'll be whispering, but this is definitely something and not sweet at all."

"Tell me before my salad starts to wilt."

"The Bureau has made some deals. The new man in charge of the Croatian government has decided to be cooperative with concerned foreign interests. He has agreed to give us access to the lab where this all allegedly started. We can interview the guy in charge of it. Our ability to cross the border into the country has already been arranged."

Her eyes lit up. "Finally. Now we're getting somewhere."

"We leave first thing tomorrow. We'll need to work on a list of questions."

She leaned back and set down her fork. "Back to work it is."

It was a long drive to the lab. On the map, it looked closer. Roads in this part of the world never ran straight for long, Collins concluded. Curves were mandatory. Crossing the border had gone surprisingly well, at least.

"Turn here," she finally said. "The lab should be on our left just a short distance down."

"Great. I'm starting to lose the feeling in my legs."

A sprawling, grey brick building came into focus. Collins pointed at the sign. "This is it."

"Nice place. It looks like they know how to generate positive revenue."

"Military contracts will do that for you."

Specht turned in and began to look for a parking spot. "Not as full as I would have expected."

"Don't complain. We can park right up by the door."

They soon found themselves in a spacious lobby. A receptionist watched them approach.

"Hello," Specht said. And then, "Do you speak English?"

She smiled in response. "Some."

About the best we could hope for, Specht thought. The person they were here to meet supposedly spoke it as well. "We are Agents Specht and Collins. We have an appointment with… Luka Karmic." He hoped his pronunciation would be sufficient.

"Yes. You can go in. He will meet you in the hallway straight ahead."

"Thank you." Specht nodded before walking through the now open access door.

"So far, so good," Collins said discreetly.

"Now comes the important part," Specht replied.

A blond-haired, middle aged man approached. "Hello. You must be from the FBI?"

His English was decent, and Specht wasted no time extending his hand. "Yes. I'm Specht, this is Collins. Thank you so much for making time for us."

"You got here very quickly. Please, follow me."

He led them through an open door into a spacious room which was obviously a cafeteria. "This is our lunch room. I hope you don't mind if we use a table here for our meeting. None of our employees speak English, so there are no concerns about being overheard."

Specht was doing a visual scan of the room. "This is fine, thank you. By any chance, do you have coffee here?"

"Yes, absolutely. Please allow me to serve you. How do you take your coffee, Agent Specht? And what can I get for you, Agent Collins? We have some breakfast items if you are hungry."

They were soon seated with drinks and muffins before them.

"Again, we appreciate you treating us so graciously at a time which must be very difficult for you," Specht said as he hoisted his mug.

"I will help you as best I can. If you can come up with any viable ways to deal with this, we would all be very grateful."

"I'm going to let my partner ask most of the questions."

Luka repressed the sudden urge to let loose with a loud sigh. Instead, he put on a brave face and smiled. His orders had been very clear. He was to be open and cooperative. It was a dramatic change in direction, but General Horvat was no longer in charge. "As I said, I will try to help in any way I can."

Collins gave him her most penetrating stare. "Can you start by telling us about this virus? Any specific details would be very helpful."

"Of course. As you already know, it is a variant of rabies. We made it transmissible by air. That meant we could weaponize it, and then disperse it in a manner such that large groupings of troops could be infected very quickly. It was to be used as a deterrent, of course—something that hopefully would never actually be deployed, but the threat of it would give leverage to negotiations that involved military or potential military actions of any sort."

"And you have a vaccine?"

"Yes. It can be given orally, so a quick remedy to exposure is easily accomplished. There is a problem, however. This variant moves very quickly once it enters a new host. The victim has only a few hours to get vaccinated, opposed to a few days with the original disease."

"That is a problem," Collins replied, understating her response so as not to be insulting.

"Since it's spread through the air, and not an animal bite, the victim might not even be aware of the exposure. Hence, they would not seek the vaccine until symptoms appeared days later."

"When it would be too late," Collins said.

"Unfortunately, yes."

She continued to take notes. "Do you know how the virus was released outside the lab?"

"I believe so. We had caged birds here for a time. It was silly, in retrospect, but they served a double purpose. Firstly, they're very susceptible to airborne contaminants. They would show signs of a reaction before humans would be harmed. We work with all sorts of chemicals and other compounds, so even though we have modern sensors that continually check air quality, we figured this back-up wouldn't hurt. I think it gave our workers an additional feeling of security.

"Secondly, the workers liked the birds. They became like pets to them. Morale went up and everyone seemed happier. I know it sounds trite, but management at that time believed it was true."

"So you had a bird escape?" Collins asked.

"No. We had a change of upper-level management. The new person in charge wanted to get rid of the birds. He thought they looked unprofessional to any visitors we might have. So, they were removed. Originally, we were going to euthanize them, but the employees nearly rioted when they found out. It was eventually decided that anyone who desired to do so could take them home to become family pets."

"Oh shit," Collins said softly.

"Exactly. Keep in mind, rabies only affected mammals prior to this. We weren't aware of this mutation. It wasn't planned or even imagined. Anyway, within a week after the birds were sent home with the employees, one of them called in sick. Because of what we do here, whenever that happens the employee must give a detailed, accurate self-diagnosis of any and all symptoms pertaining to why they cannot attend. This man's symptoms alarmed us to the point where we had additional tests performed immediately."

"And he tested positive?" Collins asked.

"Sadly, yes."

"How is he doing?"

"He's in hospital. They are keeping him isolated and as comfortable as they can."

"It's too late for the vaccine?"

"Yes. And it gets worse. He was infected through a peck on his hand that broke the skin. The bird had become aggressive and easily irritated at that point, but of course he had no idea why. His daughter was helping to care for the bird. She also got pecked."

"Oh no."

"She is also in hospital. Our carelessness has all but wiped out that nice little family."

Collins sensed their host needed a moment to compose himself.

"How did it spread outside their home? Did they breathe on other people after infection?"

"The answer to your question is, we don't know. Even though the virus can spread through the air, our tests in the lab indicate it isn't all that likely. The virus seems to drop out quickly. Of course, very close contact could do it, or a kiss, a direct cough, close proximity in an enclosed space…something like that."

"But it still has military application?"

"Oh yes. If we mechanically vaporize it, that's a different story. The proper dispersal can result in a very high probability of catching it."

And that brings us to where we are now, Collins thought. "Was the cattle attack because of your virus being leaked?"

"We don't know for sure. We haven't had a chance to test any of the animal remains ourselves since it happened outside the country. The carcasses have now been cremated."

"Can you think of any reason why cattle and pigs would be infected at a high rate?"

He shook his head. "Sorry, no."

"You got anything, partner?" Collins asked.

"Can we get your number so we can call if we think of anything else?" Specht said.

"Certainly. Ask the receptionist on your way out. She will give you a card."

Specht, coffee and muffin both finished, started to stand. "Again, thank you. If we come across any information that could be helpful to you, we will also call back to pass it on."

"Best of luck," Luka said. In the midst of this disaster, he really meant it.

23

A colony of monk seals had taken up temporary residence on a remote, rocky beach. The island, located off the northwest coast of Italy in the Tuscan Archipelago, was too small to support a human population, but the seals found it quite to their liking.

Birds came and went as well, depending on the season and amount of food available. It was not uncommon to see various species flying about, or walking along the shore in the same area where the seals were resting. There was no conflict or natural antagonism between the two and any sort of skirmish was rare.

But today, one particular gull had trouble written all over it. It was stumbling along, looking rough and dishevelled. It had been a participant in an unexpected and vicious attack by another gull several days ago. The result was that some feathers had been pulled out. Also, pecks hard enough to break its skin had been administered in several places on its body. Finally, out of desperation, the gull had taken to the air and flown away until the aggressor ceased chasing it. The wounds were minor, and it wasted no time getting back to normal behavior.

At least, that was, until the disease started to manifest itself. Now the bird had trouble standing still. Its balance was off, and everything had become awkward. Its brain was under siege and normal behavior was drifting away. For reasons unclear, the seals were infuriating it. Ultimately, the reason didn't matter. It simply couldn't tolerate them anymore.

The bird took to the air, flying in a clumsy manner, squawking loudly. It landed on a nearby seal (which one really didn't matter to the gull at this point), and proceeded to peck it furiously. The seal, a much larger creature than the gull, with thick, leathery skin, initially couldn't be bothered to react. But as the bird continued with its frenzied onslaught, the seal finally rolled over and took a half-hearted nip at it. The gull lunged forward, pecked it with great effect on its nose, then half flew, half flopped its way to the next nearest animal and started all over again.

The bloody nose was annoying, but not a major problem. Ignoring the uproar from the nearby attack, the seal rolled back over and resumed its nap.

The gull, meanwhile, managed to infect three seals before one of them actually caught it in its mouth and put an end to the fuss with one bone-crushing bite.

Now there was a problem. These three animals would develop symptoms in less than a week. And that would lead to another, even bigger problem.

Although rare, sightings of orcas, or killer whales as they are better known, did occasionally occur in this area. Several days later, one pod happened to be hunting nearby (seals were a favourite food source) and came across the victims of the gull attack. The infected animals were swimming slowly, awkwardly, and didn't have the razor sharp reflexes and escape skills that the rest of the animals had. Sensing this, the killer whales made quick work of all three. It was a tremendous feast, the high fat content of these animals providing much needed energy.

But now there was another issue.

Orcas were also mammals.

The larger islands in the archipelago were too perfect not to have a tourist component to their economy. Beautiful beaches and clear blue waters brought visitors in by the boatload. In the Tyrenea Harbor, six tourists had paid for a kayak adventure.

Their guide, Danica, was relieved that all of them had previous experience operating this type of craft. She didn't want to be trying to save somebody after they dumped their kayak several hundred yards from shore. Winds were light, the harbor was calm, and this promised to be an easy outing.

"Everybody, follow me. Nice and easy."

She dug her oar into the clear water and began to glide across the surface. A quick over-the-shoulder glance confirmed that everybody was following.

"Think we'll see any fish?" a middle-aged man asked.

"Not likely," was the unwelcome response. "They don't usually come near the surface. I think the kayaks spook them a little."

"You could definitely troll from one of these," the man continued, talking more to himself than anybody else.

Danica looked forward and saw some slight disturbance on the surface of the water. Maybe she was wrong with her answer. Maybe some fish were going to show themselves. How perfect! She decided to move in that direction.

"We're making a turn. Be careful, everybody."

There was some derisive conversation about her concern over such a simple maneuver. Did she think they were incompetent? Danica didn't mind. She had heard worse and it was her job to keep everybody safe even more than to provide entertainment.

That was when she saw it. A sleek, black snout slipped up out of the water. Soon a huge dorsal fin appeared. It fired off a loud burst of spent air through its blowhole, and there could be no doubt what she was seeing. It was an orca!

She turned to her group. "Hey, look everybody! It's a Killer Whale. They're very rare."

Half seemed excited, half seemed concerned about their safety.

Incredibly, two more orcas surfaced. The trio hovered in place, almost motionless.

Danica wished she could take a picture. She turned around. "Anybody got a phone with them? I'd love to get a shot of this."

"We were told to leave our devices on shore," somebody grumbled.

"That's all right. Let's not get any closer."

Cedric Tallin had a camera. He was on shore, watching the kayaks. He decided to take a few photos from there. The colorful hulls made a nice contrast to the blue water. With the sun shining on them, they seemed to glow.

"Let's make this a video," he said to himself as he adjusted the controls. He would need a steady hand, but under a low zoom setting, he should be able to manage.

Through the viewfinder, the image came into focus. Cedric immediately saw something new and unexpected. A large black fin was moving alongside the kayaks. Soon a second and third fin became visible. He had no initial idea what they could be, but did come to one conclusion. They seemed to be circling the people in the small boats.

As he watched, a large black head bumped one of the kayaks, a lime green model with what appeared to be a slender young man aboard. The head was huge and easily tipped the narrow boat, depositing its former occupant into the cool water. There was some sort of thrashing, but Cedric couldn't discern what was happening in great detail. The sounds of screaming reached his ears. Through the viewfinder, he saw all the kayaks making a run towards shore.

Another was hit and tipped, and the rider disappeared like the first. Now there were five left. Cedric stopped shooting, set his camera down by the bag he carried it in, and ran towards the pier. Maybe there was something he could do to help.

By the time he got to the spot where they had launched, there was but one kayak still operational. The young lady in it looked like she knew what she was doing. Paddling furiously, she approached at a fast speed.

"Take my hand!" Cedric yelled, leaning over and extending it for her to grab.

An orca had approached unseen. It popped up at the very edge of the pier, effortlessly reached Cedric's extended arm, clamped down on it and pulled him into the water directly in front of the remaining boat.

Cedric went under without a sound, never to resurface.

Danica scrambled from the kayak onto the pier and wasted no time taking several steps back. Straining, she could see all the kayaks. But try as she might, she could see no people.

What had just happened?

For the first time in her life, she fainted.

24

As they drove through the beauty of the mountains, a peaceful expression made its way across Collins' face.

"I know you love this scenery," Specht said. They were in Slovenia, back on the job.

"We have to give Peterson credit," she replied, changing the direction of the conversation. "First an interview at the lab where this all originated, and now a chance to talk to the Slovenian military unit that intervened in the attack of the killer cows. Rather impressive."

"Not the entire unit, just the commander," Specht corrected.

"Still…"

They drove on for several minutes. Collins was staring out the side window, now uncharacteristically quiet.

"Are you all right?" Specht asked.

She held up one hand as if to indicate that she didn't want to be interrupted. And then, "Pull over."

She said it so casually, Specht hesitated.

"Pull over!"

Motivated, he did so with reckless abandon. The tires skidded in the gravel as the car ground to a halt. "What is it?"

"Hold on." She looked down and located the button to lower the window on her side. It slid open with a soft hum. "Look at those cattle."

He leaned closer and slightly forward to get an unimpeded view. In the pasture, a short distance from the road where they now sat, a herd grazed peacefully. "What am I looking for?"

"The third cow from the right. See it?"

Specht did. All looked normal. "What's wrong with it?"

"Nothing as far as I can tell. But look at its back. Can you see it?"

"What about it?"

"There's a bird on it."

Specht squinted to sharpen his focus but saw nothing. The significance also eluded him. At that moment, the small bird flew off. Due to the movement, it came into view. "Wait. I see it."

"Does that mean anything to you?"

Slightly frustrated, Specht couldn't perceive any meaning. "Why? What are you thinking?"

"Birds can now spread rabies. We know cattle and pigs have been infected in large groups. These stationary animals are so big that they would hardly notice a little bird pecking away at their backs."

Specht digested her theory. "Maybe."

She turned from the cattle and looked at her partner. "In some parts of the world, birds are welcome on the back of all kinds of large animals. They eat certain pests. It's a perfect symbiotic relationship."

Specht was rooting through his memory. "It's certainly possible."

"It fits with what we know to be true."

Specht snapped his fingers. "I've got it. There's a bird…I believe it's called an ox-picker."

"Oxpecker," she corrected. "I don't think they're native to this area, but it makes a valid point. Large grazing animals, at least some of them, are pre-wired to allow that type of behavior by birds. They instinctively know that it can be helpful for them."

Specht stared out at the pasture. "So an infected bird flies from animal to animal, pecking away, and they basically ignore and allow it."

Collins nodded. "Creatures in the wild would be elusive and solitary for an angry bird to attack."

"But domestic animals that live in herd formations would be clustered together and less likely to evade or even defend themselves," Specht added.

She shrugged. "It's a theory."

He nodded. "And it's a good one. Also, the only one that anybody has been able to come up with so far to explain the mass animal infections. Good work!"

"I'm not sure how it helps us."

Specht put the car back in gear. "It's another step down the path we're on, and that can only be a good thing. Text Peterson and pass that on. Make sure you take full credit for it. He might as well know I have the smartest partner in the entire organization."

That put a smile on her face. "Aw, you're only saying that because it's true. Now, if you would just acknowledge my stunning beauty, I'd be able to put perfect trust in your observational skills."

Specht pulled back onto the road. "Don't push it."

"I am Captain Draco Hudak."

The trim but muscular man extended a strong hand and shook with the two of them. His accent was pronounced enough that communication would require full attention on their part. At least he spoke English.

"I'm Special Agent Specht, this is Agent Collins."

They stood on the sidewalk in Curragh, back where it all started.

"Would you like to see where the firefight happened?" Hudak asked. "It is only a short walk from here."

Specht was glad that Hudak wasn't dressed in a full military uniform. Hopefully they could be in public without attracting attention. "Yes, we would like that. If you don't mind, we can talk on the way."

Collins noticed his bold, piercing eyes. He looked like someone who would be at home in battlefield conditions. "Did you know what was happening here when you were dispatched?"

He nodded. "I had been briefed, but the story was so strange, I had doubts. At least, until we arrived and saw for ourselves."

"Give us an overview," Specht said.

"We choppered in. Drop off was maybe a quarter click south-east of town. We ran from there and found temporary cover. At that point, we had seen nothing unusual except there were no people on the streets. Clearly something was wrong.

"We dispersed into two groups. At the main street, my team turned to the north, Lieutenant Morina's team went south. As luck would have it, she made first contact. We heard a shot being fired and started moving in her direction. I then got a short radio call, followed by lots more firing. We ran towards them, and when we arrived, they had taken a position on a porch in front of a church. They were surrounded by a herd of cattle. The animals were doing their best to reach them, even though many had already been gunned down. We attacked from the rear, and between us, we were able to eliminate the entire herd."

"How many animals in total?" Specht asked.

"I never heard an exact count. It was more than fifty, I have no doubt of that."

"Were there any civilian casualties?"

Hudak was grim. "Yes. Again, I don't have an exact number. There were multiple people down, trampled on the street. It was worse than any battlefield I've ever seen. And I've seen some action."

"Was your entire team able to get out?"

"We were fortunate. If there had been many more animals, we would have run out of ammo. That would have been very bad for us. The animals were large and very aggressive."

They turned at a corner.

"It was just down here. You can see the church to your left."

Everything looked normal. *Leave it to the military to clean up a mess*, Collins thought.

"You can't even tell," Specht remarked. He then lowered his voice even though no one was near them. "How is your team now, Captain? Any effects from exposure to the animals?"

Again, Hudak had his grim face on. "No, thank God. Time of quarantine has expired and everyone is well. We were very lucky. We had no respiratory protection because we didn't know what we were dealing with."

"I'm glad to hear everyone is okay," Specht said.

They stopped as a group and stared at the site, each deep in their own thoughts.

"Any other questions?" Hudak asked.

"Have you been called out to any more of these attacks?" Collins said.

"No. I have heard rumors and crazy stories, but this is the only attack I've been involved in."

"You were no doubt debriefed afterwards?" said Specht.

For the first time, Hudak was somewhat reluctant to answer. "Of course."

"Did you get the impression that they knew what was going on here?" Specht figured he wouldn't get much of an answer, but thought he'd try regardless.

"It was all questions, no answers." Hudak gave no indication that more details were forthcoming.

Specht looked back towards where they came from. "In that case, there's just one more thing."

Hudak waited patiently.

"Can you help us place an order at that café we parked in front of?"

Hudak smiled, his face relaxing. "Of course. It would be my pleasure."

"The bureau is buying, so make sure you order something for yourself."

Specht and Collins sat in the rental car, still in front of the café. Specht was in no hurry to drive off.

"I hate doing this, but it's necessary. Give me a couple of minutes." He dialled his boss, pretending to forget about the time difference. He was sure that Peterson was still in bed when he answered the phone. That made him feel better.

"Well? What's next?" Collins asked when he finally hung up.

"Doug the Slug has been busy. Now that he has a better idea what to look for, he's been able to find a number of very recent, very disturbing animal attacks which seem like they either are related to this, or certainly could be. He gave us one to investigate."

"How far away?"

"It happened in Hungary."

"Can you believe I didn't do well in European geography when I was in school?"

"It's a five hour drive from here."

"I can live with that. Who would have thought that I'd ever miss air travel?"

"The incident is rather disturbing. Would you like to be briefed?"

"Can it wait until we arrive? I love surprises."

"No. Do you want to drive? That way I can fill you in on the way."

"Fine." She reached for the handle to open the driver's side door. "At least with me behind the wheel, we'll get there faster."

25

The zoo was closed—a prominent sign said it would reopen in two days. Specht and Collins approached the gate and were checked by a security guard. After giving their story and showing their ID, they were allowed to enter.

Collins hadn't gone far when she stopped in her tracks. "So that's the EcoDome," she said, looking to their right. "I've never seen anything like it."

"It's bigger than I expected," Specht acknowledged.

"I think I want to live in it."

"You might change your mind after we do this interview," he said. "Come on, we're running a touch late."

They were met in the entranceway by a dark-haired woman who was almost as tall as Collins. She appeared to be mid-thirties and was beginning to show the facial signs of a stress-filled occupation.

"I'm Cadena Jovani. I'm afraid I don't have a lot of time to spare you. We're scrambling to be ready to reopen and my slate is rather full. Please follow me to my office."

"Could we walk and talk?" Specht asked. "We'd like to see the actual place where the incident happened if possible."

She hesitated, and then, "Very well. Follow me, if you please."

They fell in beside her. "Forgive me," Specht said, "but it's going to be difficult to do this interview without asking questions that are going to be uncomfortable, or worse, may seem insensitive."

"I've already been put through the ringer," she said. "I doubt you'll ask anything I haven't already answered."

"You've never had an incident like this before, I assume?"

She raised her eyebrows. "Like this? No, certainly not. All zoos have minor accidents, but this was beyond anything I've ever heard of."

"Only one of your elephants was the aggressor, correct?"

"Yes. Hercules, our bull. There were four other animals in with him, but their behavior was normal. They were trying to get away from him the entire time."

"He attacked them as well as the staff?"

"Unfortunately. They'll all recover, but one cow and one calf were injured."

"Bitten?"

"He seemed intent on butting and trampling, not biting."

"Interesting. Has he been tested for the disease?"

"Absolutely. It came back positive for rabies."

"And do you have any idea how he might have contracted it?"

"That's the big mystery. He lived here in the dome for the past five months, even before it was open to the public. None of our other animals anywhere in the zoo have tested positive, at least not yet, nor are there any signs of illness. We have no idea how he was exposed."

Collins had been rubbernecking, checking out the interior of this fascinating building. "We have recently come up with a working theory on how the disease is being passed on, especially to grazing animals."

Their host stopped walking. "If you think there's any chance that you could explain what happened here, then please share."

Collins looked at her partner and got a non-committal shrug. She took that as a green light. "We think birds were involved."

Cadena immediately thought of the zoo's own collection. "These elephants would have had no contact with any of our birds, except those specifically placed here in the dome. And they, in turn, would have had no contact with any of our animals or birds from outside sources. We've been disease free in the EcoDome prior to this. It's quite impossible."

Collins made a show of looking up at the roof of the dome. "Is it?"

Specht and Cadena followed her line of sight. At the very top, a tiny sparrow was flitting around the support structure, some grass and branches visible from where it had been constructing a nest on top of a beam.

"What about her?"

Cadena didn't have a quick answer. "We have a few outside strays. We suspect they come in through the loading dock into the warehouse where all the food and supplies are stored. From there, it's an easy move to get into the main structure."

"Have your staff found any dead ones?"

"None have been reported."

"Would they report it if they did find one?"

"I…suppose not. But I'm not intimately familiar with every operational directive the former manager used. He, unfortunately, was the victim of the attack." By now, they had resumed walking. "If you look to our left, you will see the elephant habitat."

The fence surrounding it was robust, the agents immediately noticed. Beyond was a spacious, clean environment with an artificial stream and plants of all sorts and sizes growing.

"It's very nice," Collins said.

"So, Hercules was able to break down this fence?" Specht asked, marvelling at the very idea.

"Just past where we're standing, there is a gate. Although it is made of the same materials as the fence, the connection points are vulnerable. That's where he broke through."

Specht nodded. He had decided not to ask questions about the bloody attack itself.

Cadena turned so that she faced them both. "Should I have those stray birds caught and removed? Is it safe with them in here?"

"We're not experts in that line," Specht said. "But if you can't think of any other way that the animal could have been infected, then…"

"Oh my. Another stumbling block between us and opening. But, on the other hand, if it would eliminate a potential source of contamination…"

"If you're all right with it, we can see ourselves out." Specht smiled as a final gesture, a sign of appreciation. "You're obviously very busy."

"That's fine. I appreciate your promptness. I have some calls I should be making."

"Thank you for your time," Specht said, releasing her back to her other duties.

Collins was slow to reach the entrance, looking around with fascination all the way out. "You were wrong," she said. "I still want to live in there. I could pitch a tent beside the pond."

"I was thinking of a trailer near the water in Islamorada, myself," Specht replied.

They reached the exit and walked back outside. "Did we learn anything useful?" Collins asked as they strode along.

"This disease is moving by leaps and bounds. It shows up randomly in unexpected places. How long before it gets outside of Europe?"

Collins pondered that disturbing question. "At least the Americas are protected by two huge bodies of water."

"Research that. I think you're wrong."

"That's depressing." She picked up her phone and started to type. She needed an answer to a specific question.

"If birds are the key to stopping the spread, what can we do about that?" Specht asked.

"Well, you can't kill them all. It wouldn't be possible, plus they're essential to our ecology. And their movement can't be controlled."

"We've got trouble. Maybe it's time to go home and talk to some experts. The longer we wait to form an action plan, the more this will spread."

Collins looked at her phone. "Here's disturbing news. The Northern Wheatear, whatever that is, flies from Africa to Alaska and parts of Canada every spring, then back to Africa in the fall."

"So much for isolation."

They reached the car and climbed inside.

"Tired of living out of a suitcase?" Specht asked.

"I'm open-minded on the issue."

Specht hesitated, and then pulled out his phone. "I'm calling Peterson. It's his decision ultimately. I'll update him on what we've found and see what he wants us to do."

"Fair enough. And I'll drive us out of here at a ridiculous rate of speed. Good luck concentrating on your call."

Specht rolled his eyes. "I'll mention that you want a transfer."

26

"Come on, help me!" Antwon had the front of the inflatable raft right where he wanted it, sitting in the water at the very edge of the rocks as waves lifted and lowered it rhythmically. But to get in without losing his grip, or letting the small boat drift away, would be a move he needed assistance to do.

"But it's slippery!" Vyra protested. She didn't want an accident to deposit her awkwardly in the choppy water. Her shoes worked fine on dry land, but on the slippery slope of the surf-soaked rocks, they came up wanting. She had dressed for comfort and to look pretty. A death-defying climb was not on her agenda.

"Here!" Antwon tossed the light, nylon rope in her direction. "Just hold it. I'll climb in and hold it steady, then you can join me."

Vyra picked up the rope, giving it a suspicious glance. Her current boyfriend made an ungainly entrance into the bright yellow raft. He grinned at her the moment he was settled, displaying the physical prowess and confidence that a young man in his prime was likely to do.

"Come on! Just move slowly to the edge. Pull the raft closer with the rope and I'll help you in."

Vyra was imagining how her hair would look if she got dunked. She was a good swimmer—drowning wasn't the issue, it was appearance. Currently, after some hard work in front of the mirror, she knew she looked stunning. Topped off by a cute pair of shorts and a clingy top…she would get stared at no matter where she went today (assuming she could stay dry). "If I fall in, you're taking me back home right now. Do you understand?"

The confidence was still on full display. "Oh, come on. Grow a pair, will you? It will be worth it, trust me."

Reluctantly, she edged closer. "I already grew a pair. Are you blind?"

"I never noticed," he lied, grinning.

She was as close as she could get to the edge. A large wave would get her feet wet from here. She leaned forward, then seemed to think better of it and pulled back. "Now what?"

He extended his hand. "Just climb in. I'll keep you from falling. Do it before it starts to drift away."

She hesitated, calculating the likelihood of success as she measured the distance to the bobbing raft. "You'd better."

Once the decision was made, she threw caution to the wind and half stepped, half leapt into the raft. It was a good thing he was ready for her, as she would have overshot in her enthusiasm to stay dry. Antwon grabbed her just enough to keep her in the boat. "I told you!" he cried, as happy as could be.

Vyra was less enamoured with the successful result. "I'm not doing this again. If you want me on a boat, get a bigger one."

He settled in and lifted the oar. "Stop complaining. Just wait until you see this."

She had heard of the blue grotto. She had some doubts that she would find it to be as awesome as advertised…but at least after today she could say that she'd seen it.

Antwon was working hard to maneuver the small craft as it bobbed and slipped in the surf. He could see the narrow entrance and knew the raft would fit. It was a little too choppy to do easily, however. Some last second adjustments would have to be made, and they might seem concerning to his fussy passenger.

"Don't hit the rocks!"

Vyra was good looking, no doubt. But her self-centered entitlement was getting on his nerves. She wasn't the first girl who had shown an interest in him. A re-think about their relationship might be in the near future. "Relax. We're almost at the good part."

"I hope so." She grabbed the side of the raft as best she could, trying to add more stability to her seating arrangement. "Are you sure we are going to fit?" The edges of the craggy rocks were too close for comfort.

And then, in a mere moment, they were in.

"Told you," Antwon said with no small degree of satisfaction.

Inside was an entirely different environment. The waves and wind were gone. The water was calm and gave off a soft blue color because of the sunlight that filtered in through a submerged fissure. The luminous light radiating from the water made it appear that the sea itself had turned into an enormous, glowing lamp.

Even Vyra was impressed. "It's beautiful," she said softly.

"Did you know tourists are starting to come here?" he asked. "It's getting to be famous."

It was quiet in the cave. The outside surf was a barely audible murmur. Vyra could hear water dripping somewhere inside, but the sound had its charm.

"And do you know what the best part is?" Antwon asked.

She caught the suggestive tone in his voice. "Nobody can see us from here?"

"No!" He feigned mild indignation at the insinuation.

"What then?" she asked, enjoying pestering him.

"The best part," he said in a lower voice, "is how beautiful this light makes you look. You should see yourself right now. Your skin is glowing, just like the water."

This line of conversation was in her wheelhouse, as Antwon thought it would be.

"Really?" This thought obviously pleased her. "Can you take a picture of me? I want to see it."

It had been risky bringing his phone due to the potential of water exposure, but Antwon had gambled. "Sure. Give me a good pose."

She had plenty of experience with that, earned while taking untold selfies since making the discovery that she was good looking. She struck one of her favorite poses.

Antwon took three quick shots, each from a slightly different angle. He previewed them quickly, wanting to show her the best one. If she liked it, she might agree to more pictures. He had been thinking about where her ego might let him lead her.

"Here, check it out."

She accepted his phone. "Oh, that is nice." She continued to overestimate the influence that her looks would provide her. This shot would be a perfect addition to her currently posted photos. *Let's see the other pretty girls match this*, she thought.

She returned the phone. "You should take some more and then send them to me."

This was going exactly where he wanted it to. "Sure. I mean, who knows when you'll ever be here again, right? Might as well take advantage."

"Try this." She tilted her head a certain way, and struck a flirtatious smile.

"That's nice," Antwon said in encouragement as he clicked away. "Maybe I should be your official photographer."

She considered her next pose. "I could use one." She abruptly looked back over her shoulder. "Did you just hear something?"

Things were going too well to allow any distractions. "Nope. There's nothing to worry about in here. Hey, I have a suggestion."

"What?" Her voice was more impatient than intrigued.

"If this blue light makes your skin glow in such a pretty way, you should show more of it."

And there it was. Clunky and predicable, as always. As she considered her response, the sound returned. "There it is again. You can't tell me you didn't hear it."

Now Antwon did. A high-pitched squeaking was coming from the upper part of the cave. He had been in here before, but never heard that. "It's nothing."

A thought flashed across her mind. "What about bats?"

This was all kinds of trouble. No girl was going to succumb to any kind of romantic scenario if bats were included. Truth be told, Antwon was starting to feel creeped out too. "I've never heard of them being in here."

The sound was ramping up. Vyra was looking at the ceiling, eyes locked on the direction of the source. And then, "Bats!"

Antwon looked, and there could be no doubt. They came pouring out of some hidden access point, hundreds of them appearing in the blink of an eye.

"Get me out of here!" Vyra screamed, now in a full blown panic.

We'll be all right, Antwon thought. He had never in his life heard of anyone being attacked by bats. It surely wouldn't happen now. But he was wrong.

The sick animals dropped on them in waves, landing and biting. The small, needle sharp teeth easily punctured flesh, which they started to do with fevered enthusiasm.

Vyra was screaming hysterically, while Antwon was trying to get the raft to move back towards the entrance.

But being bitten, over and over again, proved to be a supreme distraction. New pain and injury was inflicted every second that ticked by. Antwon forgot about paddling the raft—a concept that now seemed completely unobtainable. Instead, he acted on the one cognitive thought that occurred to him in the most trying moment of his life. He rolled out of the raft and submerged in the cool water. He didn't think bats could swim and therefore hoped this might save him from further attack.

Vyra, despite her beauty, was also temporarily forgotten.

27

Specht and Collins were back stateside. Their weekend was spent recovering from jetlag, and moving back into their normal routines. Monday morning found them on their way to a meeting where they would be discussing their findings while in Europe.

Collins gave Specht a critical look as they walked side by side down the broad hallway. "Please tell me I don't look as tired as you do."

Specht fired back out of routine. "Bypassing makeup this morning, are we?"

"Ouch. So, are you prepared for this meeting?"

"As much as I need to be, with my trusty partner by my side. I know you'll step in if necessary."

"In other words, you're planning to hand this over to me?"

"I didn't say that," he responded vaguely.

They reached the door. "After you," Specht said.

Once they got seated, there were five people in total around the table.

"Good morning," Peterson, their boss, said. "You don't know these two gentlemen. To my right is Tony McLaren, assistant director for the CDC, and on my left is Aaron Klein, from the Department of Health and Human Services."

Specht and Collins both nodded in acknowledgment.

"This is Special Agent Robert Specht and Agent Jan Collins. They have just returned from some time in Eastern Europe, investigating this outbreak. Before we start, is there anything anybody needs? We have coffee and snacks coming."

Everyone seemed content.

"Very good. Rather than spending time on a broad overview of everything the agents have seen and heard, I would prefer to have them answer specific questions. Hopefully we can pinpoint our use of time in a way that will be quicker and more efficient. Tony, would you care to start?"

Tony was mid-fifties, carrying some extra weight, and had a perpetual serious look on his face which was being exaggerated by the aging process. He had notes on the table in front of him which he now scanned.

"There's no problem coming up with questions. I think the issue is where to start. How about this—tell us about the interview you had at the lab where this all originated."

Specht organized his response before speaking. "I think the main issue brought forward is the avian component. That was the big, unplanned surprise. That's how the virus escaped from the lab, and seems to be how it is spreading so quickly and unpredictably. As it was not one of the goals of the project, it caught them by surprise."

Tony shook his head. "Sounds sloppy to me, especially for something as fraught with risk as this was."

"As a point of interest," Peterson interrupted, "Croatia is a NATO member. We won't be focusing on any violations of law or treaty agreements in this matter. Our focus is on minimizing the spread and effects of this new virus. It's already having profound economic impacts around the globe. Mitigation is the key and top level government wants answers and advice. Let's stay focused on that."

Tony seemed unruffled by the rebuke. "Do they have a direction, or even a potential plan to stem the spread of the disease?"

"Nothing specific was shared with us. My impression was that the on-site manager at the lab had no idea how to fix it."

"Then let me ask you this," Tony said. "Do we move forward assuming that any sort of resolution is unlikely to come from the source? In other words, are we going to have to fix this ourselves?"

Specht chose his words carefully. "That would be speculation on my part. I would go so far as to say that a quick, effective solution does not seem to be in the workings. I could only read concern and frustration when the topic was brought up."

"Tell us about the spread. Information presented in the media is out of control, so it can't be trusted as a reliable source. How fast is it really spreading, do you think? And aren't mammals confirmed as the primary source? Has there been a single confirmed incident caused by birds?"

"All the attacks on humans, documented and confirmed, have been by mammals," Specht said. "And as you noted, if we want to stay in the realm of what we're certain of, most alleged attacks now being reported simply cannot be trusted. Testing is being performed as we speak on other animals that have exhibited unusual behavior or been involved in an attack. I would anticipate there'll soon be a more accurate answer to your question. But as an unconfirmed theory, my partner and I believe that birds are spreading the virus to these animals that participated in these attacks. We believe they're likely to be the original source."

Tony consulted his notes again. "What about the vaccine? Did you get specifics about it?"

"The fact that it exists is good news," Specht answered. "It is, however, fraught with shortcomings. Firstly, this variant of rabies has a much faster effect on human physiology. The vaccine must be administered within hours of exposure in order to be effective. This is going to cause a lot of issues, even though, on a somewhat brighter note, it can be taken orally. But getting exposed through the air means you probably won't even know it happened and therefore won't seek the vaccine regardless of how easy it is to take. Secondly, it seems to be mutating beyond what they expected. I'm no expert, but I wonder if that will eventually render the current vaccine ineffective."

Tony contemplated the answer for some time before continuing. "This virus can also be transferred through air to air contact, correct? That was the initial intent. Should we not be primarily worried about that? If that's not an issue, won't this be easily containable?"

"You're drifting away from our area of expertise," Specht said. "But I can tell you this. We were told that transmission between two living mammals during normal breathing is fairly unlikely. They claim the virus drops out of the air quickly."

"Is there anything else you think we should know, based on your findings?"

"Isolation is of upmost importance," Specht said. "Animals cannot travel easily from Europe to North America. Some birds do have an intercontinental migration path, which we can't do much about. But if you can keep the birds and animals from coming in through man-made channels, that should go a long way toward containing this. If you can slow the spread long enough, hopefully more permanent solutions can be found in the meantime."

"What about person-to-person transmission?" Tony asked.

Specht didn't really have an answer. "As far as we know, that hasn't happened yet."

"All right." Tony pushed his notes out of the way. "Just one more question. It's perhaps a little less official. What was the actual result of these attacks? Was it as awful as the media says?"

Peterson had the answer, but since he made no attempt to step in, Specht spoke up. "My partner and I interviewed an officer in the Slovenian military. He'd been involved in the first large-scale attack that we're aware of. He told us that the results were worse than anything he had ever seen on the field of battle. I know that's not super specific, but you can draw your own conclusions."

Tony leaned back. "I think that's all I need to get the ball rolling on my end. Thank you, Agents. I appreciate your help."

Peterson looked at the other gentleman at the table. "Aaron, how about you? Any questions for the Agents?"

"No, thank you anyway. I think my end of the conversation will be exclusively with Tony."

Peterson dismissed them and they were both glad for the short duration of the meeting.

"That went well," Specht said once they were back in the hallway.

"What's next for us?" Collins asked.

"We have some reports to write. But you know what? I'd like to visit Doug the Slug. I'm very curious to find out what he's been digging up."

"Excellent! Mind if I tag along?"

Specht almost looked confused by her question. "I was counting on it."

"Wait a minute. You know Doug. We should bring coffee and donuts if we want to get his full attention."

"You're right. Nice to know you're still on top of your game."

"Apple fritter for me," she said.

28

Chessa Radoslovich was chief of police for the town of Zadaril. She stood on the polished terrazzo floor, listening to the sobs and other worse sounds coming from the room where the girl was being treated. No good thing ever came from hanging around a hospital.

"Chief?" A burley deputy handed her a vending machine coffee in a paper cup.

"Thanks."

"Any updates on the girl?"

She shook her head, and then lowered it to take a sip.

"Is she going to make it?"

"It looks that way. Unfortunately, she's facing some recovery time and probably reconstructive surgery on her arms." The girl had been an oozing, bloody pulp when they recovered her outside the cave. If the boy hadn't pulled her out and swam her to shore, she surely would have died. The boy was bitten up too, but not as badly.

"Think it's that new rabies thing?"

"If not, it's one hell of a strange coincidence," she replied.

"So what are we going to do about the cave?"

"It's blocked off for now. Tomorrow, we'll gas it with the most toxic stuff we can lay our hands on. Then some lucky clean-up crew can recover the bodies of the creepy little bastards and we'll have them tested."

"By clean-up crew, do you mean low seniority cops in hazmat suits?"

She smiled in response. "We'll contract that part to professionals. You can relax." This deputy had been hands-on involved in the recovery of the two victims. He had been traumatized enough.

"And what about a vaccine?"

"Apparently all major hospitals have had some delivered in case of emergency. These two have already had it administered. They should be fine."

"That's good."

The chief let loose with a burst of air, a hiss that was easy to hear. "The problem is her appearance. Apparently she was a very pretty girl. She'll have some scarring, that much is certain. But, most of it will be on her arms. At least she's likely to fully recover, healthy and strong, with her entire life still ahead of her."

"Poor thing." The Deputy had an infant daughter at home and was feeling empathetic.

"Looks aren't everything."

"That's easy for you to say, Chief," the Deputy responded. Despite being in her early forties, the Chief was still a very attractive woman. She tolerated only occasional, tasteful teasing about it. She wanted more important things on the minds of her officers.

"Never mind," she said, feeling guilty that the comment still made her feel good even after denouncing such a mindset. She consulted the wall clock. "I was hoping for a late update from the doctor, but it looks like that isn't going to happen. I think the two of us should get out of here."

"No argument from me."

She knew exactly how hard this young man's day had been. He still had blood on his uniform. "That was some good work you did earlier. You won't often have to function under worse conditions. I'm proud of you."

"Thanks, Chief." The Deputy felt a little emotional but kept a handle on it. He respected the Chief and liked working for her.

Looks had nothing to do with it.

Specht found Collins in a friendly conversation with Doug. That was a good sign. Specht was hoping that he would be entirely forthcoming and not hold any information back.

"Here's the refreshments," Collins said, stating the obvious. "Even if their arrival falls under the *better late than never* category."

Specht didn't want to turn the conversation in an antagonistic direction. Relaxed and congenial was the way to go. "I got both of you the same thing…apple fritter."

Doug was already reaching. "Thanks, Specht. I was getting hungry just thinking about it."

Drinks and donuts were distributed.

"I was telling Doug that he should vacation in Slovenia," Collins said after a sip of mint tea. "It's the best scenery I've ever seen."

"If it wasn't for the rabid animal attacks, I might think about it."

Specht challenged himself to come up with something funny to say in response. "Stay away from herds of cattle and outdoor dining venues and you should be fine."

"Not according to my research," Doug said just prior to taking a bite of fritter.

Collins noted that some crumbs were deposited on the lower portion of his handlebar moustache. She decided not to comment. "That's why we're here, Doug. Any way you could give us a rundown of the most recent, confirmed attacks? It would help with the construction of our hypothesis as far as the spread of the disease is concerned."

"Does Peterson know you're down here?" he asked.

Specht decided to handle that one. The fact that he asked the question seemed to indicate that Peterson had placed a lid on Doug's ability to spread any findings about the case. "We just came from a meeting with him. The CDC had lots of questions for us. Your input could help."

Doug jumped to an incorrect conclusion. "In that case, let me wipe my fingers off and I'll bring you up to date."

Doug was prolific at the keyboard, and soon his fingers were flying. "I'll filter out anything that has no supporting evidence to prove it's valid. There's a ton of weird shit out there."

Collins looked at her partner. "Should I take notes or can we commit sufficient information to memory?"

"Let's just listen for now. I don't want to hold up Doug any longer than necessary." He also didn't want Peterson to randomly stroll in and ask them what they were doing there, although it was still arguably work-related.

"This is going to be in no real order. Maybe a little chronological, but don't hang your hat on it."

"We're not worried about that," Specht replied.

"All right. What have we got here? Let's start with elephant attack."

Specht didn't want to derail Doug, but neither did he want to waste time. "We actually investigated that one while we were over there."

"Did you know the animal tested positive for the new variant?"

"Actually, no. We knew it was positive for rabies, and made an assumption. Thanks for the update."

"Next is a cougar attack. Heard of this one?"

"No. That's new to us," Collins said.

"It happened in Croatia. There was a small, privately owned 'zoo' which was really a combination animal park and petting zoo. Anyway, the owner had a cougar in a fenced-in enclosure. Had it for years, apparently. He went to feed it and the cat charged out of its sleeping pen, managed to catch the guy before he could get out, and mauled him to death."

"Oh, gross," Collins said.

"Apparently it was," Doug agreed. "Anyway, the animal was euthanized and has since tested positive for the new strain."

"Do they know how it was contracted?" Specht asked.

"No. Or at least that information hasn't been circulated yet."

"Okay. I felt like I had to ask."

"No problem. Let's see…again, lots here, but not much confirmed. Oh, here's the other good one. This is going to blow your minds. There's a company that takes tourists out on short kayaking trips located along the Croatian coast. They came across a small pod of orcas the other day."

"Orcas?" Specht said. "I wasn't aware they lived in those waters."

"Same thing I thought. So I researched it. Turns out they're very rare, but it isn't unprecedented. The wild thing is, the orcas attacked the boats, flipped them over and killed everyone but the guide, who somehow managed to get back to shore."

"And this is a confirmed case of rabies?" Collins said with skepticism in her voice.

"They actually found one of the animals dead shortly after this happened. They tested it on a hunch and it came back positive for both rabies and the new variant."

Specht had fallen deep into thought. "Killer whales are mammals," he said to no one in particular.

"But how would they come into contact with it?" Collins asked.

Specht was stumped. The idea of birds getting and spreading the disease had been terrible enough. But now this. "They would have to be bitten by an infected animal," he said. "But that would be almost impossible."

"Or eat a dead animal that was already infected," Doug said. "I looked it up. It's a thing. Something like a dead bird on the water's surface could do it."

Specht was remembering the time he and his wife went to Sea World. The orca was the star of the show. Now he was imagining that huge, toothy creature with rabies, crazed and bloodthirsty.

Doug read his expression. "It's the stuff nightmares are made of, that's for sure."

"We asked for it," Specht responded.

"Partner," Collins said, "I think we should ponder this new information while we get caught up on paperwork."

Specht stood up, coffee in hand. "Thanks, Doug. Appreciate your time and everything you do."

"I'll let you know if anything that's super strange and confirmed crosses my path."

"Thanks, Doug." Collins gave him a big smile that he was sure to remember as she walked out.

29

"You know what my problem is?" Specht said from behind his desk.

"How much time do I get for this?" Collins responded. "Because it could take a while."

Specht carried on with his original thought. "I'm looking for an immediate solution. I want this virus thing resolved in its entirety and in the next few weeks, or less, if possible. I'm beginning to realize that's not likely going to happen."

Collins was surprised that his expectations had been that recklessly optimistic. "I don't know what to tell you, partner."

"Sorry, I'm just frustrated at the moment."

"Talking about people being killed by orcas can have that effect," she said. And then, "You know, I think I might understand what you're going through and why."

"Please enlighten me."

"You're conditioned to solve cases that mirror police work. More complicated, maybe. Farther reaching impact, probably. But still having this main characteristic—once you solve it, it's over. Somebody gets convicted, goes to jail for murder, or kidnapping, or embezzlement…or whatever. Then the problem is resolved and goes away. This whole issue is structured completely differently. No matter what we do, or how well we do it, it won't be possible for us to fix this and make it go away—at least not quickly, and certainly not on our own. This is going to end up requiring a drawn-out, inter-agency, multi-national resolution." *If we find one at all*, she thought.

"That way of thinking," Specht said, "carries with it some very demoralizing side effects."

"People dying and economies crippled—I know."

"Then don't you think, with stakes this high, we need to push on with some degree of optimism that this can be resolved in some way, at least partially by our input?"

"I'm sorry, partner," Collins said. "I didn't mean to say that we should give up. I guess what I meant was that we might have to be satisfied moving forward one step at a time. It won't be a one time, hit-it-out-of-the-ballpark resolution."

"I can live with that."

"Good. Can I make a proposal as we stand at this crossroad?"

"I didn't know that's what this was," Specht said. "But sure…why not?"

"Let's put our noses to the grindstone and get these reports written. Then, we can find some flimsy excuse to get out of the office and do what we do best."

"Drink coffee and goof off?"

"Tempting, but no. Let's clear our heads and brainstorm the crap out of this problem. Just no holds barred, free range thinking. Who knows what might appear when our intellects are left to wander without restrictions?"

Specht refocused on his desktop. "I'm in."

The largest of the infected orcas finally succumbed to the disease. Its body washed ashore on a remote stretch of beach in northwest Croatia. A multitude of nature's mechanisms for cleaning up just such a scenario kicked into action. One such participant was the white-tailed eagle that was nesting in the area.

With a wingspan over eight feet, it was one of the largest raptors in the world. Fish and sea birds made up most of its diet, but the gigantic buffet provided by the killer whale was too good to ignore. For several days it feasted from atop the carcass. Other birds tended to give the eagle a wide berth and simply left it to its business. This was one book that *could* be judged by its cover. The massive bird was as ferocious as its hooked beak and sharp talons seemed to indicate. Even surprisingly large animals were not off the menu when it was hunting.

The disease soon began to manifest itself in the bird's fast-moving metabolism. Eventually, enraged by the effects, it killed its own chicks. Then it took to the air, flying aimlessly as its life-clock ticked down towards the inevitable end.

Raul Penulate was one of the rare adults who continued on with the hobby of kite flying after childhood was long passed. He found it to be both fun and challenging. Also, by necessity, he had to be in the great outdoors to do it. Today he was utilizing the stiff breeze to try out his newest kite, a dual-line beauty. With it, he could do spins, dives and even figure 8s. As it was over five feet in width, when the wind gusted, he had to really hang on. Of course, that was all part of the fun.

His corgi, Max, had come with him. They had just arrived, so Max was busy checking out the new environment. Raul didn't know what Max could discern with his ever-active nose, but he was giving the place a good sniff. If he spooked up a rabbit, things would get exciting.

As the kite soared, the sun shone through the lime green polymer, making it glow against the early morning sky. It resembled a miniature version of the kites used by windsurfers. Raul found it fascinating.

The eagle came out of nowhere, its wingspan dwarfing the kite. It descended with great speed and struck it violently. Raul had never seen this before. As the bird disentangled from the kite, it was apparent much damage had been done. The material was shredded and the kite dropped to the ground like it had never been intended to fly.

"Thanks a lot!" Raul yelled skyward, frustrated by the attack. But the bird was dropping again, another target in its sights. Raul felt his blood turn cold. "Max! Watch out!"

The domesticated dog lacked the razor sharp instincts and reflexes of a wild creature. The raptor slammed into it, pushing Max to the ground as its claws curled into the flesh to establish a death grip. Max shrieked as Raul had never heard before. Infuriated and afraid for his pet, he dropped the kite string and ran towards the melee.

"Hey!" he yelled to no effect. "Get off of him!"

It was terrible to watch. Wings beating to keep its balance, the huge bird clawed and pecked at the helpless pooch.

"Son of a bitch!" Raul reached them and without thinking, kicked the eagle as hard as he could. The impact hurt his foot.

Instead of flying off, the bird turned its full attention to Raul. This was a most unexpected reaction and Raul had no idea what to do.

With its massive wings propelling it forward, the bird reached him quickly. It managed to get just far enough off the ground that its claws could reach Raul's thighs. It latched on and dug in, the needle sharp points burrowing into the flesh. The beak was snapping, biting wherever it made contact. Raul had to sacrifice his arms and hands to protect his face. The bony edge of the wings struck hard, like he was being hit with a golf club. Raul might have outweighed the bird significantly, but that wasn't going to help him in this fight. He was already in trouble. And there was no time to think—only react.

He spun away from the bird and ran. Maybe he could draw it away from Max. And maybe, if he was lucky, he could reach his car.

After several encouraging steps, the bird hit his back. It didn't seem as bad as the frontal attack, and Raul kept his footing. Onward he ran, hearing the enraged squawks of the large predatory raptor as it regrouped somewhere behind him.

The eagle hit him twice more before he reached the car, but it couldn't knock him off his feet. Raul yanked the door open and jumped inside. He had no sooner shut it than the bird hit the glass, talons clicking with obvious bad intent.

Raul sat, gasping for breath. He noticed blood, and lots of it, running down both arms. But it wasn't enough to kill him (he didn't think) and now he had the security of an automobile.

"Max!" He fumbled the keys into the ignition and started it. He drove across the grass towards his beloved pet. He could no longer see the terror from the skies.

He pulled up close to the dog, swung his door open, jumped out and scooped Max up as fast as he could. Soon he was once again behind the wheel with his best friend on his lap.

"Hey, buddy, are you all right?"

Max whined, but his tail was wagging. Raul could see wounds and lots of blood, but he didn't think any of them would be fatal.

Come on, pal," he said as he put the car back in gear. "Let's go get you some help."

30

"How did you ever find this place?" Collins asked.

The Italian restaurant was hidden behind a narrow, unimpressive front. Collins would have guessed from the street view that it housed a pawn shop or a fake business where you could bet illegally. Inside were six tables, a modest counter and several plants that looked like they were being held hostage against their will.

But the owners, a husband and wife team, seemed determined to make this experience the best ever. From the moment the two agents walked in the door, they had been greeted like they were long lost friends, or relatives visiting from out of town. They were ushered to their table with a flourish, and drinks were immediately discussed. No alcohol was ordered at that time, but the wife was smiling and winking as if a bottle of wine to go with the meal was a foregone conclusion.

"I didn't find it," Specht said. "A friend brought me here and I've been hooked ever since. Fair warning—they make their own pasta from scratch after you place your order. It'll be the best meal you've ever had, but it won't come quickly."

"For the best meal ever, I can wait," Collins said. "Besides, we're here for another reason. We'll have lots of time to think about our little problem."

"About that," Specht replied. "When you eat here, you'll be the centre of attention. We'll only get short intervals of peace and quiet. It's almost like they put on a show for each individual table. But on a brighter note, by the time we leave, you'll have two new best friends."

As if on cue, the husband walked out of the kitchen, flour on his arms. He smiled warmly. "So, Robert, this beautiful young lady is your partner? Who did you have to bribe to make that arrangement?"

"It was more of a punishment, really. You'd have to know my boss."

"Punishment? No!" He turned his attention to Collins. "Jan, we need to talk seriously." He lowered his voice as if Specht wouldn't be able to hear. "He is too old for you. You need a much younger man, more like me."

His wife breezed past, whacking him on the shoulder as she did. The smile never left her face. "Older men are not so demanding, and they try harder." It was her turn to lower her voice. "Older men will buy you things, Jan. Young men are too cheap."

"Based on experience, I'll be lucky if he buys me a tea," Collins replied.

The husband, Antonio, waggled his finger in Specht's direction. "Don't worry, Jan. We will put this all on one bill and make sure he pays for it."

"Oh, I'm paying for it, you can be sure of that."

The joking went on, and then Antonio returned to the kitchen. The aroma of food cooking soon made its way to the dining area.

"Tell me again about the food," Collins said. "That smell is kick-starting my appetite."

"All the pasta, all the sauces—everything is made fresh from scratch after you decide on your meal, all by hand. The ravioli you ordered will literally bring tears of joy to your eyes. You will find yourself lamenting the meals you could have had here if you'd known about it earlier in your life. This is the real deal."

"I'm getting excited. Why didn't you bring me here sooner?"

"Don't make me answer that."

"I insist."

Specht squirmed and readjusted his position. "Only my best partners ever get brought here. It's not just a meal, it's more like a rite of passage. It's the closest thing to a promotion that I can give a co-worker."

Collins stared, surprise and happiness blended in her expression. "Aww, Robert…that's the nicest thing you've ever said to me. You old softy…thank you!"

The wife, Roberta, walked over. "Look at you two. You're getting along better now, yes? A good meal can do that, you know."

She proceeded to regale them with chatter that ran in all directions, until some new customers walked in.

"Specht, if the food and service is this great, why isn't it busier in here?" The question had started to bother her.

"Think about it," he responded. "It's early afternoon on a Monday. If you want to dine here in the evening, or on a weekend, you'd better have reservations or forget it. Lunch is slow because the food takes too long. People are usually on some kind of schedule, revolving around their return to work."

Collins perched her chin on her hand, her arm supported by the table. She smiled an artificially sweet smile. "Not like us."

Specht grimaced. "Let's hope Murphy's Law doesn't kick in. If we get a call from Peterson, the whole experience will be ruined."

"Don't be so pessimistic," she chided.

Roberta returned, this time focusing on Specht. "The usual, Robert?"

He strained visibly, making a difficult decision. "I can't have a meal here without it. Will Pinot Noir work for you, Collins?"

The smile hadn't left her face since the smell of cooking reached her nose. "Damn straight it will."

Soon two steaming plates arrived. "Enjoy!" Antonio said as he presented them.

Collins bent down and got the full aroma. "Oh my, that smells awesome!"

"Buon appetito," Specht replied, his mouth watering over the spaghetti and meatballs now sitting in front of him.

Halfway through her food, Collins finally took a full breath and let her attention shift. She had being making small moaning sounds of pleasure throughout the eating process. "I can only hope nobody ever brings me here on a date. Between the food and the wine, I'd be apt to make a bad decision or two."

"Just enjoy the meal. I don't need you to regale me about your amorous fantasies."

"You can really talk dirty when you put your mind to it."

A sip of Pinot cut the conversation short, for which Specht was relieved.

Finally, after turning down a second bottle of wine and several mouth-watering dessert options, the agents left, waving goodbye as they went out the door.

"You were right about that place," Collins said as she put on her seat belt. "I could eat every meal for the rest of my life there."

"If you call for a reservation, when you give them your name, they will remember you. They might even guess it's you by the sound of your voice over the phone."

"That's awesome. But how do they make any money in a place that small?"

"You noticed they don't give you a menu? Your choices are given verbally with no mention of the price. If you have to ask how much it is, you can't afford to eat there. Also, they have some very expensive bottles of wine. Be careful what you order or you may get a shock when the bill arrives."

"I can tell you one thing—price notwithstanding—I'm going back first chance I get."

"Make your reservation in advance. Way in advance."

"Too late for this weekend?" Collins asked.

Specht smiled at that. "Holidays book up a year in advance. You should give yourself a one month buffer, at the least, for a normal weekend. If you want to go back, call tonight and take whatever's available. Weeknights are a little easier."

"That won't work. I can't drink two bottles of wine on a weeknight."

Specht shook his head. "I wonder if Peterson should have the company psychiatrist run you through basic screening."

"I wouldn't recommend it if I was you. You'll still have to work with me afterwards."

"I'll take you back to Antonio's again and all will be forgiven."

"I can't think of an argument," Collins admitted. "I do have a question, though."

"Fire away," Specht said as he maneuvered through downtown traffic.

"We didn't fulfil our agenda at all. Not a single word about the virus was exchanged. Doesn't that seem unproductive?"

"No. It was part of the plan."

"You know I hate it when you pretend to be smarter than me. What are you talking about?"

"Pretend?"

A dirty look was the only response.

"Here's the thing. Sometimes, even when you change things up to get a fresh perspective, the ability to brainstorm stalls out. I find that you have to do more—or perhaps I should clarify and say less. Force yourself to think about something different. Clear your mind of the problem. Let the subconscious do the thinking for you, while you enjoy a great meal, as an example."

"You are a world-class rationalizer," Collins said.

"Let's get back to the office before Peterson wonders where we are. A breath mint to cover the Pinot, then we'll go to my office, close the door, and see if the lack of active brainstorming gave us any results."

"If it does, can we go back to Antonio's more often?"

Specht smiled. "In the name of productivity? Talk about rationalizing. But sure, why not?"

Collins nodded. "I'm officially motivated. Let's go."

31

Touring the Eiffel Tower was one of the highlights of Janet's entire life. She wished it could have happened while she was younger, but life doesn't always give you exactly what you want, when you want it. The trip to France, Paris in particular, was for their thirtieth wedding anniversary and had been everything she'd hoped for.

She insisted on going up to the third floor, the smallest one at the very top of the tower, despite her husband John's aversion to heights. He had tolerated it, and those moments spent enjoying the view over nine hundred feet above the ground formed memories they would both keep and recall for the rest of their lives.

The late afternoon tour was followed by an excellent supper at the restaurant located on the first floor. Views were spectacular from their table, and as the sun slowly set, Paris, and the tower itself, lit up.

After an amazing meal and a bottle of excellent wine (she made an effort not to think about the cost), she and her husband John left the tower and went for a romantic stroll along the Champs de Mars. It was a park that had been established over two hundred years earlier, a refreshing strip of green running through the heart of Paris. There was so much to see and marvel at as they walked along. Janet made a point of grabbing her husband's hand, and leaned against him as best she could as they sauntered casually along.

"Do you think Paris is a city where an old gal like me has to worry about being molested?"

"What? What did you just say?"

"You know. Is it possible that I'm going to be ravaged before this night is over? Like after we get back to our room, for example."

"Oh." She caught him off-guard but now things came into focus. "Well, I think Paris is as safe as any major metropolis."

"I'm not sure, darling. Sometimes I'm just asking for it; you know what I mean? What if I was wearing something improper and revealing far too much?"

"I've seen it happen."

"And so you will again."

"In that case, perhaps this would be a perfect time to say happy anniversary, and…I love you."

She smiled. "It is. I love you too."

John was reconsidering his current priority. "Should we walk faster? I'm now feeling an urge to get back to the hotel."

"Are you?" she asked. "Well, that's promising."

"As a matter of fact, if I think about it anymore, walking may become awkward."

"Don't think about it."

He then noticed a man who, by all appearances, seemed likely to be homeless. He was off the walkway, shabbily dressed, staring intently at a flower garden. It was really holding his attention.

"What is it?" Janet asked.

"Nothing. I was just wondering what was catching that man's attention over there. He must be a real flower buff."

"They are quite stunning."

The man took several tentative steps backward, like he had been frightened by something. His gaze never left the plants. John could see nothing out of the ordinary.

"Does that seem odd to you?" he asked.

Janet seemed unfazed. "Typical big city stuff, I suppose. Drugs or alcohol may be involved."

The man took another step back and yelled something at the ground John couldn't make out.

"Is there some kind of movement there?" he asked. "Can you see that? It's right at ground level."

Now Janet was more interested. "What is that?"

The man screamed, took two clumsy steps and fell to the ground. He looked to be struggling, flailing his arms, but John couldn't tell why.

"Stay here," he said.

"John, what are you doing?"

"I just want to see if he needs help." John jogged over on the soft grass.

"Be careful!" Janet yelled after him.

As he approached the squirming, screaming man, John noticed to his surprise that he seemed to be covered with a grey blanket of some sort. Drawing nearer, he saw the blanket move of its own accord. The man was being enveloped by rats—hundreds of them.

John, horror stricken, had no idea what to do. That was when he saw even more of them, moving through the grass in his direction. He stepped back.

"What is it?" Janet yelled.

The poor man was being eaten alive. His grunts and moans were almost worse than the initial screaming. It meant he was growing weaker, succumbing to the attack. More rats were now pouring across the lawn. John made a hard decision and jogged back to his wife.

"What's happening to him?" Janet asked.

"Rats. There are thousands of them. They're eating him alive!"

Janet recoiled. "What? Are you serious? What can we do?"

"Run," John said in a serious voice. "They're coming this way."

She hesitated, so John gently pulled her into action.

"Come on, we'll find a policeman or somebody to tell."

"What about that poor man?" Janet asked.

John hated to think about it. "Let's put some space between us and those rats."

Finding someone who was willing to engage and be of real assistance was harder than they thought. Some of the romance had gone out of the City of Lights.

Specht and Collins had just settled in when Doug the Slug called.

"Listen," he said the moment Specht answered, "I've got a good one for you. It's fresh off the wires. Come to my office."

"We're on our way," Specht replied.

Collins was already on her feet. "What is it?"

"Doug seemed really worked up about something. I think we should hear it."

"Lead on."

In five minutes, they were in Doug's office, door closed behind them.

"Okay," Doug said. "Let me start with a couple of observations. First, this thing is really spreading quickly."

That was the last thing they wanted to hear.

"Where did this one happen?" Specht asked.

"Paris. Downtown, in the touristy area. Right at the base of the Eiffel Tower."

Specht and Collins both processed that information on an imaginary map of Europe in their minds.

"That's the farthest yet," Specht said solemnly.

"Now, before I continue, I have to reiterate that this happened not very long ago. Therefore, involvement of the new strain hasn't been confirmed. But hey, come on."

"What exactly happened?" Collins asked.

"Some poor guy was overwhelmed by a massive wave of rats. They pretty much devoured him based on the preliminary reports."

That revelation made the room grow silent.

"No one else was hurt, but they had to evacuate the area."

"This is getting out of hand, partner," Collins finally said.

"I know." Specht looked at Doug. "Thanks for the update. I'll be thinking of you when I can't sleep tonight."

"That's somewhat disconcerting, depending on how I take it. And you're welcome."

Specht opened the door. "Come on. We've got lots to talk about."

32

The Kamchatka brown bear is the largest species in Eurasia. Thought to be the ancestor of the giant Alaskan Kodiak bear, it lives primarily in the rugged, remote eastern region of Russia.

This particular bear, a male known to the locals simply as *Bolshoi* (which means 'big'), had passed all normal growth expectations, even for this large species. Weighing over sixteen hundred pounds, it towered well beyond ten feet tall when standing on its hind legs. Currently, Bolshoi was concerned only about finding something to eat.

As he scoured the forest floor and sniffed the breeze for any sign of food, he stumbled across something that was new to him.

Alerted by movement, he shuffled closer for a better inspection. There, amongst the leaves and saplings, a red breasted merganser was flitting about. This species of duck was known to have the fastest recorded flight speed of any duck—one hundred miles per hour! But this male wasn't setting any records. Something was clearly wrong…besides the fact that they never land in the forest. Its dark green head turned towards the bear.

Bolshoi had never been attacked in his life, except for minor skirmishes with other bears when he was younger and smaller. He was caught completely unprepared when the duck uttered a strange squawking sound and flew directly into his face. The merganser gave a good account of himself, at least until Bolshoi swatted it with a paw that was capable of killing a moose. He bent his huge head down and sniffed at the twitching bird.

He had killed it, fair and square. And he was hungry. He decided to eat the duck, although it would only be a snack. It didn't take long, but the duck turned out to be quite tasty. Sadly, it didn't do much more than whet his appetite. He shuffled off in search of other food. He had no idea about the virus that he had just consumed.

Peterson looked up from the page he was reading. "This is it?"

Specht assumed he was referring to the size of the document. "We felt it was better to have information flow incrementally rather than wait until it builds up, so it's a little abbreviated."

"I already came up with most of this on my own." He dropped it on his desk. "I have to admit, though, I like the idea of prioritizing development of the vaccine for animals."

"Giving it to wild animals might be impractical," Collins said, "but since livestock is particularly vulnerable, farmers could pre-emptively protect them."

"And in the process, stop attacks like the ones we've already seen." Peterson seemed to enjoy finishing her thought, as if to prove he was one step ahead.

"Exactly. And some of the other traits of the vaccine need to be improved as well."

Peterson looked away, turning his attention back to desktop papers. "Stay on top of this. I'll pass several of these suggestions on."

And take credit for them, no doubt, Specht thought. "Thank you, sir."

He and his partner wasted no time extricating themselves from their chairs and exiting the office.

"Charming and supportive as ever," Collins said, once a safe distance had been reached.

"Don't get me started."

"You're right. Back to business, then. Let's do a walk and talk."

"What's on your mind?"

"A young girl died from the new strain early this morning. It's all over the news. She's the first known human to die directly from the disease."

Specht frowned. "Anybody we're aware of?"

"Her father worked at the lab."

"The pet bird?"

"That's right."

They walked in silence until they reached Specht's office.

"Feel like working independently?" he asked.

"Maybe for a little while."

"It's a good idea. We need time to mull this over. Let's meet later and we'll compare notes."

"All right. Send me a text when you're ready, partner."

Greg Scollard sat in the raised blind, wondering in an abstract manner if he was the first brew master to ever be in this exact spot. Probably, he guessed. There weren't all that many of them around, in comparison to the general population at any rate. His mind then wandered off in a different direction.

A week of hunting wild boar in Russia was an expensive proposition, but it had been on his bucket list and he'd finally saved the extra vacation time. His wife agreed to it, no doubt to stop him from constantly dropping 'subtle' hints and whining. Still, he owed her one. An expensive tropical vacation would be his penance. Could be worse, he supposed.

The promotional videos he had watched made it seem like the action was going to be non-stop; but after two hours, no hogs had yet to appear. His guides, Oleg and Gregor, had warned him to stay alert. When the hogs were flushed out, they would be coming in hot, at an all-out run. Lining up the shot at a moving target, between the trees, would be a challenge and he would only have a few seconds before the opportunity passed. If he missed the shot, he was the one losing out on a freezer-full of pork. And they also promised to rag on him severely if that happened.

He was unaware of it, but there was a good reason for the lack of action. The wild hogs had sharp senses and knew the path that led past the blind was not a safe place to be. It wasn't Greg they were avoiding. There were worse things in the dark woods today.

Greg was jolted out of his daydream by a new sound. It was a soft chuff, a breathing sound made by an animal. He looked around, eyes now refocused, ears straining for any other signal of approaching game. He heard it again, softer this time, less pronounced. Nonetheless, he did manage to figure out one important thing. It was coming from behind him.

He turned. A massive bear head was right there, level with the blind. Bolshoi was so large, he didn't need the ladder to reach the platform. He just stood there, foaming at the mouth.

"Shit!" Greg's movements were choppy and bungled by fear and surprise. The bear's black eyes and menacing teeth filled him with the ultimate terror. His new Weatherby .300 Win Mag fell from his bumbling hands. It could have easily resolved this situation, but was useless lying on the rough wooden floorboards.

The bear lunged with a mighty, blood-curdling roar. It easily sank its fangs deep into Greg's lower leg, then yanked him violently off of the stand. Greg no sooner hit the ground, a process which knocked the wind out of him, than Bolshoi tore into him. Being mauled to death triggered an attempt to scream, but with no air in his lungs, Greg could only wheeze. He died horribly and silently.

When the guides returned, they found a bloody mess. Not only had they never seen anything like it before, they had never even heard of such a thing. On top of all the reasons to be horrified of what had happened, they came to the realization that they would have to call his widow and break the news.

There would not likely be a quick end to the trail of terror caused by the massive bear. He would not succumb as easily as the weaker creatures. His metabolism was unusual, capable of revving up or shutting down if either was of benefit. It would fight the disease, while he raged through the forest. His legacy was about to get a boost.

33

The Babanin family had been running a modest farming operation for many generations. Located along the edge of the taiga forest in the Kamchatka area, crop production was marginal. But in this cool region, the pasture was good enough to raise sheep and cattle. A modest vegetable harvest could be coaxed from the garden with enough hands-on care. Trapping in the cold months, and preserves made from wild berries in late summer and early fall helped to supplement their income. Add it all together and life was possible.

But the Babanin family now had a financial ace up their sleeve. Ivan, the youngest son, had decided to stay home and work on the farm after finishing his education, while the two older sons and one older daughter had made their way westward in search of romance and prosperity.

Ivan was a smart young man, and had done well in the schooling he had received. He knew the farm was struggling, and that there were many unchangeable reasons why. Yet, he felt there must be something else which could be added to their income stream. After some research, he found it.

Samogon is the Russian equivalent of moonshine. With prices of liquor climbing in stores, homemade spirits were enjoying a significant increase in popularity. Distilling equipment was readily available and of good quality. It was illegal to sell samogon, of course—but not to make it for home consumption. This created a bit of a loophole, and production around the country was climbing.

Ivan had everything he needed. There was sufficient space in the big, old barn on their property to set up the operation. He could access local grain with no problem. And a quick, casual survey of the neighbors indicated an interest in the final product.

Since its original inception a short time ago, his distillery had already tripled in capacity. Business was good, and even some of the local authorities became regular customers. Interference from the government didn't seem likely now that they were buying it for themselves, and the distillery brought in income equivalent to the entire revenue generated by the rest of the farm. Soon, he intended to branch out into specialty, flavored liquors that some customers had been expressing an interest in.

Ivan, confident in a brighter future, had started assessing the local girls for a potential wife. He could afford one now.

On this particular morning, Anton, Ivan's father, was first to head out to the barn. There were chores to be done there, and then the pastures needed to be checked. First, out of a curiosity that hadn't yet waned, he walked into the distillery at the side of the barn. He loved the smell, and the look of the shiny metal distillers. He had only a basic grasp of how it worked, but no matter—

Ivan took care of this part of the farm. He enjoyed a brief walk-about, thought everything looked to be in good order, and then exited to get on with his chores.

As he walked around to the other side of the barn, he noticed something was wrong. After a moment, he upgraded his initial response. Something was *very* wrong.

The wooden door had been ripped off of its hinges. It lay a short distance away, broken into several pieces. Anton stood motionless, assessing.

Who could have done this? There were no major population centres anywhere near them. All the neighbors had known each other's families for generations, and got along well. The chances of a random person looking for trouble ending up here was negligible. So what had happened?

Anton stood still, listening as hard as he could for any sound that was out of the ordinary. He heard none. If anything, it was too quiet.

The barn had been built on a raised foundation to keep it dry during times of rain. It had rained two days prior, and there was a low spot that always held water not far from the door. Anton walked very slowly towards it, alternating his view from where he was going, to what he could see through the doorway. He craned his head and looked at the mud settled in this low spot. There was a paw print clearly showing. It was huge and it was bear.

Anton's blood ran cold. He had an old, double-barrel shotgun in the house. It wasn't much to look at, but two shells of 12 gauge buckshot will win most arguments, even with a big bear. That put yet another idea in his head.

"Bolshoi," he whispered. Of course he had heard of the bear, but no one had ever mentioned it causing any trouble for the people in the region before. But something had happened here and there was more yet to be investigated. He decided to risk entry to the barn without the old gun. He felt it likely the bear would be gone now that the sun was up.

He walked ever so slowly towards the open doorway, measuring and carefully placing each step. His eyes focused as much as possible on the interior of the barn, but because of the contrast created by the early morning sunlight, it was difficult to see into the relative darkness.

One step, stop and listen. He repeated the process until he had reached the doorway. He braced himself and stepped quietly inside.

Even in here, he could hear no sound. That was bad. There were three pens to his left. One was temporarily empty, the other two held a horse and a bull respectively and they should have reacted to his appearance. To his right was a stack of bales, both hay and straw. Everything on that side looked normal.

On the left, it was a different story. The door to both pens had been forced open. Fearing the worst, he went first to the horse pen.

The animal lay on the ground, its hide partially torn off, and its side so mauled that organs were sagging out onto the floor. Its head was at an impossible angle…obviously some damage to its neck had occurred.

"Damn." Again, Anton kept his voice to a whisper. Reluctantly, he made his way to the last pen.

The bull had suffered a similar fate. It lay on its side, torn and bleeding. Worst of all, it was still drawing the occasional ragged breath.

Anton had been wrong. He would need the shotgun after all.

34

"You're not going to believe this."

Collins looked up to see Specht in her office doorway. That wasn't too surprising. The look on his face was. He never exhibited excitement or emotion. "What's going on?"

"We've been requested at another high-level meeting."

That wasn't good news. "So why are you excited? Personally, I'd rather take a pass. Can you tell Peterson I'm not feeling well?"

"Are you sick?"

"No! I thought you were more perceptive than that. I just don't want to go to the meeting."

"It's in Paris."

"When do we leave?"

He nodded. "That's better. The plane's getting fueled up as we speak. The meeting is tomorrow morning."

"But, I haven't got caught up on my laundry from the last trip. I'm low on clothes. How long will we be there?"

Specht shrugged. "As far as I've been told, just tomorrow. But that could change, as you well know."

"Then I guess I'm ready whenever you are."

Knowing they would lose some time flying east, they both managed to sleep during part of the flight. Once on the ground, they barely had time to check in to their rooms before leaving for the meeting.

"Do I look or smell like I missed my morning shower?" Collins asked as they taxied towards the address where the meeting was to be held.

"You're fine," Specht assured her.

"You need to hone your lying skills—or at least put more effort into it."

"No one will notice one way or the other."

"Oh, that's way better. So, what's this meeting going to look like? How many people will be there and who will they be?"

"I honestly don't know," Specht said as the taxi rolled to a stop in front of an older looking stone-fronted building. "I expect representatives from a variety of countries. Probably all middle management government officials."

They both exited onto the sidewalk.

"Sounds horrible."

"We'll soon find out." They walked in and asked for directions. After a brief wait, a man approached. He was so broad across his shoulders, Specht wondered how he ever found a suit jacket to fit.

"*Bonjour*," he said in a deep voice. "Follow me, please."

Small talk didn't seem to be on the agenda, so they followed in silence. They took the elevator to the third floor. From there, he escorted them to an open door.

"The meeting is in here."

"Thank you," Specht said as Collins and he entered.

It was a large office, lined with bookshelves on two sides. The far wall was almost completely glass, allowing sunlight to pour in. A long table, with no one sitting at it, sprawled in front of the bookcase to their right. In front of the windows was a single desk. A woman sat behind it. She looked up, analyzed them for a moment, and then stood, smiling as she did so.

"Hello. There are two chairs in front of my desk, if that is not too formal for you. Please, take a seat and make yourselves comfortable."

They both hesitated. "Are we in the right place?" Specht asked.

"Yes, of course. Why do you ask?"

"Are we too late…or too early?"

She consulted a wall clock. "You are perfectly on time. Have these surroundings offended you in some way?"

"No," Specht quickly said. "Confused us, perhaps. We were expecting a larger group, that's all."

"I see. Well, this will be a rather intimate meeting. There is one more person coming, but he will be somewhat late. Would you prefer the table to my desk for seating?"

"Not at all. Excuse my uncertainty."

He and Collins sat, trying to look comfortable. They had both expected to be in a corner listening, while a plethora of government officials argued the day away. Now they were the center of attention.

"I don't believe we've met before. I am Juliette Moreau, Prime Minister of France."

Specht was stunned. "Agents Specht and Collins. I must admit, we were expecting someone a little lower on the chain of command."

"We are of the belief that this problem requires immediate, high level attention. I understand that you two have recently been to both Croatia and Slovenia, correct?"

"We did a preliminary investigation there."

"Then you are exactly who I wish to speak to. May I ask some questions?"

"Absolutely."

"How bad do you think this is going to get?"

That was unexpected and blunt. Specht hesitated.

"That would require a lot of speculation," Collins said, filling in the conversational gap.

"I understand. Our response, to no small extent, will reflect the level of danger this virus presents. There is a shortage of experts in France, at least those who have any first-hand experience. Even speculation would be helpful to us at this point."

"It's the speed of the spread that concerns me," Specht said. "It seems to be jumping over large distances in short time periods."

"Are you aware of our recent incident?"

Are we supposed to be? Specht wondered before answering. "Yes. At least, I assume you mean the rats."

"That is correct. Agent Collins, what are your thoughts on all of this?"

"You mean about the spread?"

"About any aspect. Are you confident that this will soon be resolved?"

"I have hope, but no concrete evidence to support it. Right now it feels like we're trying to carry water with a sieve. I don't think any successful effort has yet been made to slow the spread, let alone fix the original problem."

"And what do you think could or should be done...either of you?"

Collins was happy to let Specht resume talking.

"I think vaccination is the key right now. The Croatian version can be taken orally. I wonder if it shouldn't be manufactured in large quantities, and then have the general population get protected by taking it. It's not an injection, so it would be fairly painless and easy."

"You know what the likely reaction would be after suffering through the same issue with COVID," the Prime Minister said. "Forced vaccination will not be popular."

"It beats getting rabies. And I think we could move forward under the assumption it would only be for a short time until this gets brought under control."

"When and how?"

Specht shrugged. "You should ask a biologist."

"If you could give me any advice at this time, what would it be?"

Specht pondered. "Croatia needs to share every bit of information they have with the European Union and the world. This needs to be a collective solution."

The Prime Minister shifted her gaze to Collins. "And you, Agent Collins?"

"Well, a lot of the spread seems to be associated with domestic animals. They can be vaccinated fairly easily. Farmers already do that on a regular basis. A version of the vaccine for that purpose needs to be manufactured as quickly as possible also."

"Do you both agree that birds are the likely cause of the swift expansion of the disease?"

"I think it's self-evident," Specht answered while Collins nodded.

The Prime Minister shifted the direction of their conversation. "I spoke to your supervisor a short time ago—Mr. Peterson."

This can't be good, Specht thought.

"He has agreed to have you participate in a joint French/American operation. I have assigned a French agent to go with you. We need answers. We need them to be complete, accurate and confirmed."

"We're at your service," Specht said.

"Good," she replied. "The real meeting is happening this afternoon. You don't need to attend. It will be full of posturing, bluffing and hedging of bets. Information will be exchanged, deals will be agreed upon—but to know what is truth and what is fabricated...that will be open to interpretation. I need you to supplement any information put forth, and also confirm or deny its veracity.

You already have contacts. I will ensure that you will have full access to whomever and wherever you need."

They were interrupted by a soft knock on the door.

"Ah, here is you new, temporary partner," the Prime Minister said, looking quite happy about it.

Specht and Collins, while keeping their feelings to themselves, felt somewhat the opposite.

35

The cab seemed infinitely more crowded than before. Specht sat behind the driver's seat while Collins, next to him, occupied the middle. On the passenger's side sat the French agent, Andre Gagnon. Collins hadn't been able to find a seating configuration that precluded her from rubbing shoulders with him.

"*Pardonnez moi,*" he said in a smooth voice. "Agent Collins, is it? I seem to be making you uncomfortable."

"Not at all," she lied. "You're fine. I'm just not used to being so close to my partner."

Gagnon's age was a bit obscure. He had a significant bald spot in the center of his head and the rest of his hair was salt and pepper in color. Both of those traits could make a man look older than he was. But his face had no lines, his features were pleasant enough, and his teeth were perfect. Overall, not a bad presentation. Best of all, at the moment, he was casual, friendly and relaxed.

"Once we pick up our rental car, I can drive and leave you two with lots of room in the back."

"We'll rotate driving to make it fair," Specht responded. "But I may have to warn you about my partner's driving habits first."

"No, no," he said, waving off Specht's concern. "I live in Paris, and the drivers here are all crazy. I'm sure it will be fine."

"Your English is excellent," Collins said. "That makes things easier."

"It is the most widely spoken language in the world. Many times it makes my job easier. I am currently learning Chinese."

"That could come in handy at some of the restaurants I like," Collins said.

Gagnon nodded. "*Duo xie.*"

Collins smiled. "I appreciate the effort, but I don't know if you're being polite or telling me to pound salt."

"In that case, English it is."

They pulled up to the rental agency and left the cab behind. Collins wasn't sure how to respond when they discovered that they had been booked into a minivan.

"We shall have lots of room," Gagnon said.

"Hopefully no high-speed car chases," Collins added.

"Wait a minute—isn't your personal car a Prius?" Specht asked.

"And it really flies," Collins responded defensively.

Gagnon stepped forward. "Please, allow me to sign for the car and get the keys. I believe it was my government that made the arrangement, so why don't you two relax and let me take care of this."

Collins watched him walk towards the counter.

"Initial assessment?" Specht asked.

"He seems okay. Polite, for sure. Not the typical arrogant Frenchman I was expecting."

"I wonder if he's thinking something along those lines about us," Specht said.

They were soon loaded up and ready to go. Gagnon ended up behind the wheel due to his familiarity with the city of Paris.

"Enjoy the sights," he encouraged.

Collins sat beside him on the passenger seat, while Specht, suffering from jet lag, ended up in the back and was soon snoring.

"Is this your first time in Paris, Agent Collins?"

"Yes. The problem with work travel is that there's no time to see the good stuff."

"It is a beautiful city. I sometimes think the planners did a better job two hundred years ago than they do today."

"There's nothing like a period of rapid industrial expansion to mess things up."

He didn't respond, as he was maneuvering onto a busy, six lane highway. Once established in a suitable position, Collins once again commanded his attention.

"How long have you been an agent, if you don't mind me asking?"

"It's no secret. I've been working for the bureau for six years, four of them doing outside investigations, three of those working with my current partner. How about you? How long have you been doing this kind of work?"

"Forever and a day, I think," he said, followed by a rueful smile. And then, "Forgive me cynical attitude, Agent Collins."

"As long as we're in a casual environment like this, just call me Jan."

"Short for Janet?"

"Janice."

He nodded. "Jan it is. I regret to say my name isn't conducive to a short form. Andre I was named by my parents, and Andre I'm still called."

"I can make up a nickname for you, if you like."

"Should I trust you to do that?"

"Definitely not. Unless your feelings aren't easily hurt, that is."

"Then you will be Jan and I will be Andre."

"I think that's best." Collins was momentarily distracted by some interesting architecture as several older buildings went past.

"So, tell me, Jan," Andre said, "What have you and your partner learned about this virus?"

"Not nearly enough. I can give you the condensed version. It won't take long."

"Would you, please? Perhaps I can learn something that could help with this case."

"It started in a research lab in Croatia. A military experiment, designed to weaponize the rabies virus, went awry. The new virus accidentally transferred to a bird, which they didn't plan or anticipate, and it consequently escaped out into the natural environment. From there it spread surprisingly fast, resulting in some horrific attacks.

"As of now, we know it's in Hungary, Slovenia, Italy—and of course, France. Our research guy tracks it daily, and I wouldn't be surprised if it hasn't spread beyond that.

"There's a vaccine which apparently is effective. It can be given orally, which makes things easier as well. The problem is the speed factor. This disease establishes itself much faster than the original virus. The vaccine must be administered within hours of exposure in order to be effective. And with the possibility of airborne transfer, a person may not even be aware that they've had contact."

"So no reason to get the vaccine," Andre said.

"Exactly."

"Can you tell me about the attacks?"

Collins asked herself the same question. If they were working together with the blessing of their boss, she couldn't see any reason not to.

"A herd of cattle stampeded into a quiet little town in Slovenia and trampled a number of people to death. The military actually got called in on that one. Then, a waiter at a restaurant in Rome was gored to death by three wild boars that had caught the disease."

"How could that happen in a restaurant?" Andre asked.

"They had an outdoor dining area. Apparently it's not uncommon to see wild hogs in Rome."

"*C'est horrible.*"

"And then there's your incident with the rats."

"*Oui.* Nothing to be proud of."

"I'm sure there's more. As a matter of fact, let me check in with our *guru of the gruesome* and see what he's turned up today."

Andre turned towards her briefly. "I'm not sure if I should thank you or not."

"Just doing my job," Collins replied.

"In that event, *merci.*"

36

"You still with us?"

Specht sat up, trying to resist the urge to rub his eyes while his partner stared. He finally gave up the struggle. "I am. I've been working on a cure for jet lag, apparently." He looked around in an attempt to reorient himself. "Where's our new French friend?"

"Andre had to take a call. And we needed gas anyway, so here we are."

"Anything noteworthy happen while I was out of it?"

"I got an update of the macabre nature from Doug. A couple of young people were chewed up by bats in a cave."

"Are they testing positive?"

"The bats, yes. The kids got vaccinated in time."

"Where did this happen?"

"Croatia."

"Hmm. Well, if there's any good news in that, at least it's not indicative of another big jump geographically speaking."

"I wouldn't get too excited. Doug's tracking all sorts of weird things all over the place. They just haven't been confirmed yet."

"Should I ask what the furthest one away from the epicentre is?"

"I don't recommend it. Here, have a pastry."

Specht accepted it. "Where did this come from?"

"Andre bought some a while back. You slept right through that little maneuver."

Specht smiled. "On a first name basis now, are we?"

"We're working together," Collins replied. "So why not? It's an effort in diplomacy."

A little defensive, Specht noted, planning to retain that for future reference. "This is good," he said as he took his first bite. "I suppose if you want a man who knows pastry, make sure he's French."

Andre returned to the van and resettled behind the wheel. "Anybody else want to drive?"

They didn't.

"I just got a call from the Prime Minister. Our immediate agenda has been set."

"And what exactly is it?" Specht asked.

"We're off to Croatia. We will visit the lab where this all started and talk to the on-site manager. We will get an update on the various alterations being done on the vaccine. Then, we report our findings."

"And after that?" Collins asked.

Andre started the van. "I don't know, Jan. They are, as you say, *still working on it*."

They arrived early at the lab after a long night of driving. Specht got out and took a few tentative steps.

"I need to stretch, amongst other things."

Collins seemed to have come through the ordeal in better shape. "Once again the signs of advanced aging manifest themselves. It's hard to watch."

Andre walked around the back of the van. He stretched his back and then rolled his head. "Don't worry. I suffer the same malady."

"Thanks for the support," Specht replied. "Maybe if we stick together we'll stand a chance against her."

"Against Jan? No, not necessary. She is too nice."

Specht frowned. "Don't be fooled. You're going through the honeymoon phase right now, so to speak. As soon as she gets comfortable around you, the truth will come out."

"I can't believe it," Andre said with a smile.

"If the two older gentlemen would be so kind as to grab their walkers and follow me, we can get this show on the road," Collins said from around the other side of the van.

"Told you," Specht added.

"My, my."

The trio walked into the lab, ready for the interview.

The interview had gone as expected. A few updates had been revealed, and at least that had value. As things wrapped up, Andre leaned in extra close to Luka, the manager.

"Listen, outside of the official interview, I wonder if I can ask you a question of a different nature."

Luka just wanted this to be over. He was, however, still trying to be polite. "How can I help?"

Andre lowered his voice. "Do you have a shower room here? We have driven straight from Paris and need to freshen up and put on some clean clothes."

"We have several emergency showers used for exposure to dangerous substances. They would work, I suppose."

"Is the water heated?" Collins asked.

"It should be comfortable enough. The only problem is that they're out in the open. They need to be quickly and easily accessible in case of an accident, you see."

That was a show none of them wanted to put on.

"Wait. I have an idea. Please give me a moment. I'll be right back."

Collins was hoping this was going to work out in their favor. "Great idea, Andre."

"Some labs have showers to avoid carrying contaminates on your skin or clothes," he said.

Luka returned quickly. "Good news." He had made a deal. "There is a shower in one of the labs that is not being used today. It's at your disposal. I will inform our employees that the room is off limits until you are finished and also ensure the door remains locked. Will this be satisfactory?"

Andre couldn't keep from smiling. "Yes, thank you so much for this, and all of your other cooperation."

Luka turned toward the door. "Follow me. I will show you the way."

"I'll grab all of our bags," Andre said.

"We have towels here," Luka added. "You may use them."

Collins was walking in a position that indicated she would be the first to use the shower. "I feel better already."

It was a refreshed group that settled back into the van. Collins was behind the wheel this time. Andre had volunteered to sit in the back.

"I feel like a million bucks," Collins said. "Now, if we could find a four star restaurant…"

"Let me report in first," Andre said. "Then we can find somewhere to eat." He exited the van again for some privacy.

"I vote we let the French guy choose," Collins added.

Specht opened his door. "I'm getting a call from Peterson. I'll be right back."

Suddenly she was alone in the van. "That was unexpected."

Andre was the first to return. "That part is done."

"What now?" Collins asked.

"I think we're about to find out," Andre replied, reading Specht's expression and body language as he returned to the van.

"Good news and bad news, folks," he announced.

"What's the good?" Collins said.

"We'll soon be out of this rental van."

"And the bad news?" Andre said in a sombre voice.

"We're headed to the nearest airport."

37

Specht gave them a briefing as they drove along.

"Really? Russia?" Collins didn't seem thrilled. "I've never flown Aeroflot before."

"The plane will be fine. Don't worry." Andre spoke as if from experience. As always, he seemed completely unconcerned. "But I'm not familiar with the airport where we will be landing."

Specht handled that one. "Andyra Airport is in the eastern Kamchatka region. It's a combination military and commercial setup. It's in good shape as far as the runway is concerned, but there won't be a lot of people coming and going—at least compared to the American airports we're used to. Anything you might want to purchase will probably be in limited supply."

"Kamchatka?" Andre had a hint of concern in his voice for the first time. "Something has happened there? That is a long way from here."

"And not far from Alaska," Specht added.

Collins, now driving, tried not to get distracted. "The new virus has jumped that far? Has that been confirmed?"

Specht frowned. "I know I don't need to say this, but I must relay what Peterson told me. It's a small miracle that Russian officials have agreed to let us come in and investigate. None of this must ever be talked about outside the three of us. If it somehow leaks, it would constitute an international incident that could have negative consequences on our relationship with one of the most influential countries in the world."

Andre didn't act offended. "Of course. Understood."

Collins nodded. "I'm in."

"Good. The rest, however, is bad. Let me start with the original incident which led us to this. It began with an American who was vacationing in the area where we're going."

"Who vacations there?" Collins asked.

"The area is well known for hunting and fishing charters. This man went there to hunt wild boar. They're prolific in the region, and grow very large. There are several companies that organize hunting expeditions."

"You would be surprised," Andre added, "but wild boar is delicious."

"The two guides got him situated in a raised blind. From there, all he had to do was shoot a hog when it runs past. The guides take dogs, find the hogs and drive them toward the hunter. The worst thing that can happen is that the guy is a crappy shot and misses. Normally, at any rate.

"On this day, there is no shooting. The guides return and find the hunter on the ground, torn to pieces. Based on tracks and other evidence, the killer was a bear. Based on other evidence, the bear was enormous.

"During the clean-up and investigation process, the local coroner, who, like everybody else in the world, is now aware of the new rabies variant, gets ambitious and has swabs taken from some of the bite wounds. These are tested and come back positive."

Collins was astonished and confused. "How did it ever get there? How far away from here would that be?"

"That's not good news either," Specht admitted. "It measures out at nearly five thousand miles."

Collins was incredulous. "That's impossible! Five thousand miles through rough territory in a country where borders are protected and in this short amount of time? Why isn't there a trail of confirmed transmission between here and there which explains the movement?"

"All valid questions. And all reasons why we need to go and investigate."

"Partner," Collins asked, "how far is this place from Alaska?"

"A lot less than five thousand miles," he said.

"How much less?"

"Under a thousand."

"Can we assume the water will act as a buffer?"

"The Bering Strait," Specht replied, "is only fifty miles across at its narrowest. And we don't yet know how it jumped to Kamchatka so fast. If it was on the wings of a bird…we're in real trouble."

"How far is this place from the airport?" Andre asked, more familiar than the others with Russian topography.

"That's another issue," Specht admitted. "It's a long way, through mountains and forest."

"So what's the second portion of this plan?" Collins was not optimistic that she would like what he said next.

"It'll be another first for all of us, or at least I'll make that assumption on Andre's part. Aeroflot also has helicopters in their fleet. There will be an Mi-26 waiting for us. They'll fly us in to the camp where the attack happened."

"This is getting exciting," Andre said, sounding like he meant it.

"And how long will we be staying at this hunting camp?" Collins asked.

"Overnight. Peterson had to give them a definitive time and he wasn't sure how long we'd need to do our investigation. This was the best guesstimate he could come up with on short notice."

"So…we'll be sleeping where? Please don't tell me on the ground."

Andre held up his hand, as if volunteering to answer a question during class. "They will have cabins, or at the worst, large heated tents. They tend to feed people well, and they will have vodka, count on that."

"Sounds almost civilized," Specht said.

"Almost," Collins muttered more or less to herself.

"If we are lucky," Andre continued, "we may get to eat some wild boar."

"Look," Collins said, "If these guys didn't see the attack or the bear that did it, how are they going to help us?"

"The coroner is coming out to meet us. He may have something helpful to say." Specht fought off a desire to sigh out loud. He needed to maintain a positive outlook. This was important, and it was his job. "It's our responsibility to come up with good questions. Try to play along, Collins."

"Excuse me if I think somebody has to be pragmatic."

"Jan," Andre said in his smooth, unflappable way, "Don't worry. I have done these kind of excursions before. I would bet you twenty euros that you'll have a wonderful time. It may be rustic, but it will be the kind of fun you can only have when you go back to nature. If our hosts are agreeable, I will cook the supper meal. I bet an additional twenty euros that you'll love it."

"I'm not sure what I can buy with forty euros, but I'll be happy to take your money. Should we shake on it?"

Andre needed a brief moment to filter her response through his knowledge of English. "Oh, no. Not necessary. We have a valid verbal contract; your partner is the witness."

Collins now seemed distracted from her negative feelings about the upcoming trip. "Hope you brought cash. I don't want to start breaking fingers or anything like that."

"I would dislike that as well," Andre replied.

Specht sat quietly now, content to observe. He liked the way Collins responded to this man. And he respected how Andre could sense what needed to be said in order to get her back in a good frame of mind. *Maybe he's not so bad, after all*, he thought. And then, *I hope nobody gets offended if I don't drink straight vodka.*

38

Frank and Madeline Fisher were celebrating their first anniversary. They'd been together for nearly forty years and married for thirty six of those—but that wasn't what they were celebrating. It had been exactly one year since they both retired from their individual jobs, a noteworthy event coordinated to happen on the same day.

Frank had a walking mail route and Madeline had been an elementary teacher. They created a stable, middle income life for themselves, but now—with their children grown and the two of them firmly ensconced in the arms of both private and government pensions, they were in the process of fulfilling a life-long bucket list item. They were touring England, top to bottom and side to side; particularly interested in visiting the lesser-known places. The costs tended to be less, crowds smaller and they got to see things they didn't even know existed.

Today, they woke in the Regent Royal Hotel, located in the town of Stauffer. Notably, it was the easternmost point of the entire country of England. They walked a short distance to the pier, which ran out over the waters of the North Sea. They picked up a tea and a scone and meandered along, listening to the gulls cry and the waves break along the shore.

"This is nice," Madeline said.

"And we're the only people here," Frank added.

They had tickets for a play at the Marina Theatre later that evening, and a reservation for supper at a highly recommended restaurant. Other than that, the day was theirs to enjoy without agenda.

"Are we driving or walking, once we start exploring the town?" Frank asked.

"A bit cool for a long stroll, isn't it?"

"We're out over the water now, after all. Probably more cozy inland."

"I don't want to catch a chill."

Frank knew it was time to compromise. "Driving it is."

"You're a sweetheart," Madeline conceded.

"It must be true, everybody says it."

She gave him a casual swat that only becomes acceptable after reaching a point of extreme familiarity. "None of the people I know do."

"You're obviously hanging around a lower class of individuals."

"Debateable."

"Agree to disagree."

"The very definition of debateable," she replied. And then, Madeline pointed with her free hand, tea safely held in the other. "See that?"

Frank looked and he did. "A bit early for migration, wouldn't you say?"

"I don't know, but regardless, that's a big flock."

A mass of birds was moving across the water, nearly black due to the sheer density. It expanded and contracted with no real pattern to the movement, undulating in a strange rhythmic manner. It was hard to tell how big the flock really was, as the distance between them was uncertain. Individual birds were indistinguishable in the dark blob.

Madeline had a friend who was into the hobby of birding. "You know who would love to see this? Mary Elizabeth."

"Oh yes. She's bonkers over this sort of thing."

"Take out your phone and get a picture of it. We can send it to her later."

Frank was willing, but not thrilled. "Fine. I'll gulp down my tea, first."

After scorching his throat, he pulled out his phone and braced his arms on the railing. "Might as well get a steady shot."

"I still can't tell what they are."

The flock was moving in their direction.

Frank zoomed in as he looked at the viewfinder. "I hate to disappoint, but I think they're just starlings."

"Oh, is that right? Still, to see such a big group is rather intriguing."

"I'll take a video of them as they fly past. That might be a better presentation than a photo."

"You're a good lad," Madeline said.

Frank made a last adjustment to the camera. "I've been trying to tell you that."

Rather than respond, Madeline stared, eyes riveted on the approaching flock. "They're going to fly right over us," she observed.

"Yeah." Frank was now feeling a little uncomfortable for the first time. Shouldn't they be veering off? They weren't very high, either. He waved one arm in the air. "Hey, we're right here. Piss off!"

"Frank!" Madeline seemed shocked by his outburst. "Don't say that. You'll get it on the video. Mary Beth will tease you for the rest of your life."

The birds were now closing fast. Frank hadn't heard them make so much as a single squawk.

At the final moment, the sound of thousands of small, beating wings could be discerned hissing through the air. *That is so odd*, Frank thought, and then they were upon them.

They immediately enveloped both of them, covering them with a blanket of living birds. Pecking furiously, they attacked every inch, whether clothing, hair, skin or individual features like ears, eyes, nose and even lips.

The experience for Frank and Madeline was like falling into a vat of acid. Everything hurt to the point of utter distraction, and they lost contact with every thought except for the pain. If not for the rail, they would have both fallen into the sea below. As it was, they soon toppled over and lay squirming in agony on the walkway. The birds, seemingly satisfied with the results of their attack, flew towards the beach and then moved on into town.

Anything that moved became a target, and was overwhelmed by sheer numbers. The town would be under siege for hours before they moved off and flew further inland. They left behind a trail of pain, injury, fear and confusion.

It was an attack unlike any that had ever occurred there before. And the day wasn't over yet.

39

Flight 446 from Heathrow was a 737 MAX with one-hundred-and-eighteen passengers aboard. It was a short flight, and as it approached Norwich International Airport, landing conditions were perfect. The setting sun was still providing enough light for unlimited visibility, and winds were light.

The co-pilot was flying the aircraft, while the Captain kept his experienced eyes on everything that was transpiring. They had turned final and were losing altitude rather briskly, but completely according to plan. The runway lay open before them, and there was absolutely no indication that the worst air disaster this airport had ever seen was now moments away.

"Landing gear down," the pilot said. "Flaps are set. Altitude looks good. Let's not spill any drinks."

"Shouldn't be a problem," the co-pilot replied.

As the plane dropped below a thousand feet, a black cloud rose up towards them. They were now less than thirty seconds from touchdown.

"What the fuck is that?" the co-pilot asked, concern apparent in his voice. The black blob was large and already blocking their approach.

"Turn us away," the pilot said briskly. "Abort landing. Go around."

"Roger." The plane, however, was sluggish at this speed and flap configuration.

"More throttle!" the Captain urged. "Turn, don't climb!"

The co-pilot had his hands full. "Shit! We're going to make contact!"

Thousands of birds were all around them. Dozens began to get sucked into the two engines. The windshield was being pummeled.

"What do I do?"

The Captain reached for the yolk. "I'm taking back control. Give me full throttle."

Alarms were now buzzing. "Both engines are out!"

At this altitude and speed, that was an issue from which they couldn't recover.

"Try restart!" the Captain screamed.

He couldn't see through the windshield. A quick glance at electronic instrumentation gave yet more bad news. By now, they had drifted over a residential area.

The Captain never swore in his life, but his last words were an exception. "Oh fuck."

The plane plowed into a row of houses at a little over two hundred miles per hour as the passengers screamed in horror. An enormous fireball immediately engulfed the entire area.

The end results were all too predictable.

"You see?" Andre asked. "The plane is both safe and comfortable, no?"

Collins sat beside him, 'enjoying' a window view. Specht was in the aisle seat directly across from them.

"It's fine if you don't talk about the in-flight meal or movie options."

Andre turned to Specht. "Is she always like this?"

"Yes," he answered with an enthusiasm she didn't appreciate. "I thought it was just to annoy me. It's somewhat comforting that you're suffering the same fate."

"Keep talking like that and you'll both learn what suffering really is."

"Perhaps," Andre suggested, "we could discuss sports or the weather instead."

"No offense," Specht replied, "but I'm going to get some sleep. These eastern flights are killing me."

"A good idea." Andre looked around for an attendant. "I think a relaxing drink is in order first."

"Make it two," Collins said. "Then we can all pass out."

"Vodka and orange juice?"

"Sounds perfect. I'll try to mellow out my attitude in exchange."

Andre, as always, remained calm. "Two screwdrivers it is."

Collins couldn't help but be disappointed with the Andyra Airport. The landing had been smooth, and it had everything a traveller needed—as far as she could tell. But it looked shabby, like a cheap knock-off of a real airport. There were abandoned aircraft strewn here and there on the grass and remote paved areas, and others that were optimistically positioned while waiting for replacement parts and service. The workers were friendly enough, but all seemed to be covertly preoccupied with sneaking off to have a smoke or nap or something.

Inside, at the approach to the lobby, was a stuffed bear assuming an aggressive, upright position, teeth bared and claws extended.

"That's appropriate," she said.

Andre went to the counter, and returned soon to announce that the chopper was almost ready for them.

"Should I risk buying something to eat here?" Collins asked.

"Have you travelled in Russia before?" Specht asked Andre, not knowing the answer to her question.

He was noncommittal. "If you lower your expectations a little, everything is fine."

"A pack of gum and a chocolate bar should get me through. I want to stay hungry for eating all those wild animals later."

"You're funny," Andre replied as she walked off.

"Would anyone here speak English?" Specht asked.

"I don't know. But it should be fun to watch her order and try to pay. We have no rubles. They might not want euros here."

"Will a credit card work?"

"Probably."

"She'll figure it out."

"I speak a little Russian. If she gets in real trouble, I'll bail her out."

It wasn't long before they were being escorted to their waiting chopper. The Mi-26 was a big machine, with room to move equipment and supplies, and an eight blade prop overhead.

"Are we delivering elephants as a side-hustle?" Collins asked when she saw the size of it for the first time. "I could use the extra money."

"It's designed for military use," Specht said. "It was adapted to commercial applications."

The formerly open back area was now rigged with several rows of seats. They didn't look comfortable.

"At least we're not sitting on the floor," she said.

"It might be loud," Andre warned. "Anything you want to say, perhaps should be done now."

Collins took advantage. "I'm asking for a raise when this is over. Can I count on your endorsement, partner?"

Specht shook his head. "How about I retire and you can take over my job?"

"Are you kidding? Do you think I want to start every working day thinking about you at home, drinking coffee and reading the paper in your pajamas? That would be torture for me."

"But you make it sound appealing from my perspective," Specht said.

The engines began to whine as the turbines spun up.

"Did you know this thing generates twenty-two thousand horsepower?" Andre asked.

Collins shook her head. "I doubt the question ever makes its way onto Jeopardy."

"Have a good flight, both of you." Andre began the process of buckling in.

"What's the safety record of this thing?" Collins now had to yell for her partner to hear.

Specht had no idea. "Outstanding. Relax and enjoy the flight."

Collins looked at the seat with distrust. "How could I not?"

40

The chopper ride was loud and full of vibrations. Specht found the seat unsuitable for sleeping and suffered through the two hour flight fully awake. The most interesting thing that happened the entire time was Andre undoing his straps and walking up to the cockpit area. That was surprising, but nothing compared to the fact that he carried on a long conversation with the pilots, much of it spent laughing as if they were exchanging jokes.

"I thought English was your second language," Specht yelled when Andre returned.

"I work throughout Europe," Andre said. "I pick things up along the way."

"I pick up loose change when I drop it," Collins responded, "Not foreign languages."

"Europe is diverse—what can I say?"

"Learn anything of value?" Specht asked.

"We will be landing shortly. The pilots were able to talk to the hunting guide on the radio. He is at the base camp, waiting for us."

"Is the coroner there?"

Andre shrugged. "It never occurred to me to ask."

I guess you're human, after all, Specht thought. "No problem. It doesn't change our itinerary one way or the other."

The chopper tilted to one side.

"This is our approach," Andre said, settling back into his seat.

A minute later, all sensation of movement stopped. A gentle bump heralded contact with the ground. As the turbines began to wind down, Collins was already out of her straps.

"Let's get out of this thing."

Andre opened the side door, and waved at the pilots. They returned the gesture.

"Okay, we're good. Let's go."

They were in the midst of a large, grass-covered area. All around the perimeter was forest, towering trees as far as the eye could see. To their right was the camp. A large tent had a stack protruding out of the roof from which a lazy plume of smoke issued. A big man was walking towards them as the helicopter flew off. He raised one hand and waved.

"*Privet!*"

Andre turned to his companions. "Shall I handle this?"

"Please do," Specht said.

After a brief conversation, the guide broke out in a smile. "I speak English, yes. Many clients have it. I am Oleg."

They all exchanged handshakes. Oleg's eyes lingered longest on Collins.

"You are agent too, no?"

"Proficient in shooting and hand-to-hand combat, so don't get any ideas—I don't care how long you've been out in the bush."

Oleg looked stunned for a moment, but then burst out laughing. "Oleg likes you. You are kick-ass American girl. You should hunt boar since you are here. You know, we eat the heart. Then you are legendary hunter for life. It is better when raw, yes?"

Collins looked slightly nauseous. "I'll pass."

Oleg looked to be in his forties. He hadn't shaved recently; bathing was an issue as of yet unresolved…they hadn't gotten close enough to know. He had a prominent nose that was just off-kilter enough to suggest that it had been broken sometime in his past. He looked a little rough, maybe ex-military—certainly at home in a barroom brawl. But he clearly liked what he was doing and had a good sense of humor. "So, tell me. Where are you from?"

"I'm French," Andre answered. "And these two are American."

"No, no. I mean, where are you from today? The place from where you came, you know?"

"We started in Paris and it gets kind of blurry after that," Collins said.

Oleg raised his eyebrows in surprise. "Paris? You come a long way." He showed sympathy to their situation. "What do you need? Food? Drink? Rest? Maybe a walk to stretch out?"

Collins was starving. "What do you mean by food? Do you have anything that comes from a box or can, rather than a fresh animal corpse?"

Andre intervened. "This is Russia, and the boonies to boot. Your suggestion might not be as good as you think."

"Then what do you have in mind? I have to eat. We all do."

Andre curved his right hand and tapped himself in the chest with the tips of his fingers. "I am French. I am a man. I can cook."

He got some puzzled looks, one of them from Oleg.

"Oleg, my new friend, would it offend you if I used your kitchen to cook some food?"

Oleg smiled. "Less work for me? I am okay with that."

Andre actually looked a little excited. "Show me what you have."

Oleg gestured for all of them to follow. "Come. You can cook—you can drink—you can sit or lie down and sleep. I will share Russian hospitality now."

The tent was quite spacious. Mats were placed on the ground inside. There were no walls but different areas could be determined by the furniture, storage and overall layout. Heat from the small stove made it feel quite cozy.

"Sit," Oleg offered. "Would you like drink maybe?"

"Too soon for vodka," Collins said. "Do you have anything non-alcoholic?"

Oleg took a few steps and opened the door to an old looking fridge. He pulled out two bottles of water, and then gave them to Specht and Collins.

"Where do you get your power from?" Specht asked.

"If you look southeast, there is road not far. You can hear if big truck goes by. New power lines follow road, so now, we have power too." Whether the hook-up was professional and legal or not wasn't part of the conversation.

Andre opened the lid to a chest-type freezer, hinges squeaking loudly as they moved. He leaned in and rummaged before emerging with a package in his hand.

"This is an excellent start," he said. "Oleg, do you have any spice, or sauces…anything like that?"

Oleg checked out the frozen package. "Good choice. Soon we will see if you can cook." He pointed to a free-standing cupboard. "Look in there."

Andre did. "We're in business," he declared.

"You can cook on hot plate, or stove. You see pots and pans hanging, yes?"

As Andre busied himself in the 'kitchen', both Collins and Specht decided to lie on a cot, just to check it out for comfort.

They were both snoring within minutes.

41

Collins woke and rediscovered her appetite. She had been dreaming about food. A tempting aroma was wafting through the tent.

Specht was already up. "I knew you wouldn't sleep through a meal."

Her hopes for some decent food had just sky-rocketed. "Andre, what've you got there?"

"Meatballs in a spicy-sweet sauce over a bed of rice."

"In that event, just one more question…is it ready?"

Now he was smiling. "Yes. Allow me to make you a plate. Oleg, can you be in charge of cutlery?"

The big man was soon handing Collins a knife and fork. "We may keep Andre here as camp cook, I think."

Andre served Collins first, a steaming plate with a good-sized serving.

"Should I ask what kind of meat this is?" she said.

"Think about where we are," Andre replied.

She scrunched up her nose. "Not wild boar?"

"Try it," was all he said.

She had to—it smelled awesome. She cut a meatball in half with her fork and placed it tentatively in her mouth. It was mild and sweet. With the sauce and rice as accompaniments, there could only be one conclusion. "Andre, this is delicious!"

He was serving Specht as she delivered her positive review. "Thank you, Jan. A chef always likes to be complimented."

She was too busy eating to respond.

They had just finished their meal when a man walked through the flap at the entrance to the tent. Oleg hailed him with a wave. They had a brief conversation in Russian.

"This is Dr. Volkov. He is here to answer questions."

Specht walked over and shook his hand. "Thank you for coming. We appreciate your time."

The doctor nodded but that was the only response.

"He speaks no English," Oleg said.

"I can interpret," Andre volunteered.

"I will clean up then," Oleg offered. "After all, you cooked."

The four remaining people sat in a makeshift circle on folding chairs.

Andre spoke in Russian for nearly a minute. After the doctor responded, Andre switched back to English. "He says he will tell us everything he knows. He will talk a little, then pause so I can translate. Will that work?"

"Perfect!" Specht declared. "Thanks to you both. Please proceed."

The doctor spoke and even though neither of the other two agents could understand a word, they enjoyed the rich sounds of the language.

When the doctor finished his presentation, and Andre had translated, he made one last brief comment directly to Andre.

"He wants to know if you have any questions."

Specht thought it through. "Is this is the only attack he's aware of?"

Andre continued to act as the doctor's voice once he had finished speaking. "Yes."

"No other incidents of unusual animal behavior?"

"He says that is not his line of work, but none have come to his attention."

Specht nodded. "How about you, partner? Anything come to mind?"

Collins had been listening attentively. "Nothing that he would know the answer to."

Andre thanked the doctor on behalf of all of them, and then dismissed him to return to town…wherever that was.

"Did anything that he just said help us?" Andre asked.

Specht had been thinking about the same question. "He confirmed some things, and that has value. But the big questions, I'm afraid, are still unanswered. What we need as much as anything right now is to know how it spread here so quickly."

Collins stood up from her chair. "I think we know the answer."

"Keep talking," Specht encouraged.

"If the timeline for the accidental release of the virus that we know is even close to being accurate, there's only one way it could have been brought here so quickly. It must have flown here on an infected bird."

Specht nodded. "That might make sense, but leaves many other questions. For example, if it was transported here that way, how did a bear in the middle of nowhere catch it? Bears don't have birds on their diet, and I wouldn't think an animal that big and dangerous would allow a bird to peck away at it."

"If the bird died and the bear stumbled across it…he might eat it."

Specht fought some mild frustration. "I suppose they eat carrion. But what are the odds?" He turned and looked over his shoulder. "Oleg? Can I ask you a question?"

Oleg, just finished with his cleanup, strolled over. "If you want to know about vodka supply, it is good." He stuffed an unfiltered cigarette into his mouth.

"Well…no. But tell me this. Have you noticed any strange bird behavior? Or maybe seen sick or dead birds around this area?"

"No, I have seen nothing like that."

"Did you, after this attack, try to track the bear?"

He nodded. "My partner and I try. Tracks went straight off and just kept going and going. We had to turn around."

"How far can a bear like this one travel?" Specht asked.

"As far as he wants. He is king of forest. Perhaps all the way to Moscow."

"How big was it?" Collins said.

"I answer any question for you." There was a joking tone to his response. "This bear was very big. Client was in blind when attacked. No claw marks on ladder and blind is eight feet off ground. So, the bear was reaching him by standing."

"He reached over eight feet up?" Collins asked.

"Easy, yes."

"How big do these things get?"

"Kamchatka bear…very big."

"Okay. No walks in the forest for me," Collins said.

Oleg shook his head. "They not bother you. Just stay away. They fear people, yes? They know what hunters do. But…"

"This was a very dramatic exception to that rule," Collins said.

"This time different. It was sick, yes?"

"The woods are not as safe as you might think," Collins said. "Especially now."

Specht decided to step in. "With what we know about this virus, and how fast it works, I think it's a fair assumption this animal is either incapacitated, or dead by now."

Oleg snorted. "That is a thing we cannot change. Now, how about a drink, my new friends?"

42

Bolshoi wasn't dead. He was suffering—but not yet incapacitated.

All sub-species of brown bear hibernate in winter weather. Despite their size and strength, there simply isn't enough food available to sustain them. So, they find a safe, suitable den of some sort, get comfortable, and sleep the cold away. Once things begin to thaw out in the spring, the bear awakens and restarts its normal life.

During hibernation, the bear's respiration, heartbeat and temperature all drop. The reserves of fat are sufficient to sustain it until it can resume hunting and foraging.

This virus had put Bolshoi's metabolism under severe stress. As the massive beast stumbled through the trees, nature made a decision for him. Confused and angry, the bear nonetheless responded to the urge to bed down and hibernate, even though the season was wrong. The changes brought on by hibernation would make life difficult for the virus, maybe even impossible and conceivably save the bear's life.

He eventually found a den previously used by another bear and unceremoniously claimed it for himself. He settled in as best he could and was soon snoring.

Evening had fallen, blanketing the forest in a blackness which is only possible with complete isolation. There were no city lights here to add a glow to the sky. The moon and stars, when available, filled that role.

The four had gathered in a loose circle around the stove, talking and laughing—bringing life to new relationships that would likely and unfortunately dissipate forever when the helicopter returned the next afternoon.

Specht's phone rang; the sound of technology foreign in this place. He looked at the screen and didn't recognize the number.

"Excuse me," he said as he got up and walked over to exit the tent. He stepped outside and was immediately rattled by the inky darkness. "Specht here."

"Yes, hello. This is Luka Karmic. From the lab, you remember?"

"Yes, of course."

"We have been continuing with our research. We discovered something today. Something new and unexpected. I feel compelled to tell you."

Specht thought he heard a stick break somewhere in the direction of the trees. With the image of the giant, rabid bear in his imagination, he fought to ignore it. "I'm listening."

"We were asking the question about how the virus became transmissible to birds. The answer was somewhat elusive, but the research led to another breakthrough."

"And what was that?" Specht asked.

A pause made Specht wonder if the signal had been dropped. But then, "If birds can get it, what about other classifications? So we tested fish, reptiles, amphibians…even insects. Results are only preliminary now, but so far it seems that none of them can."

"Thank God." Specht had been terrified of the direction the call was going.

"Except one species of reptile."

Specht forgot about the forest sounds. "What do you mean?"

"In the lab, but not yet in real life, it seems there is some acceptance of the virus to cells of the order crocodillia."

"It can be spread to crocodiles?"

"It hasn't yet been confirmed. I would only say that the virus continues to exhibit qualities we didn't expect."

"That's stunningly bad news. Anything positive? What about the vaccine?"

"We're working on that. Breakthroughs are not likely to happen this fast, unfortunately."

A thought flitted through the back of Specht's mind. *It's the end of the world as we know it…*

"Are you still there?"

"Yes. Thank you for the update. Keep working on it."

"Have a good evening, Special Agent Specht."

He disconnected the call and stared at the phone in disbelief. When he walked back inside, it didn't take long for the other two people who worked in the spy business to see that something was wrong.

"I don't like the look on your face," Collins said. "Did you miss a payment and your Netflix got cut off?"

"Let's just say it's not good news. But it isn't confirmed yet, so I would suggest we ignore it for now. I can't see how additional stress could help us with our challenges."

"You see?" Oleg said. "Oleg lives in the woods and has no troubles. The world blows away and I won't even know. I will be sitting by fire, eating wild boar and drinking vodka, just like tonight."

"And smoking cigarettes made from scraps found in a landfill, by the smell of it," Collins added.

"Actually," Specht said, "I think I'm ready for a shot of your famous Russian vodka."

Collins nearly fell off her chair.

Oleg held up one finger in a universal *just wait* gesture. "I have surprise for you. It might be better for American taste." He walked over to a storage cupboard and rummaged around. When he returned, grinning, he held a bottle full of brown, not clear, liquid.

"Is that what I think and hope it is?" Specht asked.

"Scotch," Oleg confirmed. "A gift from a client."

"Not the poor chap who was killed by the bear?" Andre said.

"No. This one went happy back home."

"I'm in," Specht confirmed.

"I'd love some myself," Andre added.

"Two shot glasses." Oleg looked at Collins. "What about you, pretty agent lady?"

"I'm sure there's a rule about not mixing vodka and scotch."

"Oleg has not heard of it."

"Well, it's more of a guideline, really."

"Three glasses?"

"You Russians can really negotiate."

"Oleg will be the best host, tonight." He went to the narrow counter to get glasses and pour on a stable surface.

Andre reached inside his jacket and pulled out a small case. "If you're drinking scotch, you should consider a cigar to go with it." He pulled out a slim, elegant smoke. "I'm definitely having one. How about you, Agent Specht?"

"Let me do a quick calculation. Okay, my wife is about five thousand miles from here. I'll chance it."

"If you tell me you didn't offer because I'm a girl," Collins said, "I'm going to stake you out in the grass as bear bait."

Andre smiled. "Forgive me. As I am unsure if you are serious or not, let me just say, of course you are welcome to partake."

Oleg returned and distributed the glasses.

"Would you like a nice British cigar?" Andre asked.

"Only one way for Oleg to know." He swapped a glass for a smoke.

Andre passed around his fancy lighter, and then everyone settled in.

"A toast," Andre proposed. "To international cooperation, and my new drinking friends."

"*Za lyubov'*," Oleg exclaimed as he raised his glass.

Andre snickered, raising Collins' suspicions.

"What does that mean?" she asked.

"In the interests of maintaining international relations, I'm going to pretend that I don't know." Andre raised his glass in her direction and took a sip.

"You're all on dangerous ground." She took a puff and managed to look elegant doing it.

"What did I do?" Specht asked.

"Remains to be seen," she said. "But as a good agent, I'm always proactive."

At that, Specht had another sip.

43

Despite their unique and unusual appearance, giraffes are one of the most graceful and photogenic animals in the world. When Ray and Andi decided to book a safari in W National Park, they did not expect to see one. The Northern Giraffe had been, by all accounts, absent from the park for some time now. It was clinging to existence only in small, remote pockets outside of the sanctuary.

The 'W' in the park's unusual name originated from the shape of the meandering Niger River that formed part of its border. Although not widely known to the outside world, the park actually covered a massive four thousand square mile area split between the countries Niger, Benin and Burkina Faso. An abundance of wildlife called it home. Andi had suggested this location as it wasn't as busy as some of the better known parks. Ray, not a fan of crowds, readily agreed. At the very least, it would be an adventure. As he was now in his forties, and this was his first trip to Africa, he was up for almost anything.

As long as they had fun doing it.

Their guide had been driving slowly along a dirt trail, scanning the gently rolling hills for noteworthy animals. But it was Andi who saw them first. She grabbed Ray by the arm.

"Ray, look at that!" She pointed to be sure that he would see them.

"Giraffes? I thought there weren't any in the park."

The driver turned around. "You see them?"

"Yes! Can we get closer for some pictures?" Andi was vibrating with excitement.

"Of course," the driver agreed. "But don't make any sudden moves. And don't yell. They won't be used to having people around."

"Is this common?" Andi said.

"No," the driver responded. "I've never seen them here before."

Andi gripped Ray's arm for the second time. "Ray, there's three of them!" She forced herself not to raise her voice, but the excitement was evident.

"One's a calf!" Ray was now equally excited. "We need to get some shots of this before they spook off."

"I hope my battery is good," Andi lamented.

They approached at a snail's pace, trying Andi's patience. They both started taking pictures using the telephoto option.

"Two adults and a calf," Ray said in disbelief. "How lucky are we?"

"Oh, my battery is over half," Andi said while consulting her display screen. "I'll take video, you take stills."

"Roger, Captain," he said with a slight sarcastic edge. He would still allow Andi to push him around. He'd been head-over-heels about her since they met three years ago. So far, the flame was still burning brightly.

"Ray, look!"

The mother and calf had started to run. The larger male was not far behind them.

"Did we scare them?"

Ray didn't think so. "No. They're actually coming toward us."

Their driver turned around to face them. "I'm going to stop. Maybe you can get pictures as they run past."

"If they keep coming this way." Andi was still in disbelief over their luck.

They stayed the course. Mom and calf were close together; the male was trailing behind but was gaining on them slowly.

Something suddenly changed. The male stopped chasing them. The cow and calf now veered away from the safari truck and ran past a short distance away. Andi pointed at the bull. "I think something's wrong with him."

He took several sideways steps, stumbling to the point where it looked like he would fall over. He recovered his balance, and stood with his head hanging close to the ground, swinging in a pendulum motion. His mouth foamed as he stood.

Ray and Andi had heard of the new rabies variant. This animal's condition looked very much like it was infected.

"I think we should go," the driver said after a moment's contemplation.

"Wait!" Andi was thinking furiously. "Get a picture of it foaming like that. People need to know this is happening here."

Ray did so.

Andi leaned closer to the driver. "What about using your gun?"

He looked shocked. "Yes, for emergencies. Self-defense only."

"You're going to let it suffer? What if it attacks the calf and mom? What if it spreads the disease throughout the park?"

He hadn't thought about that. "But I can't." A charging lion was one thing, but if he shot a protected species like a giraffe in the park, and it turned out not to have the disease, he would be fired, and possibly face jail time as well.

The male giraffe raised his head, settled his eyes upon them, and then charged without any other warning.

The guide seemed to develop second thoughts about using the gun. He fumbled with the straps that held it in the rack behind his seat.

"What should we do?" Andi asked.

"Stay in the truck!" the guide yelled.

Ray recognized the kind of confusion caused by extreme duress. "Just drive away!"

The guide now had the gun, freshly extracted, in his hands. Why hadn't the driving option occurred to him? He hesitated between the two choices. The indecision proved to be fateful.

The giraffe, even with some unsteadiness in his gait, reached them quickly. He lined up with the front driver's side seat.

The safari vehicle was a pickup truck that had the original roof and doors removed. In their place, a hard top roof on four metal pillars had been installed for protection from the sun. The sides remained wide open to allow for unimpeded viewing. After all, the guides were armed and since the animals in the park were used to visitors, they ignored the vehicles.

The big male giraffe kicked with a very long front leg and hit the guide on his shoulder. The impact almost knocked him out the other side of the vehicle, breaking bones and crushing flesh in the process. The gun fell and was forgotten as pain and fear took over. The guide knew that giraffes were capable of killing lions.

The big male tried to give him another kick, but the roof now protected him. It couldn't quite reach. The gangly beast shuffled sideways to access the back seat.

Ray, sitting on the far side, knew what was about to happen. He grabbed Andi and yanked her as far as he could to his side. The hoof lashed out and just missed making contact. The giraffe made a grunting sound, and then lowered its head.

"Come on!" Ray yelled as he continued to pull Andi away from the immediate danger.

"What are you doing?"

He pulled her completely out of the truck, while the big giraffe's head extended into the vehicle, attempting to reach her. It swung around wildly, horns clanging into whatever they made contact with.

"Climb under. Hurry!"

The truck sat high enough to allow for driving off-road. They both dropped to the ground and scrambled under.

"Watch the exhaust!" Ray warned. "It's going to be hot."

They both disappeared under the vehicle, careful to pull their feet and arms all the way in. They could hear the giraffe still thrashing about inside the truck.

A new set of feet hit the ground. The guide had decided to follow them. Unfortunately, in his befuddled state, he dropped onto his injured side as he prepared to crawl under.

"Yeaaa!" He rolled unto his back and tried to lift his injured side with his good hand, leaving himself exposed and announcing it with his screams.

"Ray, help pull him under!" Andi hissed.

As Ray wiggled into position to do that, a large hoof crashed down on the guide's fully exposed head, crushing it with a sound that was both sharp and wet. Andi would have nightmares about it for the rest of her life. Ray, despite the warnings in his mind, couldn't stop himself from looking. After all, maybe there was still hope and it would be worth the risk of pulling the guide under the truck. His head was destroyed, his face distorted into a Halloween mask visage, and blood intertwined with other internal parts oozed out onto the sandy ground.

The attack continued. Hooves struck again, pounding and crushing what remained of the man.

Ray turned away from it, refocusing on Andi as she sobbed. "Shh, stay quiet. It can't see us or reach us under here."

"What can we do?"

Ray wasn't sure but felt like she needed to hear something encouraging. "Wait until it's over. We can see its feet, so we'll know when it leaves. Then we'll drive ourselves out of here and back to the park office."

She continued to sob. "But, what about him?"

"Don't look." Ray could still hear the sound of hooves pounding flesh. "I'll try to pull him into the back seat, okay?"

It was going to be a gruesome task. Ray was already steeling himself and building resolve as best he could.

"I'll try," he repeated.

44

Oleg was up and fussing in the tent. His actions resulted in noise, and that resulted in the agents waking up. Sunshine was already illuminating the canvas walls. The time for sleeping in the Kamchatka woods was over.

Collins sat up, swinging her feet onto the ground. It was obvious that Oleg was tending to something on the stove. "Is that breakfast I smell or are you planning to waterproof your boots?"

Oleg smiled as he continued to slowly stir the pot. "I will miss you, pretty agent lady. You make Oleg smile."

She stood and stretched. Sleeping on a cot was apparently possible if you're tired enough. "That wasn't an answer." She walked over to investigate. The pot was filled with a cream-colored gruel. She recognized the smell. "Oatmeal?"

"Good way to start day," Oleg affirmed. "I have powdered milk, orange juice and I will put on pot of coffee."

"Sounds great," Specht piped up as he arose.

"Brown sugar?" Collins asked.

"We have it."

Andre was now upright. "Is there any protocol for the order in which we use the outhouse?"

"First come, first go," said Oleg, still smiling.

"Ladies first?" Andre suggested.

"Here's an agenda suggestion," Collins replied. "The men go in any order that suits them, and I'll hold it until I get to my apartment back home."

"We could be here for days," Specht said, knowing she wasn't serious.

"I'll deal with it. Mind over matter."

"You can go in woods, if you prefer," Oleg said. "But I would say, watch for poison ivy."

"And bears," her partner added.

"Pass. Thanks anyway."

"This is ready," Oleg announced as he stepped away from the pot. "Come. Help yourselves."

In the fresh air, even oatmeal tasted good. As they ate, Specht voiced a question.

"Oleg, I want to tap into your hunting expertise."

"You want to hunt boar? You make reservation, come back again and Oleg will take good care of you."

"That does sound like fun, but I think my days of tramping around in the woods are behind me now."

"No, no. Oleg does tramping. You sit, enjoy nature, then shoot boar."

"I'll ask my wife. For now, I do have a question about animal behavior."

"Oleg will answer."

"The bear that killed the hunter…I know you tried to track it and the trail went on too far, correct?"

"*Da.*"

"From what little I know, I would speculate that by now, the animal is either dead or incapacitated by the virus. Do you think there is any chance that it could have moved back in this direction before it died? Would it be possible to find it this morning before the chopper picks us up?"

Oleg didn't seem enthusiastic about their chances. "Oleg does not know, how do you say…what makes animal do when sick. Why would it come back?"

Specht had no idea. "Would it remember the hunter and return to see if anybody else was here?"

"Oleg doesn't know. Sorry."

"Can you show us where it happened? Who knows—maybe there will be some sign of it."

"Oleg will show you, yes. First, coffee."

That suited Specht just fine.

Andre looked at Specht while they finished eating. "What are you hoping to find out in the woods?"

"Almost certainly nothing. It's a shot in the dark, that's all. A way to kill the last few hours before we fly out of here."

Andre nodded while he ate. "Fair enough."

"I feel like we came all this way, and really didn't get any information to justify the trip, or improve our situation. Maybe a little more effort on our part and fate will reward us."

Andre nodded again. "I think I understand."

"You do?"

"Too much scotch last night."

Specht laughed. "Thanks for some motivation."

"For what?"

"To prove you wrong."

Andre finished his last spoonful of oatmeal. "I'm happy to help."

The woods were dense enough to make walking a chore. Fortunately, a path had been worn over time due to the repetitive journeys to the blind. Oleg led while the rest followed in a weaving line.

Collins pushed a thin twig away from her face just in time to avoid a scratch. She peered up at the sky, looking like it was being held in place by the towering trees. "It's like a unique microclimate in here. There's no wind at all."

"I think if we weren't walking and talking," Andre said, "there would be no sounds either."

"It is quiet because we are here," Oleg replied. "You would be surprised at the forest sounds when people leave."

"At least I haven't seen a mosquito yet," Collins said.

"Come back in spring," Oleg invited. "They will fly off with you, never to be seen again."

"No spring hunts I take it?" Specht asked.

"*Nyet.*"

As they walked, Specht allowed his thoughts to wander. He didn't expect to see the bear, but was hoping for any signs of how the disease might have been spread. That kind of information would add real value to the trip.

Fifteen more minutes went by, everyone stepping along on the soft mulch. Oleg stopped without warning, turned his head slightly like he was looking at something beside him in the leaves, and stood motionless.

Collins gave Specht a *what's up with him* look, to which Specht shrugged in reply.

Andre was the first to catch on. "Maybe it's not so quiet after all," he whispered.

Specht and Collins strained, and then they heard it. It was distant and faint, but there was no doubt that a sound was being generated by some living thing. It was too erratic to be mechanical.

Specht stepped slowly closer to Oleg. "What is it?" he whispered.

Oleg looked puzzled. "Ducks, I think."

"You have ducks this time of year?"

He was noncommittal. "Some, yes."

"Do you have them in this exact spot usually?"

Oleg slowly shook his head. "No."

"Can we take a look?" Specht asked.

Oleg turned to face him. "If you want. You are boss."

"Do you think it's a good idea?"

"Oleg would like to see."

"That settles it. Where are they?"

Oleg pointed. "There is pond this way. Not far. Follow me, okay?"

Specht turned to the others, unsure if they had heard the conversation. "Side trip. Follow the big Russian."

Collins looked concerned. "Bear?"

"No. Ducks."

Puzzled, but relieved, Collins joined in the march.

"Duck for lunch would be amazing," Andre said quietly, unsure if it was safe to speak at full volume.

As they walked along at a steady pace, the sound became more pronounced. Soon, it transitioned into a full-blown racket—a chaotic, ear splitting cacophony of squawks. It sounded like a stadium full of ducks rioting because their team lost due to a bad officiating call.

"Is that normal?" Specht asked, sensing they were close.

Oleg used the interruption as an opportunity to check the readiness of his rifle. "No. Not normal."

"What is it, then?"

"Maybe something attacks them. Maybe that is why they make so much noise."

Specht immediately thought of the bear. "Do bears do that sort of thing?"

Oleg was ready to continue the approach. "No. But, what is normal now?" He started walking again, this time slightly hunched over, his profile closer to the ground. He was walking slowly, methodically—all the while keeping his vision laser focused on what was ahead. The others followed in similar fashion.

It wasn't long before they could see movement through the branches of the trees. A blur of flapping wings and streaking bodies heralded the source of the noise.

Their approach almost ground to a complete halt, maximum stealth now the priority. They snuck past the last tree trunk, emerging from the low branches, and stood exposed and unprotected.

The area above the waters of the small pond looked like a tornado had picked up a thousand ducks and whipped them through the air in a bizarre melee of feathers and bodies, punctuated by loud, crazed squawking. Specht looked and couldn't see the source of the mayhem.

"What's causing this?" he yelled at Oleg.

"I don't know," he yelled back.

Collins stepped up beside her partner to facilitate communications because of the noise. "Should we be here?" she shouted at her partner.

"Maybe we could step back into the shelter of the trees and watch from there."

Oleg heard and turned to face them. "That is good idea. Get back behind some branches, okay?"

They all hunched over and took shelter under the lower boughs of a large pine. From there, they continued to watch the spectacle unfold. Collins whacked Specht on the shoulder to get his attention, and then pointed, grim-faced, to the edge of the water directly in front of them.

"See that?"

A duck had fallen out of the swirling flock and landed on the grass at the edge of the pond. It was injured, and flopped and flapped desperately to no avail. Other ducks were flying past it, pecking at it as they did. One landed on top of it and began a furious barrage of snapping and hitting it with its wings.

"Why are they doing that?" Collins yelled.

Specht had already come to a conclusion, although he wasn't absolutely certain. "Rabies?" he asked at full volume.

She blanched before his very eyes. "If it is, we're way too close. I'm not sure I want to watch this anyway."

As if on cue, a solitary duck flew into the branches in front of them, flapping its wings feverishly in an attempt to reach them. The needles on the pine branches thwarted the aerodynamics of the wings and the bird fell awkwardly to the ground, flailing as it went.

Even Oleg was shocked by that. "We need to pull back. But only use the big pines—we need branches to keep them from flying into face." He pointed to another tree about fifty feet away. "That one! We will go together, yes?"

They were all in agreement.

"Run!" He led the way, moving surprisingly fast for a man of his size. Motivation was a wonderful thing. Some scratches were accumulated in the process, but they all got into the shelter of the branches without contact with the birds. They watched and listened as the chaos continued over the water.

"This is insane," Collins gasped.

"Is this the disease we are chasing?" Andre asked.

"At a guess, I would say yes," Specht answered.

Oleg met his gaze. "This is it? The sickness that makes you crazy?"

"I think so, yes."

"What do you want Oleg to do now?"

Specht thought about the answer. "We should go back to base camp. I'll see if we can get the chopper to pick us up later than planned. We can come back before we leave if things settle down and have a good look at the scene."

"I heard the word *leave*," Collins said.

Oleg nodded. "Leave is good. Follow me."

45

The chopper was postponed by a day. The agents had one more night to spend in the Kamchatka woods. And Oleg had one more day before he would need his facilities available for the next paying client, a fortunate coincidence. He was hoping the ducks disappeared before the client arrived.

It was early afternoon. The day had turned out to be beautiful and they were all sitting outside, enjoying the views and sounds of nature. Collins was visualizing her next hot shower. Without warning, the flock of ducks came pouring out from over the tree tops and flew directly over their heads.

Oleg held out his hands, fingers splayed in the universal sign for *don't move*.

They all sat silently, frozen in place. The birds sounded as chaotic as they did at the pond, making violent contact and squawking in protest. But they flew past without incident and eventually were out of sight.

"That was interesting," Andre said, breaking the silence.

"I wonder where they're going," Collins said.

"Hopefully not Alaska." Specht had never looked so grim.

"Do you know this species, Oleg?" Andre asked.

He nodded. "*Da*. I know Russian name for them."

"Do they stay around here all year?"

"*Nyet*. Water freezes here in winter. They fly south."

"Not to America?"

"I think not, but not sure. And these are crazy ducks, so…"

"Who knows?" Andre finished his thought.

"I'd like to revisit the pond," Specht said. "It seems it's been abandoned."

"Could there be some that stayed behind?" Collins asked.

"We be careful," Oleg said. "No risks for us. Oleg walks slow, and brings shotgun this time." Oleg stood up from his chair. "So, let's go for nice walk."

"Yuck." Collins emerged with the rest of the group. The pond and the narrow shore around it were spread out before them. Both ground and water were covered with down and feathers. Several carcasses floated on the surface of the pond. The shore also had dead birds in plain sight.

"Will animals come and eat these birds?" Specht asked as he stared out over the water.

"*Da*."

"Like bears?"

"Bears, yes. Wolf, fox, mink, lynx, others too…"

Specht turned and looked at his new Russian friend. "You better be careful for the next week or two."

Oleg sported a look of dismay for the first time. *"Da."* His voice was subdued. The image of the bear victim was still fresh in his memory.

Specht pulled a plastic bag out of his pocket, followed by a pair of disposable gloves he had 'borrowed' from Oleg. "I'm getting a sample bird. We can bring it back for testing, just to be sure."

Collins knew it was essential, but was disgusted nonetheless. "Don't tell the crew on the chopper—they'll never let us on. And how are you getting that thing through customs?"

"I'll make some calls. We have friends in high places."

"As long as you're not planning to treat it like carry-on."

Andre winced. "No duck for lunch today." He lowered his voice. "Maybe never again."

When the chopper arrived, they were all caught off guard by how much they realized they were going to miss Oleg. Andre, thinking about the food aspect as well, seriously considered booking a guided hunt.

"Oleg, do you have a direct number? You know, like a cell phone or something."

Oleg smiled at Andre's question. *"Da,* Oleg has cell phone. Sometimes works, sometimes not."

Specht interjected. "Do you mind giving us all your number?"

"Oleg is happy to." He went into the tent to get his business cards to exchange with the agents.

"Listen, my new friends," Andre said, "Let's all book a hunting charter and come back here together. I'll cook, and we can drink and smoke and enjoy each other's company. We don't even have to shoot anything if you prefer. What do you say?"

Both Specht and Collins were surprised to find themselves considering it.

"If this business doesn't bring the world to an end, then definitely maybe, at least for me," Specht said.

"Maybe if Oleg gets one of those outdoor showers," Collins added.

They traded cards with Oleg, shared a brief but enthusiastic hug, and were then on their way back to the Andyra Airport. A long jet ride from there would put them back in civilization.

And within reach of a clean, comfortable bed, and a hot shower.

Collins was counting the minutes.

46

It felt amazing to finally return home.

As his internal clock was a disaster, Specht wasn't even sure what day it was. But it wasn't the first time he had dealt with this issue, and he knew it would resolve itself eventually.

Collins took the longest shower of her life and then ordered Chinese take-out. Accompanied by a bottle of Chardonnay, she felt like she was in heaven.

The next morning found them both at the office, perhaps not entirely back to normal, but feeling good, all things considered.

Specht appeared in Collins' doorway. "Doug's office for an update?"

She stood. "I'd rather be there than in Peterson's."

Specht stood aside to give her room to walk out. "That's next." He had a cardboard tray with coffees in it, and balanced on top was a donut box.

"You're way ahead of me this morning," Collins admitted.

Doug the Slug was happy to see them, as well as the food and drinks. "Welcome back. How were things in Mother Russia?"

"I've got to work on a sarcastic answer for that," Collins said. "Everybody keeps asking."

Specht opened the plastic top on his coffee cup. The flap gave him some trouble. "It was weird and disturbing. On a brighter note, if you need a hunting guide in the Kamchatka area, we can set you up. How are things in your world?"

"Pretty much the same except for the hunting guide. Are you ready for this?"

"I'll eat and drink my way through it," Specht said.

"Way ahead of you," Collins agreed, raising her donut like they were supposed to bump them together in a toast.

"Then hold on to your sanity," Doug warned. He proceeded to update them on multiple animal attacks which had been confirmed as being the result of the new virus. Each one seemed more horrible and bizarre than the previous. That Doug planned it to unfold that way didn't occur to them.

"So, how about you? More creepy tales from your trip?"

Anything said in the office was automatically confidential, so there was no need to be discreet.

"We were attacked by a flock of rabid ducks," Collins said. "How's that for another day at the office?"

Even Doug, who lived in the realm of wild and strange things, was impressed by that. "Are you kidding?"

"We have hard and fast first-hand evidence of the avian component," Specht confirmed.

"Did you get injured?"

"No. My razor sharp reflexes saved me," Collins replied. "But thank God they were ducks and not eagles."

For some reason she didn't understand, that comment put a serious look on her partner's face. She wasn't sure if she should ask him about it then and there, or wait for a better moment.

Specht read her expression. "I just thought of a question."

"Is it appropriate for public consumption?" she asked, with Doug looked slightly offended at the insinuation.

"If eagles—and all birds of prey, for that matter—eat meat as the mainstay of their diet, then why don't they show up as being infected as opposed to ducks, who have a plant-based diet? And how does a huge flock get infected all at once like that?"

Collins reflected. "The answer to that could be important."

"It could be vitally important," Specht agreed. "If there's a component to how the virus spreads that we haven't discovered yet, then it could hold the key to slowing it down. It's the birds that move it around quickly. We need to know how to control that."

"There is a confirmed case of a man and his dog being attacked by a rabid hawk," Doug said.

"But the question about the birds which don't eat meat being infected is still valid. There has to be an answer we haven't considered yet." Specht tried to think.

Collins looked reflective. "Remember how this began. A bird from the research lab spreads it to two people before escaping their custody and doing who knows what after that."

Specht was following her. "And the herd of stampeding, killer cows was likely infected by birds, as far as we now believe."

"Or a bird. One very busy, very angry, very sick bird. And the same scenario seems likely for the wild boar attack in Rome."

"Okay. What happens from there? The elephant attack in Hungary, where we know from seeing first-hand there were outside, wild birds who had access to the animal."

"The killer whale attack!" Collins exclaimed. "If there were dead ducks in the water, why couldn't they have eaten them and got infected that way?"

"Birds are the key. The question is—how did the ducks, or any other non-meat-eating bird, get infected? Especially en masse, like that flock we had the pleasure of meeting."

"Want me to look up any bird info?" Doug asked. "My fingers are literally on the keyboard."

"Too vague. We don't know what we're looking for. If it was obvious at all, we'd have thought of it by now. Look up ornithologists, Doug. See if there's one in this area."

"Too easy," Doug said as his fingers flew across the keyboard.

Collins shook her head. "You're going to make more work for us."

The car ride was subdued. Neither of them expected to be on the road again so soon. Office work had suddenly become appealing.

"At least we're not getting on a plane," Specht said.

"As far as we know," Collins replied. And then, "How far is it again?"

"Maybe an hour and a half from here."

"Any chance that a bird expert will make for an entertaining interview?"

"There's a chance they may hold the key to resolving a major part of this."

"You and your common sense. How am I supposed to win any arguments?"

"Keep one eye on the GPS," Specht said. "I don't want to get lost and drag this out any longer than necessary."

Collins consulted it. "Amen to that."

The expert was Professor Hammond Cooke. He looked young, almost certainly still in his thirties. He had the most perfectly proportioned facial features Collins had ever seen. To add flair, he had grown a small moustache and let his hair grow long at the back. It had a nice curl to it, she thought, before getting alarmed at her response to his looks. She gazed discreetly for a wedding ring and saw none. *What's wrong with this guy?* she wondered. *Seems too good to be true.*

"How can I be of service?" he asked with a smooth baritone voice, flashing perfect teeth.

Oh, there's definitely something wrong, Collins thought.

"I'm Special Agent Specht, and this distracted-looking lady is my partner, Agent Collins."

"Well, that's intimidating. Did I do something wrong?" He asked the question with a smile and a light-hearted tone.

"Not at all," Specht answered. "We have some bird-related questions we hoped you could help us with."

"In that case, you're talking to the right guy. As I have no idea how long this is going to take, I feel like I should offer you a place to sit."

"We just drove two hours to get here," Collins said. "Standing works fine for me."

"As you wish. Straight to the questions, then."

Specht collected his thoughts. "I'll do my best to present this in a cohesive manner, but it might not be as straightforward as I would prefer."

"Ask away. I'm just happy to meet someone who's as interested in birds as I am."

He looks like Matthew McConaughey, Collins thought to herself.

Specht noticed that something was amiss with his partner. "Maybe you'd like to get us started, Collins?"

She smiled. *I'll just stare and fantasize*, she thought. "Go ahead. I'm fine."

47

Professor Cooke took some time before answering Specht's question.

"I'm sorry, but off the top of my head, I can't think of any way birds could pass this disease on to each other in the manner you described."

"Consider this brainstorming," Specht said. "We don't need a scientifically supportable theory, just any possibility. We know it's being passed quickly to large numbers of birds. There has to be a way they're doing it. We've got to be overlooking something."

"Is it all species of birds, or something more specific than that?"

Specht shrugged. "We don't know. No studies have been done yet. This is in the very early stages."

"We were attacked by ducks two days ago," Collins added, knowing the comment would get some attention. "Does that help?"

"Attacked by ducks? What do you mean by that?"

"We can't share all the details," Specht answered. "But my partner is right— we saw a large flock of ducks behaving erratically. One broke off from the group and tried to attack us."

Cooke seemed initially dismissive. "Geese, swans and ducks have all been known to get aggressive if they think their nest or young are in danger. It's not unusual to go for a walk in the park and see a goose chasing a dog or child away from the edge of the pond."

Specht shook his head. "This was different than that. It was hundreds, maybe thousands of ducks, all acting crazy and aggressive, even toward each other. They were literally killing themselves. I believe, if we hadn't had good cover, we would have been attacked, possibly by the entire flock."

Professor Cooke stared off into space, musing. "I have to preface anything I'm about to say by first reaffirming that I know very little about rabies, and absolutely nothing about this new strain. I do know birds and their behavior, but not in this particular context. Everything from this point on is pure speculation."

His lead-in was actually getting Specht a little excited. He was desperate for any possible explanation and was eager to hear what the professor was about to say. "Understood. We expected that before we arrived. Anything you can think of has the potential to be helpful."

"Very well. Now, most people who don't raise birds or have other reasons to become familiar with their habits probably aren't aware of this. Some species of birds, ducks being one of them, commonly eat each other's fecal matter."

Collins winced. "They literally eat shit?"

"It has to do, in the case of ducks, with their digestive system. It isn't as efficient as it could be, so there are still nutrients available in whatever they poop out. Sounds awful to us, but it causes them no harm. As a matter of fact, it's helpful."

"Where are you going with this?" Specht asked.

"I've already said that I don't know much about rabies. Ornithology is my field, and up until a very short time ago, rabies was not a bird disease. I do know that traditionally, rabies cannot be transmitted through urine, blood or fecal matter. But this is something different, isn't it? If, and it's a big if, this new virus could be spread in this manner, it could explain the mass-infection. Your mention of ducks is what triggered the thought."

"I have no idea if it's feasible," Specht said. "But it's exactly the sort of outside-the-box thinking we were hoping for. Do you have any other ideas or suggestions?"

"How easily is it transmitted through the air? Some species of birds mass together when nesting and at certain other times. Waterfowl does this during migrations, as an example."

"We don't know. As far as mammals are concerned, it's currently thought that it's not easily transmitted in that way."

"I thought that was the big fear, or at least that's how it's been reported in the news."

Specht hesitated. "Only if it's been weaponized. Under natural conditions, not so much."

Cooke frowned. "None of this is natural."

"True enough." Specht stood. "Thank you for your time. Please take my card. Call me anytime if you think of anything else that could be of help."

Collins quickly extended one of her cards as well. "Same again. Call me anytime." After saying it, she wished she'd worded it better.

"Absolutely. I wish you both all the best. Please resolve this before it gets any worse."

As they drove away, Specht made a point of staring at Collins longer than would be considered appropriate.

"What?" she asked.

"Nothing. At least you stopped drooling and put your tongue back in your mouth."

"Gross! What's that supposed to mean?"

"Like I said…nothing."

"He looked like Matthew McConaughey. What was I supposed to do?"

"Could have been worse, I suppose."

"I was perfectly professional."

"In that event," Specht said, "did you learn anything?"

"Yes. Ducks eat poop and I'm never going to a petting zoo ever again."

"The question is, could that explain our bird infestation?"

Collins refocused. "What if it does? Are we going to mandate diapers for ducks?"

"Let's make somebody who knows bird behavior aware of it. Maybe they can figure something out."

"Call Peterson and give him the poop. Information, I mean. Sorry."

"Good idea. I assume, not really knowing what I'm talking about, that it would be easy to discover if the virus is available in the fecal matter or not."

"Please do it so we can move on. The word fecal is starting to leave a bad taste in my mouth. Figuratively, of course."

Specht couldn't help but smile a little. "I'm pulling over so we can swap. You drive, I'll call the boss."

Oleg was the first one up on this day. After delegating breakfast to his partner, he went outside and got busy checking guns and ammo, making sure all the equipment was ready for the hunt.

Movement caught his eye. An animal the size of a border collie walked out from behind the tent. They weren't a common sight, but Oleg had seen them before. They were usually reclusive but this one stumbled into plain view with no apparent hesitation. It was a wolverine.

Although not the largest animal in the forest, it was one of the fiercest. They weren't known to back down from any animal, even bears. They would also tackle large prey if the opportunity presented itself.

This one didn't look healthy.

Oleg read the signs of rabies easily enough. Fortunately, he literally had a rifle in his hand. Unfortunately, the shot was going to scare the daylights out of the client. Canvas walls didn't muffle sound. Also, there would then be some residual and uncomfortable questions to answer about why Oleg did it.

But there was no choice. The animal was now moving towards him, growling as it came.

"Better you than bear," Oleg said softly as he aimed. One shot dropped the sick creature like a rock. His suffering was over.

What else had a duck dinner? Oleg wondered. The answer would present itself soon enough.

48

Luka Karmic sat facing three scientists from the bio-research division. The expression on their faces was making him uncomfortable.

"This doesn't look like good news."

The three exchanged a glance between them but didn't speak.

"All right...the door is shut and locked. Why have I been called here?" He knew they had been obsessively researching the new rabies virus, looking for ways to stop the disease or at least slow it down.

"You're not going to like this," one of them said.

A second researcher spoke up. "It could turn out to be good; we just don't know yet."

Resigned to his fate, Luka waved one hand in a *keep this ball rolling* gesture. "Give me the good news first."

The second man to speak was given the floor. "The virus continues to mutate."

"All viruses mutate," Luka said. "We already know that."

"This one is mutating a lot. It is developing new symptoms and behaviors almost daily."

"And why is that good news? With that, our vaccine may be rendered ineffective."

"If it keeps this up, the virus may someday not be transmittable at all. It may be rendered inert. We wouldn't even need a vaccine at that point."

Luka sat in stunned silence. "What? Do we have any evidence pointing to that?" For a brief moment, he felt elation.

"It's not a certainty, but we hypothesize that it's possible. The virus is much less stable than we thought it would be."

A million pounds of stress was hovering over him, still close but temporarily off of his shoulders. "Then what could possibly be the bad news?"

The first man to speak took over. "As it mutates, it's picking up new traits."

"And?"

"Recent tests have indicated that..."

"Tell me!"

"It could possibly be transmitted to insects."

Luka looked like he had slipped into a coma. He didn't move or speak for several seconds. "That cannot be possible. Their physiology is far too different."

"That's what we initially thought. The mutations have somehow made it possible."

Luka couldn't begin to imagine what this would mean in terms of the spread of the virus. There were untold trillions of insects on the planet. "Are you absolutely certain?"

"We have a specimen in the lab that has contracted it. A fruit fly."

"Whatever else you do, don't let the damn thing get loose!" Luka leaned back until the chair was on the brink of toppling over. "If this is true, then all life on Earth could be wiped out!"

It was deathly silent. Luka had never noticed the wall clock making a ticking sound before. "But there is hope— a chance—that this virus may mutate into something else and be unable to infect or spread at all?"

They all nodded solemnly.

"Two extremes running completely opposite from each other. What am I supposed to do with that kind of information? Do I pass it on as a warning, knowing it will cause a panic unlike any we've ever seen before?"

No one responded. They didn't want the responsibility of making that kind of decision, or even influencing it.

Luka was despondent. "What difference would it make anyway?" He waved them away. "Back to the lab. Keep working as before. And shut the door when you leave."

"Look at this," Collins said as she drove, holding her now ringing phone towards her partner.

Specht squinted to make out the screen. "Does that say *Russia*?"

"I programmed it in. It's our friend Oleg."

"I wonder what he wants?"

"I hope it's not inappropriate but I'm not ruling anything out. You answer it…I'm driving."

Specht took the phone. "Hello?"

"Hello, pretty agent lady. Your voice is not sounding so good. Do you have cold?"

Specht laughed, unsure if he was joking. "No, she's driving. This is her partner."

"Special Agent Specht! How are you?"

"Good. Nice to hear your voice, Oleg. All is well in Kamchatka, I hope?"

"Yes, is good. But Oleg finds something today. You will want to hear this, I think."

"Really? That sounds interesting. What did you find?"

"We have client today, so we hunt wild boar. I go with my partner. We bring dogs and let them loose. Soon, they are barking but not running. So, Oleg goes to see what is reason for this. You never guess what they find."

Specht had no idea, either good or bad. "Please tell me."

"They find bear. And not just any bear. They find Bolshoi. He is *the* bear."

"Not the one that killed the hunter in your blind?"

"Yes, that one!"

"It was dead, I assume. I hope you kept your dogs away from it."

"This bear was big surprise. It was not dead."

Specht was shocked. How could it have survived for so long after getting the virus? "You're kidding? Did it attack you or the dogs?"

Collins was looking like she needed more information. Specht was not a fan of speaker mode and she was only getting half the conversation.

"No. Listen to Oleg. Bolshoi was asleep in den. He was hibernating."

Specht was confused. He thought Oleg had either made a mistake, or possibly been drinking too much vodka. "But it's not winter. Bears don't hibernate in the warm weather."

"Oleg knows. So I call it in and men come here to see Bolshoi. They are doing tests, some right here in forest. You know what they tell Oleg?"

"I have no idea."

"Bolshoi not sick anymore. Oleg even watches him wake up, then walk off into forest."

"They let him go?"

"Yes. Blood tests negative. Bolshoi cured from virus. That is what they say."

The hair stood up on Specht's arms as a chill ran up his spine. "My God. If that's true, then…we need to have the results from those tests. Who did you call?"

"Forest Management Ministry. They come quickly when I tell them about Bolshoi."

Specht fumbled around for a piece of paper and a pen. "Oleg, could you text the number to me? I really need to talk to somebody about this."

"I will do it. I hope this is good news."

Specht's head was swirling. "Me too. Oleg, thank you so much for calling."

"Be good, Agent Specht. Say hello to Agent Collins for me."

"I sure will."

He ended the call and received *the stare* from Collins.

"What's going on? You look like you're going to faint."

"According to Oleg, he found the bear that killed the hunter. It's still alive and tested negative for the virus. Some government people let it walk back into the forest."

"So it can kill again?" Collins asked.

"I don't see how it could carry the virus this long and still be alive, let alone look like it was healthy again. I wonder if Oleg is wrong, and it's not the right bear."

"What made him think it was?"

"I didn't ask. It never occurred to me."

Collins concentrated on her driving. "Call Peterson. If this is legit information, it might change everything."

"You're right. Take your phone back. I'll call him on mine."

49

Specht had just finished his next call. Again, hearing half of it wasn't sufficient for Collins to piece everything together.

"Well?"

"They're sending in a team. They want the bear for testing. If what Oleg told me is true, this animal could lead us to a cure."

Collins drove along, thinking as she did so. "Peterson didn't tell us to go along?"

"No. And I wasn't about to suggest it. A couple days in the office is looking good right about now."

"Poor thing."

"Who, me?"

Collins fired off a derisive smile. "No, the bear. It gets sick because of what humans did, reacts to it badly, cures itself with no help from the humans who caused it, and now it's going to get hunted down and what…get shot?"

"I'm not sure. I got the impression that Peterson thought they'd bring it back alive."

"I hope so. You know what, partner?"

Specht didn't have a clue. "Tell me."

"If the bear somehow survives all this, I'm flying back to Kamchatka with it so I can watch it get released and go back to the life it deserves. I might even stay a night at Oleg's camp and drink some more vodka."

Specht was impressed with her compassion, but disturbed by his reaction to it. "Damn."

"What? What did I say?"

He watched the scenery fly past as they drove along the interstate. "If it works out that way, I'll come with you."

She gave him a huge smile, the real one she reserved for special occasions. "You're not such a bad guy after all, you know that?"

"Don't get mushy. The bear may never see the forest again. Let's go and get some paperwork caught up."

"Can I make a request?"

"I'm not helping you with your paperwork."

"Take me back to Antonio's again." The little Italian restaurant had been on her mind.

"What—now?"

"Why not? Peterson knows we're on the road. He'll be too busy to pay any attention to what time we get back and he wouldn't know the difference anyway."

"Stop underestimating him. You're going to get burned if you keep doing that. He's going to look closely at my expense report one of these days and figure it out. How will I explain that?"

"You sound like a man with a guilty conscience. Does that mean you're going to say yes?"

"Here's the deal. If you can find it from here without asking me for directions or using the GPS, then the answer is yes."

"Done! You're the best partner ever."

Specht went back to staring out the window. "You say that now."

Later that evening, Specht had to explain to his wife why he wasn't all that interested in the supper she put on the table. She was tolerant, but still clearly disappointed in his lack of enthusiasm. Not long after that she found him snoring in his recliner, the gameshow on the big screen long forgotten. She knew his travels had tired him out and tolerated that as well. She left him to his rest.

When he finally woke, he needed a moment to figure out where he was, how he had come to be there, and what time it had gotten to be. He visited the washroom, being as quiet as possible, then snuck discreetly into bed. His stealthiness was in vain.

"Hello, stranger," his wife said in a sleepy voice. "Slide on over here."

She lay on her side, facing away from him. He slid over and spooned up against her. "Guess I wasn't very good company tonight."

"Still time to redeem yourself," she murmured.

His hand reached around her. "Did you forget to put on pajamas?"

"I have decreed it to be *clothing optional Wednesday*."

"Is that what day it is?" he asked as he kissed her shoulder.

"I thought I'd sleep naked in case of emergency."

"What kind of emergency requires that?"

"Something might come up. As a matter of fact, I can feel it now."

"Seems I have a little energy left in me after all."

She rolled over onto her back. "Don't waste it."

Specht got to work only to be called into Peterson's office before he could unpack his briefcase. He figured it could only be bad news.

The door was open, and even though he was on the phone actively talking, Peterson waved him in. Specht sat uncomfortably and waited for the call to end.

"Special Agent Specht."

"Good morning, sir."

Peterson waved the words away. "Oh, forget that formal stuff. Right now, you're my favorite agent."

This was a surprise. He almost asked his boss if he was feeling all right. "That's good news. Or at least I hope so."

"It's very good news. I just found out that a team has found and captured the bear. It will be in the air within the hour, on its way back here."

"Is it still alive?"

"Oh God yes. At this moment, I daresay it is the most valuable animal on the face of the planet. It may be the one to save us all from this virus. As such, we're going to protect it like it was the President himself. I wanted to tell you to your face—that was some good work you and Collins did on this case."

Another surprise. Specht was on a roll. He would hit a variety store for a lottery ticket first chance he got. "Again, thank you. To be honest, most of the time we felt like we were just flailing away. We didn't know exactly what we were trying to find or what we should do with it even if we did stumble across something."

"But that's the whole point. It was an unprecedented problem with no clear path to a solution. So you dug around, reacted to what you found, communicated well when you deemed it necessary, and fostered working relationships that have now paid off handsomely. Again, good work."

This had transitioned to a point where it was starting to make Specht feel uncomfortable. "I do get paid for this."

Peterson managed a smile. "Pass on these congratulations to your partner. I'll keep you apprised of the testing and any results that come from it."

"Thank you, sir."

"Enjoy your paperwork," Peterson said in dismissal.

"Can I ask one favor?"

"You can always ask," Peterson said in a non-committal way.

"Collins has a soft spot for animals. If the bear gets returned to its home, she and I would like to accompany it and be there when it gets released."

Peterson gave him an indeterminable look before answering.

After that, Specht left to give Collins the latest news.

50

The flock of infected ducks flew out of the deep, isolated woods of Kamchatka, fighting and engaging in various mindless behaviors as they went. The disease continued to ravage them as they reached open water and moved eastward across the Bering Strait. Birds faltered from injury and disease, falling out of the sky. Less than half of the original flock made it back over land again.

They flew as far as the Bering Land Bridge National Preserve. At that point, disease and exertion became too much. The birds plummeted to the ground, fighting amongst themselves all the way down. Finally, they flopped and flailed pointlessly until death finally took them from their suffering. Hundreds of birds lay in a diseased pile, a monument to man's perversion of nature.

The virus was mutating, not only in the labs where it was being tested, but in the real world—where it would have a chance to affect other living things. A fruit fly in a Croatian lab contracted the disease, much to the dismay of those overseeing the tests. What was about to happen on the tundra would be worse, and on a scale infinitely larger, with no control being exercised over it.

As the dead birds began to decay under the long summer sun, hordes of flies and insects gathered for the clean-up feast. They would get more than just nourishment from this diseased meal. And worse, these birds had made their last landing in the state of Alaska.

Charlotte Andrews, who went by Char (pronounced *shar* as in shark), watched the plane gather speed as it rolled away, finally lifting off and eventually shrinking into a speck on the horizon. The sound of its engine faded and a profound silence enveloped them.

"I can't believe we're actually here."

Dave Neville, her research partner, was in full agreement. "It only took two years of planning."

Imuruk Lake was spread out below them, a beautiful blue sheet amongst the rolling green hills. As spectacular as it was, it wasn't the reason for them being here. The Imuruk Volcanic Field, one of the most unique environments on Earth, lay beyond. They were going to do research there on the various species of lichens that thrived in this strange and unique place.

As Char looked around, turning slowly to get a 360° panoramic view, what she saw took her breath away. "Doesn't it look like we're on another planet?"

"The photos don't do it justice," Dave agreed. Knowing how she thought, he added, "Should we set up camp now before wandering over to see the field?"

She agreed, but reluctantly. "I know we've got four weeks, but I can't wait to see the field up close and personal."

"You'll appreciate the camp when you need to sleep tonight, or if it rains. And don't forget, it's Alaska. Even summers have cool nights."

"And mosquitos," she added.

He clapped his hands together as his enthusiasm grew. He too wanted to see the volcanic field. "Then let's do the necessary job, so we can move on to the more interesting one."

Char surveyed the proliferation of crates and boxes spread about them. "This might take a while."

In the end, it took hours of work before the job was done. Dave, tired and a little achy from exertion, stood with his hands on his hips surveying the result of their efforts.

"It looks good. Really good."

"Everything is anchored down and stored properly," Char agreed. "Problem is…now I'm starving. Who cooks on the first night?"

"If it's a can of beans, I'll volunteer." Dave wasn't kidding.

"Here's what we'll do," Char replied. "Tonight, in the interest of good nutrition, I'll cook. You're up tomorrow and I don't want beans on the menu."

"I'll figure something out."

They had a limited supply of fresh fruits and vegetables. Knowing they wouldn't keep long without refrigeration, Char took advantage and threw together a nice supper with plenty of fresh food. They ate outside, looking at the landscape that would be their home for the next month.

"It's so awesome to be here. And not a sight or sound from another human being." Char actually finished off her plate before Dave did his.

"Couldn't agree more," he said between bites.

"Are we going to have time to walk down to the field before dark?"

"We could. But we won't have time to do much more than just get there and immediately turn around."

"That's disappointing—but under the circumstances, let's wait until morning. I don't want to twist an ankle in the dark."

Dave nodded. "We'll get a good night's sleep, then we can get an early start."

Char was all smiles. "Tomorrow will be a day worth remembering!"

"Happy Friday," Collins said as she announced her presence.

Specht looked up from a pile of papers. "Anticipating a weekend off? There's a novel idea."

"Don't say that out loud. You'll jinx it."

Specht pushed the pile away. "What's on your mind?"

"Nothing. I just appreciate your company."

"If you're going to lie to me, at least make it plausible."

She smiled. "I was wondering about the bear. Any updates?"

"After getting the unexpected pat on the back yesterday, I'm back to feeling somewhat *persona non grata* with Peterson once again. No doubt the bear is on American soil by now, but other than that—I don't know."

"Is it strange that I might be more worried about the status of one animal than its potential to save the world?"

"Human nature," Specht replied. "We respond more emotionally to things as we get closer to them. You can hear about an earthquake killing thousands in some remote corner of the world, but if you get a phone call after that telling you your great-aunt Irma who you haven't seen in thirty years passed away, that will hit you much harder."

"Irma? If she was alive when they were handing out names like that, she must be ancient anyway. But I get your point."

"How's your paperwork coming along?"

"Just finished," Collins said with a smile. "Time to flip the page on my to-do list."

"Me too. Perhaps it's time to review where we are with that embezzlement case."

Collins scrunched up her nose. "Sounds bland compared to what we just went through."

"But with much less jet lag."

"Always looking on the bright side. Your office or mine?"

Specht had to think about that. "Yours. If I remember correctly, you had the original files."

"Please keep in mind that my cleaning lady didn't show."

"Why not?"

"Some flimsy excuse," Collins said. "Let's just focus on our job."

As it was Friday afternoon, Specht had some doubts about whether that would be possible.

51

The volcanic field was enormous, covering nine hundred square miles. Their research would be mostly in several isolated, smaller pockets. But random, unplanned exploration would happen as well. No one could lay claim to knowing every inch of this unique environment and some discoveries might lie outside the predetermined areas. Spending nights away from the base camp was a real possibility. Dave, the more paranoid of the two, had started to worry about that eventuality.

"Keep an eye out for bears," Dave said as the two of them hiked along.

Char knew it was a joke. They had no weapons save a can of bear spray. Their best defense was understanding the behavior of the wildlife around them and not making any mistakes that could put them in harm's way. "I can outrun you. I'll be fine."

"Ha-ha, very funny. Please post the aftermath of that online. At least I'll get my fifteen minutes of fame that way." He stopped and surveyed the vista spread out before them. "I've got a suggestion. Why don't we forget about the grid search for now?"

Char stopped beside him. "But the grid is the foundation of our research strategy."

"I know. But the problem with the grid is that it's too restrictive. Now that I'm looking at this place with my own two eyes, I am coming to the conclusion it's too vast for such a plodding methodology."

Char frowned. She was a fan of structure and consistency. "Meaning what exactly?"

"Meaning…let's go where the action is. If we spend a day on a grid that's devoid of interesting lichens, isn't that wasting our short and precious time?"

"Dave, it's our first full day. Things have gone great so far, but that doesn't mean one of us isn't going to twist their ankle or come down with a cold. And what if it rains for three or four days in a row? You know that's common up here. We need structure and we need to be productive on a daily basis. The grid maximizes that."

"Summarize, please."

"I want to stick with the plan."

"Use the grid system?" Dave asked.

She gave him an open-handed swat on the shoulder. "You'll survive. Stop trying to be creative. There's a time and a place for that."

Instead of matching her as she took a few steps, he stared off into the distance.

"Now what?"

He pointed. "What is that?"

A low, dark cloud was visible. It was moving like something alive, its borders undulating as the shape changed moment by moment. Parts were translucent, the horizon visible through the floating blob. Then it reformed and the view disappeared.

"I don't know," Char said. "I'd say blackflies, but they don't congregate like that. It's definitely not smoke."

"There's nothing to burn," Dave added, standing knee deep in lush, green grass. Everything was moist from the early morning mist.

"Should we avoid it or get closer and investigate?"

Dave didn't think long. "Let's avoid it. Firstly, it has nothing to do with our research. Secondly, I think it's some kind of insect. Whether mosquitos or black flies, I don't want them to get close. Being eaten alive will make for a long, miserable day—not to mention distracting."

"They look to be heading towards the lake. Let's detour to our left. That should keep a nice distance between us."

"That puts us upwind," Dave said. "Do bugs smell?"

"Of course they do," Char replied. "But they're not predatory as such, and they don't move that fast."

"All right. Let's go. Lichens await."

A slight alteration seemed to remedy the potential problem. They refocused on keeping their feet from slipping into a hole or off the side of a damp, protruding rock.

After a few minutes elapsed, an over-the-shoulder glance revealed disturbing news.

"Char? Look at that."

The swarm had changed direction and was slowly closing the gap between them.

"Are you kidding me?" She reconsidered their options. "Well, I'm not running. Did you put on insect repellant?"

"Sure did. We should keep moving. Let's turn right this time and see if they bypass us."

"Okay. I mean, it's only bugs, right? I just hope this doesn't turn into a daily thing. We've got work to do."

The blob now revealed itself in more detail. It was larger than Char originally thought. She heard something and stopped. "Dave, listen."

A soft buzzing sound radiated out from the blob. The fact that they could already hear it was most disconcerting. That would require a lot of very tiny wings. "Are you sure we shouldn't run?"

"To where? There's no place to hide. And it's between us and camp."

The swarm was now moving faster. It seemed to flow swiftly over the ground, like an avalanche of organic life rushing down a mountainside. It was going to reach them, there could be no doubt.

"What should we do?" Dave asked, trying not to sound as panicked as he felt.

"Drop the gear. Crouch down and cover yourself with your jacket. Pull it up over your face as best you can. They should pass us by fairly quickly at the speed they're moving."

Dave didn't like the direct line the swarm was on. They were aimed perfectly to intercept them. But what else could they do now?

They dropped the gear, and then hunkered down. They pulled their jackets over their heads, protecting their faces as best they could. The swarm was on them in seconds.

It was a mixture of insects rather than just one species, something unprecedented. The diseased bugs had fed on the dead ducks and subsequently become infected. The virus stole away all natural behaviors and left them crazed and devoid of pre-programmed instinct.

The swarm enveloped them. Tiny, tenacious creatures found openings and seams to gain access. They poured in, biting as they found flesh. They also managed to reach their faces, seeking out eyes, crawling into nasal cavities and trying to gain access into their mouths.

Dave and Char both gagged in reflex. They opened their mouths to take a breath of air. Instead, they gasped in dozens of living assassins. Bugs were in their eyes, mouths, lungs…even their ears. As bad as any of those things were, the inability to breathe was the critical issue. They both stood up in panic and desperation, waving their hands and arms to swat away the bugs. It didn't work.

Every ragged attempt to put some clean air in their lungs simply drew in more bugs. They were being smothered by the swarm. The resulting weakness soon buckled their legs and they toppled over, flailing and twitching. Their attempts at self-preservation were destined to fail as they were overcome by sheer numbers. They were slowly but surely asphyxiated as their research and entire future was snatched away in a most unexpected manner.

Choking violently to the very end, they drowned on dry land.

52

Collins was seriously considering sneaking out early. She had worked enough extra hours over the past couple of weeks to cover the deficit with plenty to spare. Her plan was destined to fail.

"Boss wants to see us," Specht announced without fanfare as he returned his phone to an inside pocket.

She made a point of looking at the wall clock. "Are you kidding?"

"I wish my sense of humor was that good. Maybe I could compete with you."

She stood with reluctance. "Why the late meeting?"

He stood aside and let her walk out first. "Don't know. But Peterson sounded both insistent and dismayed."

"I don't suppose this is about the embezzlement case."

Specht fell into step beside her. "I doubt it. Hard to imagine it being this time-sensitive."

"I don't like the direction this is going."

The office door was ajar when they arrived. Peterson noticed movement, saw them and waved them in. "Close the door behind you," he said.

"Sitting or standing?" Specht asked.

"You'd better sit."

They did, exchanging a look as they lowered themselves onto the chairs.

"It's bad news." Peterson dragged his hand across his face, rubbing his eyes as he did so, as if they were the conduits through which his stress was flowing. "With all my training, education and general expertise, I still have no idea how to explain this. I'm going to throw it out there, and then we'll navigate through it as best we can.

"Simply put, we now have credible evidence that this new virus can spread to and from insects."

Specht and Collins shared a perplexed look.

"Rabies?" Specht said. "To insects?"

Peterson nodded. "Yeah."

"But it's a mammalian disease," Collins protested.

Peterson gave her a look that suggested doubts about her intellect. "What about birds, Agent Collins?"

She didn't have a response.

"What evidence is there?" Specht asked. "What happened to raise the possibility and bring it to our attention?"

"A pair of students doing research in Alaska. They were found deceased, covered in bugs. They had them in their eyes, noses, ears, lungs…they choked to death on them."

"Why does that suggest rabies?" Specht said.

"It was passed on to us earlier today that such a transfer was possible. They made it happen in the Croatian lab you two visited while in Europe. So samples were taken of the bugs, tests performed, and they just came back positive."

Specht tried to imagine the consequences. "I received a call from the lab manager while in Russia. I knew they were running some strange tests, but this was never mentioned."

"Apparently the virus is mutating faster than anyone there anticipated, and in ways they never imagined. Who knows what's next."

"And now it's on American soil," Collins said.

"One of the first things for you to do is find out how it transferred here in the first place. Sorry to do this, but I need you to get on the company plane and head for Nome."

"I think we know how it transferred," Specht said.

"How can you know that?"

"The flock of infected ducks in the Kamchatka region. It's not that far from the Bering Strait, and the water's only fifty miles or so across. I'd start by looking for signs of dead waterfowl in the area."

"I'm encouraged that you already have the beginnings of a plan." Peterson sighed. "Between you and me, I don't even know what the repercussions of this latest mutation are likely to be. It almost seems like this is slipping away from us. I can only hope we've finally seen the worst of it. We can't be proactive and get ahead of it when we're constantly scrambling to catch up. That's why I appreciate you two and the information you've been able to channel through this office. We just don't know what snippet of information might turn the tide in our favor."

"Hopefully the very next one," Collins said quietly.

"The news about insect transmission may be withheld for a period of time, or at least that's the latest report. So keep this especially quiet. I've already arranged for the plane. I apologize for doing this again and so soon after the last trip. As always, I'll have my cell with me. Call me anytime day or night if you have important information." He sighed again. "If this thing doesn't destroy us all, or make life as we know it unsustainable, I'll find a way to get you both some time off when it's over."

"Thank you, sir," Collins replied. That was one promise she would commit to memory.

"Just do what you do best," Peterson said. "Use your intuition. React as you see fit. Ask questions, make contacts…whatever helps you along the way. If you need anything you don't already have, call me. The plane is loaded with food and drinks. Good luck to you both."

Collins settled into her seat, looking around the jet as she did so. "Beats the crap out of flying commercial."

Specht already had a mug of coffee on the small table. "Can't complain about leg room."

"Partner, what are we going to do?"

"About working another weekend?"

Collins smiled, but not a happy one. "No. This virus. I think we're going to lose this one."

Specht took a sip. "Meaning what, exactly?"

"Meaning we disappear and the animals get the planet to themselves, assuming they don't get wiped out along with us. On a positive note, that would probably resolve all the pollution and war problems. But I kind of like it here, being alive and all that. I'd rather stick around if possible. Of course, I can't speak for the other eight billion people."

"I'm with you," Specht said.

"That's two."

"I could find more."

"I don't doubt that," she said. "But that's not the problem. Desire isn't going to make this go away. Mankind has finally gone one step too far. And it's not like we haven't had warning signs along the way. We can't plead ignorance."

"Let's not get too morose. That doesn't help us personally, and it certainly doesn't help us do our jobs. One step at a time, Collins—that's the way to go."

"That's armchair, old-style philosophy—not science. We need tangible, real answers."

"Let's find the birds and confirm our theory. That's step one."

"What's step two? That's the important one."

Specht unfolded a newspaper on the table and flipped to the crossword puzzle. "I'm working on it. Ask me again once we land in Nome."

She settled back, looking like a nap was imminent. "Ask me for help with the puzzle when you get stumped."

"Don't you mean *if* I get stumped?"

Her only response was a smile.

53

"You sound like an inebriated moose when you're sleeping."

Specht had been roused by the jet maneuvering into position for landing. "Where are we?" he asked, momentarily confused.

"Nome. Or at least we will be once we get on the ground."

To Specht, this was astonishing news. "I slept the entire flight?"

"And after drinking a mug of high-test coffee. I don't know how you do it."

He stifled a yawn, which became more of a process than if he'd just allowed nature to take its course. "What time is it?"

"Nighttime. As we've been flying west, I think you've created a new version of jet lag by sleeping through the time we gained. You'll get to the hotel just in time to go back to bed. Problem is—you'll be wide awake."

"You have a way of creating issues when there aren't any. I'll sleep fine."

"Amazing," she admitted. "I want your constitution, at least as far as sleeping is concerned."

"Try drinking more coffee. It seems to work for me."

"If I drank the kind and amount of coffee you did, I'd be wide awake for days on end."

Specht felt the changes in pressure as the plane lost altitude. "So what have you been doing all this time if not sleeping?"

That seemed to cheer her up. "I've been doing research. Frankly, I'm surprised you could sleep through it."

"What sort of research generates that kind of noise?" Specht asked.

"Phone calls," she immediately responded.

Specht considered her response. "Who did you call?"

"You'd never guess."

Specht growled a little. "I can see you're dying to tell me. Just spill it."

She managed to look falsely offended. "Fine. If that's how you're going to be. By the way—I'm trying to be intellectually equal to my quick-witted partner, that's all."

It was fabricated bull crap and Specht knew it, but he still felt guilty because of it. "I shouldn't besmirch the effort you put in while I'm snoring away. Please accept my apology."

She reached towards the top of the small table where her phone sat. "Wait. Just let me record this momentous occasion for posterity."

"Stop it."

"Fine. I'll stop before you reach your breaking point and have an apoplexy or worse." She savored the reaction painted across his face. "Never mind. I've been talking to Dr. Hedrick Vance, head of bioengineering at Powell University."

"Who?"

"I found him while doing online research about viruses. He and his team are pioneering a new concept for disease eradication. They call it *lethal mutagenesis*."

"Sounds dangerous."

"It is for the virus. The concept hasn't been put into use yet as it's still in the inception stage. They're creating math based formulas that can be used to predict which chemicals will force a virus or bacteria to mutate to the point where they put themselves out of existence."

"Formulas? Do they have a timeline as to when this might become usable?"

"Not yet."

"So, long-term, there may be help on the way?"

"It looks that way. Dr. Vance was both excited and confident."

"That's some good work, partner. I've never heard of this before."

"It's cutting edge stuff. And he did mention smallpox as a side note."

Specht tried to find an explanation while scanning his memory but came up wanting. "Smallpox?"

"A virus responsible for hundreds of millions of deaths over the centuries. It's now eradicated."

Specht nodded. "There's a precedent. So it can be done."

The sound of landing gear locking into place could be heard.

Collins referred to some notes she had written earlier that were strewn about the table top. "When assessing the likelihood of eradicating a disease, they look at four main factors. In no particular order, it goes like this.

"Is it easily recognizable? Is there a non-human reservoir? Is it geographically restricted? Is there a vaccine?

"So, we have good news and bad news. Rabies is easily recognizable or diagnosed—that's good. There is a vaccine—also good.

"On the other hand, there is a non-human reservoir which seems to be growing by the minute—that's bad. And it isn't geographically restricted—also bad."

"Is there a bottom line?" Specht asked.

Collins didn't seem to be in any hurry to finalize her presentation. "Bottom line? Someday we may be able to wipe this thing out. I think that's where it ends."

The jet touched down with a thump.

"That's still good work, partner. We need to keep digging. There's got to be an answer out there somewhere." He noticed a look cross Collins' face. "What is it?"

"After we check in, want to find a restaurant and have some late supper?"

He smiled. "Your life revolves in no small way around food. And I thought you were having a work-related thought."

"I did. But since we're about to get kicked out of the plane, I figured we'd take care of some logistical things first. Then we can find a comfortable setting for the next round of talks."

"Okay, I'm in. I haven't actually eaten for some time."

"Good. Like you always say, brainstorming gains inspiration by being removed from the immediate situation."

"When did I say that?" Specht asked.

"I'm paraphrasing. Frankly, I thought it was a nice summary. And it rhymes."

Specht stood up and stretched. "Agreed. Let's give Pilot Dave our congratulations on another safe flight and grab a rental car."

"Check in and then supper?"

"What's our topic of conversation, if I may ask?"

"I want to talk about a bear."

54

Specht was delighted when the waitress informed him that they served breakfast all day. He ordered scrambled eggs, toast and bacon.

Collins opted for a chickpea salad and a small glass of white wine.

"I assume that it's Oleg's bear you want to discuss," Specht said.

She seemed to have lost some enthusiasm. "It is. Really, it's more of a summary which the bear plays a role in." She chewed on the inside of her lower lip, a sign of deep thought. "I have an idea. Instead of talking in a random fashion and then trying to tie it together in some meaningful way, why don't we do a simple 'good and bad' list?"

"I'm game if you are." The waitress had just filled Specht's cup with coffee and he reached for it eagerly. "Do you want to start us off?"

She nodded.

"Proceed when ready. I'm all ears."

"This is still going to be random, so be patient with me and help me to sort this as I go."

"Should I take notes?"

She shook her head. "I don't think that'll be necessary."

Specht sipped in silence as his partner prepared.

"Let's start with the bear. It now seems that the hibernation process defeats the virus. It apparently doesn't tolerate lower body temperatures and/or a slowed metabolism. This is going on the 'good' list. The problem is, how would we apply it towards finding a cure?"

"I doubt it would present a cure," Specht said. "But it does present a potential treatment option. It sounds like it could be used even after the deadline for vaccination is past. But tests are still being done, so who knows?"

"Agreed. I feel like I want to make a blanket statement next. Let's think about the bird aspect. It seems to be a fair and reasonable assumption at this point that most of the spread is occurring because of birds. They can travel long distances in a short period of time, and they seem to be able to spread it to multiple hosts easily. This is bad, but if a way of limiting the bird exposure can be found, suddenly it becomes very good. I think it would be an enormous step towards a solution."

"I agree. Everything we know about the virus suggests that it wouldn't spread that easily or quickly without the birds carrying it."

"Except for the most recent revelation—the reason we're now here. Never mind the birds. If insects can carry and spread it, we're screwed...pardon my language."

"Wait," Specht countered. "Think of it this way. We haven't confirmed this, but I'm confident that the birds are the ones that spread it to the insects as well.

If so, then containing them still presents a viable solution, or at least a way of significantly controlling the overall spread."

"Should that be where we focus our attention?" Collins asked.

"Honestly," Specht answered, "I don't know. I really don't. It makes sense in many ways, but what if we're obsessed to the point that we miss something else important along the way?"

Collins took a sip of wine. "If we assume that we can't stop birds from flying around, then what about focusing on how they get exposed to the virus themselves. If they don't get it, they can't spread it."

Specht had a thought. He held his finger up for emphasis. "Let's go back to where this all started. Maybe we missed something at the very beginning. Think about the bird from the lab that passed the disease on once it was taken home."

"Okay. Where are you going with this?"

"How did that bird get infected? It was at the lab, but in the same environment that proved safe for the people working there. How did it get exposed? I think we skimmed over that too quickly."

Collins thought back to the interview at the lab. "What did the manager say? Didn't he explain in some way?"

Specht refreshed his memory. "He alluded briefly to the fact that birds were more susceptible to airborne contaminants. That's as far as it ever went."

"So does that mean the virus was in the lab, in an area thought to be secure?"

Specht shrugged. "I don't know. But how else would it happen?"

A silence ensued while the waitress appeared with their food. After the plates were delivered and no further attention was required on her part, she left to tend to other duties.

"I think this is very important," Collins said in a low voice.

"What are you suggesting?"

"We need to talk to…what was his name again…Luka! We need to talk to Luka again."

"Croatia is a long way from here. I hope a phone call will suffice."

"Make it a conference call and we're in business."

"Okay. Not a bad conclusion for a dinner meeting. Let's eat, go back and get some sleep since this is nighttime in Croatia anyway. Oh shit…"

"What is it?" Collins assumed a look of concern.

"Tomorrow is Saturday. The lab might be closed."

She chewed and thought at the same time. "We can try calling the lab. If that doesn't work, we'll call Peterson. He said anytime, night or day. Let him figure it out."

Specht prepared to go back to his food. "All right. We have a plan."

"Partner?"

Specht had a flash of concern. Collins was usually happy when they were eating. "What is it?"

"If we can't figure out this bird thing, then I think we're in it deep."

"I've never seen you with an inclination to wave the white flag before. Is that what you're doing?"

"Not yet. But we need a break. Something…anything, to go our way. We've been chipping away at this thing, and at the end of the day, it continues to get worse. Arguably, much worse."

Specht finished his food. He pulled away from the table to gain a little space and to settle into a more comfortable position. "We're not scientists or doctors or researchers. We're more like ditch-diggers in all this. Grunts, scabs…whatever you want to call us. We're running around, trying to get new information so we can pass it on to somebody who can make some miracle happen. I'm disappointed too. But you never know what little piece of information, or what spontaneous, abstract thought might bring this thing to its knees.

"We've worked hard on this. I'm not sure what else we could have done. Look, we have an agenda for tomorrow. Let's go with it, discover what we can, and go from there. What do you say?"

She emptied her glass. "Wine doesn't have caffeine so I'm going to sleep better than you."

Specht heard his phone ping. "Hold on." It was a text from Peterson. He was up late. *Join the crowd*, Specht thought.

"Anything important?"

"We have to be at the airport by nine tomorrow. Access to the area we're going can't be done by car. So, it's going to be a short night."

"Not really," Collins countered. "It's been a long one already."

55

A man in uniform holding a large German Shepherd on a leash walked towards Specht and Collins on the tarmac.

"Hope you don't have drugs or doggie treats in your pocket," Collins said.

"Just Milkbones and cocaine."

The man stopped close enough to talk comfortably, but far enough away that they had a buffer zone between them and the dog. "I'm Lieutenant Bill Driver. I think you're expecting me."

Specht knew they weren't. "Sorry, no. Who are you looking for?"

He frowned. "I'm bad for remembering names. Two agents, both FBI. I believe one is named…Cooper?"

"Collins?" Specht asked.

"That's it."

"She's Collins, I'm Specht. You gave us your name—can you tell us why you're here?"

"It's not me, so much. It's Sadie, my dog."

"Why do you think we need your dog?"

"She's a cadaver dog. She's trained to hone in on the smell of decaying flesh. Above and beyond that, I don't know. I was going to ask you."

"Who sent you?"

"My boss."

Specht felt like he should do a mime imitation of someone trapped in a box behind invisible walls with no apparent way out. "We live and die by communication or lack thereof."

Collins snapped her finger as she figured it out. "Wait. Does your dog track only human remains?"

"Typically. But she'll zone in on any decaying flesh."

Collins smiled in triumph. "The ducks, partner."

The fog suddenly lifted. "Of course. How else would we find them in the middle of nowhere? Bill, fair warning; I think you and your companion are going to be tracking some dead ducks, and I don't mean that metaphorically."

"That's fine. I still get paid."

Collins looked towards the small plane they were soon boarding. "Let's hope we can all fit in there. If there's an issue, Sadie is sitting on your lap." She smiled at her partner.

Specht looked at the large dog, currently assuming a relaxed posture and expression. He waxed reflective to previous job-related disasters. "Beats getting shot in the shoulder."

"How can you assume what Bill might or might not do if you pester his dog?"

The plane was cramped, but the flight was less than an hour and the dog was well behaved.

"Can you circle around?" Specht yelled to the pilot, over the engine noise. "A couple times if possible."

The pilot, rather than fight to be heard, simply gave a thumbs-up in response.

Collins made first eye contact with their quarry. "There!" She pointed, but the gesture turned out to be too vague.

"Where?"

"See that grayish-brown smudge? I think that might be them."

Specht nodded. "I see it now. Between your eyes and Sadie's nose, we should be able to get there once on the ground."

The plane landed on the grass. It was bumpy, but the oversized tires handled it well. Once they stopped rolling, the engine soon shut down.

"Safe to exit?" Specht asked.

"We're here. Everybody out."

The site had several shelters set up.

"This is their camp," the pilot explained, now outside the plane.

"Where did it happen?" Specht asked.

"Go left of the lake, on top of that ridge. You can see a light patch where the grass is shorter. They were found there."

Specht turned to Lieutenant Bill. "Are you and Sadie ready for a walk?"

Sadie, who apparently spoke fluent English, started pulling on her leash.

"We are," Bill said.

"You lead, we'll follow."

As they trudged through the grass, trying to keep up with the dog, they both found it difficult not to be fascinated to the point of distraction by the lake.

"Yet another place I've never heard of," Collins said. "But is it ever gorgeous."

"There's nothing else here, though." Specht could easily imagine himself sleeping in a sturdy tent and fishing the day away. He was quite sure his wife would have none of it. "You need a permit for most activities, I believe. And you can't drive here. So...to the benefit of nature, people generally don't have access."

Sadie started barking, pulling hard on the leash.

"She's probably triggering on where they died," Bill explained.

"Let's have a look at it," Specht said.

The grass was flat where Sadie was excitedly nosing around.

"I can see dead bugs on the leaves," Collins said with a grimace, pointing to a specific spot.

"That's a lot of bugs."

"Partner," Collins asked, "Is it safe to be here? If the diseased ducks are still lying on the ground and the bugs are still feasting on them, what's to stop a repeat performance?"

Specht mulled it over. "We can't be sure about anything with this virus due to the mutations. Having said that, typically the disease can't be transmitted for long after the carrier dies. The saliva dries up, and the virus disappears. It should be gone by now."

"Should be?"

"Tell you what. If you see any clouds of insects, yell and run."

"You're comforting."

Bill had heard part of the conversation. "Anything I should know?"

Specht knew this was confidential and didn't want their guide to have a nervous breakdown anyway. "Not really. We'll explain should the need arise."

Bill mumbled something about living and dying by communication, then took Sadie by the leash and led her away from the site. "Her tracking is going to depend on the wind. I may have to swing her around, but I'll try this way first. She doesn't usually go directly from one find to another, so that might confuse her."

"No problem. We're not expecting any miracles." Specht fell into step behind Bill. He swatted at a solitary mosquito that flew past his face. He turned to Collins. "You might want to ignore that."

56

Collins gagged. "No disrespect to Sadie, but I think I could've found this without any additional help."

The pile of decaying duck corpses was giving off a nasty stench. Sadie had been enthusiastic and loud since zeroing in on it. Not only did the rotting mound excite her, but she also spooked off a couple of foxes who seemed interested in a free but rancid meal.

A swarm of flies and other assorted insects hovered, waiting for an available speck of duck that wasn't already claimed. The bugs ignored the trio, much to their relief.

Specht had taken out his phone and snapped a couple of pictures. "Confirming this as the source was all we really needed. Let's get out of here."

"Should we get samples for testing?" Collins asked.

"Based on what I know, and I'll admit that's not much, the disease should be as dead as these ducks by now."

The plane ride back to Nome was too cramped and noisy to allow meaningful conversation. Specht and Collins each meditated on where they were with the investigation and what, if anything, the latest find meant.

After thanking Lieutenant Bill, the pilot and Sadie, they took the rental car back into town.

"I know I've been saying this a lot since we got put on this case," Collins said. "But what now?"

"Firstly, let's not eat right away. I'd like to let that memory and the smells fade first."

"I'm okay with that."

Specht tried to squirm into a more comfortable position. "I sent Peterson confirmation that the ducks were the source of the spread."

"Good."

They drove in silence and the minutes started to pile up. Finally, Specht said, "I don't know what to do."

"Hey, don't forget about Luka in Croatia. Let's try calling the lab and see if anybody's around."

"Good idea," Specht said. "Either you call, or we switch places."

Collins pulled out her phone. "Keep your panties on and concentrate on driving. I've got this."

As it turned out, Luka was working despite it being Saturday. Something about dealing with a threat to the entire world population that apparently made it hard to go home and relax.

Collins asked the questions and he seemed to answer as best he could. Specht caught part of it, and when she hung up, he didn't care for the expression she was wearing on her face.

"What did you learn?"

"Not much. He isn't sure how the bird was exposed. Airborne is almost a certainty, but even at that, the exact process that led to acquiring the disease is nothing more than a gigantic question mark."

"Do you think the security and safety measures at the lab were violated at some point and there's no way anybody is going to admit to that?"

"Maybe. The problem is there's no way of knowing. And once our flow of new information dries up, we become stalled."

"Does it seem like that's where we are now?"

Collins didn't answer immediately. "I guess."

Specht didn't let himself get too distracted from his driving. "Tell you what…let's change and shower-off any remaining smell of death. Then we can have a nice lunch and do another brainstorming session. If that falls flat, I'll call Peterson and see what he wants us to do."

"I don't usually shower twice so close together on the same day, but I'll make an exception for this."

Specht thought Peterson sounded almost as discouraged as he felt. The call wasn't long, and ended with new marching orders.

"Come home."

Specht gave his partner the news with mixed feelings. "Looks like we won't be working the entire weekend after all."

"Just as well. I read a brochure on local activities. You'll never guess what's at the top of the list."

"I'm all ears."

"Birding."

Specht didn't laugh out loud but it was a near thing.

Monday started with a meeting. Peterson looked at Specht and Collins with a tired face.

"That's it. I'm pulling you both off. Go back to the embezzlement case."

"Can I ask why?" Specht said while Collins looked offended.

"Don't take it the wrong way," Peterson replied. "You've both done a fine job. You went everywhere I asked you to. You investigated enthusiastically and thoroughly. Your efforts resulted in all sorts of new information…all of which was appreciated and utilized to one extent or another.

"But we've reached the point where it's in the hands of scientists and researchers. We know how it started, we know what it is. We know how it's spreading. We just need to know how to stop it, or at least slow it down until a cure can be found. And that's out of our jurisdiction and beyond our capabilities."

Specht knew his boss was sometimes privy to information that he knew nothing about. "How is this looking right now? I know the outlook is gruesome in the media, but in reality, are we moving towards a resolution at all?"

Peterson considered his response. "I wish I had encouraging news. I don't. It's like living through COVID all over again. Travel is being restricted, economies shrinking, stock markets down, layoffs…on and on it goes. The overall infection count is rising but slowly. The rate of human infection is actually declining ever so slightly. The vaccine and the awareness are making a positive difference. We need to settle in and let this play out."

Walking away from a case without resolution left a bad taste in Specht's mouth. But it was a matter he had no more say in.

He and Collins left Peterson's office in silence.

57

By mid-afternoon, Specht had to get out and go for a walk. He found himself in the doorway of his partner's office.

"I thought you needed a sulking day." Collins was looking up from a paper-covered desk.

"I did. Just taking a break from it. Making any progress?"

"Of a sort. I'm compiling a list of people to interview regarding the embezzlement case." She sat bolt upright like she had been given an electric shock.

"What is it?"

"The bear! I just remembered. Are they done running tests yet?"

"I don't know. In the midst of everything else, I forgot about him."

"I'll call Peterson and ask." Collins reached for the office phone.

Specht found a chair and sat while she had a short conversation with their boss.

When she hung up, she stood. "Come on. Peterson wants to meet us in Doug's office."

"About the bear?"

"He said we could discuss it after we meet."

"I assume this isn't about the embezzlement case."

Collins fell into place beside him in the hallway after swinging her door shut. "I don't think so. Not by the tone of his voice."

"Elated?"

"Not even close."

The three of them stood behind Doug so they could see the screen of his computer.

"Bring us all up to speed, Doug," Peterson said. "Specht and Collins don't know about this yet, so start at the beginning."

"The gist of the article is rather abbreviated, so this won't take long." Doug pointed to his screen, but the article shown was long and too hard to read from any distance away. "This ran in a Sao Paulo paper today. It'll be all over the world in less than twenty-four hours. It's not a feel-good story by any means."

"Just to alleviate any uncertainty," Specht said, "I assume this pertains to the virus?"

Doug nodded. "A researcher in Brazil has done a quick study on the potential effects of the disease spreading into the rainforest area of Amazonia. The results are horrifying. Keep in mind, this is based on preliminary information. But the science seems plausible."

"Is it the end of the world as we know it?" Collins asked in jest, momentarily forgetting the proximity of her boss.

"Let him finish," Peterson said.

"In summary, if insects remain vulnerable to catching this variant, and it makes its way into tropical South America, we're all screwed. The heat, humidity and dense foliage support a very robust population of insects. There's no winter to reduce their numbers like in the northern hemisphere. The study looks at the likely spread, assuming bugs can pass it to any mammals they come into contact with, or even worse, directly to each other. Each scenario was calculated separately, but the results were similar. Whether passing from dead, infected animals or directly from other insects, the death toll will be devastating.

"This is somewhat speculative, but nonetheless, it suggests that upwards of 80% of all animal and insect life in the region will perish."

"And what can we extrapolate from that?" Peterson asked.

Doug shrugged. "We just don't know. Certainly the balance of nature will be completely haywire. It's likely that the large, predator-type animals will be hit hardest. Perhaps the smaller species that survive will then overpopulate, causing more unbalance and unforeseen problems. As to the insects, they can repopulate quickly in most cases, but even a temporary shortage could be devastating. Think of bees and other pollinating insects as one example. If they disappear or reduce sufficiently, some food sources will be wiped out. Some insects help keep other species in check, so there could be explosions of who knows what kinds of bugs."

"What if it's not that bad?" Collins asked.

"What if it's worse?" Specht countered.

Peterson nodded. "This could have consequences like we've never seen before. And this study doesn't even touch on human casualties. If it happens quickly, we won't have time to plan a contingency for it. This could be bad in ways we haven't even thought of yet."

The room fell silent.

"If it does happen, then it will spread through Central America as well, given the similar climate." Doug sighed. "A lot of fruit is grown in that area, such as bananas. Prices will skyrocket and that's a best-case scenario. Some products simply might not be available at all."

"I know I just pulled you two off the case," Peterson said. "But I want you to spend a few days or whatever time you need to investigate this study. You can do this work from your office. Verify the likelihood of it happening. Try to find some answers about stopping it, or at least dealing with it if it happens. And hold on to your hats—when this becomes public the whole world is going to lose its collective shit."

"Sir," Collins said, "What about the bear?"

"Oh, right." He refocused for a moment. "The testing is done. They couldn't find any incontrovertible evidence that it developed immunity to the virus. It seemed that the hibernation process knocked it out. That's disappointing to us, but still good news for the bear. There were no discernable signs of the disease, so they've declared it cured. It's still here, being held at the research facility."

"Can it be returned and released?" Collins asked.

"I believe so, based on what I've been told."

"As you know, we'd like to be part of that process," Collins said.

"Right. I did approve that, didn't I?"

Specht and Collins waited for a more definitive response.

"If you go, can you still work on the virus case along the way? I think it's more important than a bear, no disrespect intended."

"We can do that," Collins said, answering on behalf of her partner.

"Very well. Doug, keep digging. I'll find out the details of the bear's release and let you two know about it as soon as I know. Meanwhile, get back on this case. As always, I'm counting on you."

Specht noticed that his partner couldn't keep a grin from crossing her face. Once again, the bear took precedent over a global catastrophe.

58

The return of Bolshoi was expedited after Peterson's call. By the following morning, Specht and Collins were on a military cargo plane flying to Kamchatka, carrying nothing much more than the crew, the agents and the bear in a cage. One vet came along to keep the animal sedated and comfortable. Collins hated it, but knew it was necessary. She couldn't wait to see him walk back into the woods, victor over man and virus.

If only the rest of them could fare so well.

Her phone rang and an unknown number came up. Some yelling would be involved if she answered it with the noise of the plane. But she felt, under the circumstances, she couldn't afford to miss a call. She got up and walked towards the back of the plane, near the bear cage.

"Hello?"

"Is this Agent Collins?" a female voice asked.

"Yes. Who am I speaking to?"

"My name is Meera Sastry, but you don't know me."

"Then how did you get my name and number?"

"I'm a graduate student at Powell University."

That made a light go on. "So you know Dr. Vance?"

"Yes. I'm working under his supervision."

Collins was trying to figure out the reason for the call, but was coming up blank. "I'm sorry for the background noise. I'm on a plane. Can you tell me why you called?"

"I'm doing research on the eradication of viruses. I think I have something you might be interested in."

What she said was startling. "What do you mean by *something*?"

"Specifically, I've been doing research on viral reproduction."

The statement just hung there. It was too scientific to mean anything to Collins. "Okay. How does that pertain to our current problem?"

"This could be a long and difficult conversation to have if we are yelling at each other."

"There's nothing I can do about that. Can you give me a brief summary?"

"I called you on my own. I'm not supposed to talk about this to anyone outside our own department. I risk getting expelled or worse if anyone finds out. I signed a non-disclosure agreement at the beginning of this project."

"Did Dr. Vance give you my number?"

"I saw it on his desk written on a pad. He spoke to me about your call in a conversational way, so I knew who you were."

"Look, I don't know where this is leading, so I don't know how to help or guide you. I'm very interested, but what happens next is completely up to you. Are you trying to tell me you have a cure for this virus?"

"It's not that simple…but potentially, yes."

Collins actually grabbed the bars of the cage with her free hand to keep from falling over. The bear didn't react. "Did I hear you right? You have a cure?"

"This is very complicated. How long will you be on the plane?"

"Another four more hours."

"May I call you back after that time has elapsed?"

"Yes, of course. I'll be glad to hear what you have to say."

"Please, don't tell anyone we've spoken. I'll need a guarantee of being anonymous."

"You have my word that no one except me and my partner will know about this. I have to include him as we are working together. He is very trustworthy."

"I'll call back in four hours. Have a safe flight."

Collins looked at her phone in mild disbelief after hanging up.

"What is it?" Specht yelled, reading her expression as she returned to her seat.

"I don't know if this is legit or not, but either way, you're not going to believe this."

Four long hours dragged by. Specht was a little upset that Collins hadn't allowed the call to proceed considering how potentially important it could be, even with the noise on the plane.

The bear had to be transferred to a chopper, which was a bit of a procedure at the remote airstrip. Finally, to their collective delight, they landed at a clearing within view of Oleg's hunting camp and set the cage on the grass. The door was opened and the bear given some time to recuperate from the sedative he'd been given earlier.

Oleg appeared and gave an enthusiastic hug to both of the agents.

"So, you bring our friend back. That is good. Is he all right?"

Collins fielded that one. "Good as new. He just has to wake up, and then he's free to go back to being the wild creature he was born to be."

"Good. Oleg is glad to see you. Can you stay?"

"No," Specht said. "Unfortunately, we're still up to our necks in the virus problem."

"You fix it, all right? Oleg knows you can. Then, you come back and stay for a while. I give you discount on price for best expedition ever."

It was hard to look beyond anything but the disaster they were in the midst of.

"We might," Collins said.

Bolshoi was up on all fours, and despite being obviously dizzy, he managed to lumber out of the cage. He looked around, then pointed his nose upwards and had a good, long sniff.

Collins couldn't help but tear up a little. "That's it. You're home again. Go back to your life—you deserve it."

Bolshoi gave her a brief glance, and then started shuffling towards the trees. They all stood and watched in joy and wonder until he disappeared into the forest.

"That was awesome!" Collins exclaimed, with a hint of a sniffle.

"Hey, partner," Specht said. "How long until your new best friend calls back?"

"Anytime now. Although, I don't know what a stickler she may or may not be when it comes to timeliness."

Specht strolled over to the chopper and had a brief conversation.

"They can give us another half-hour," Specht said when he returned. "After that, we've got to go. It's going to get noisy again after that."

"I can't call her back. The number was unlisted and she wants to be anonymous. I don't want to risk calling the wrong person and tip them off."

"Let's see if Oleg will give us a seat in the tent. We can talk until our time is up, and if she calls before that, all the better. I don't think we have to worry about Oleg ratting her out."

They had been chatting for perhaps ten minutes when Collins' phone rang. It came up as unknown number.

"Quiet, please," she said. Then, "Hello?"

"Agent Collins. It's me, Meera."

"Hi. I'm so glad to hear from you again. Good timing—we have some peace and quiet for a few minutes."

"Very good. So, where do you want me to start?"

"Why don't you tell me about your research?"

"Then I will start with a question for you. What do you know about how a virus spreads?"

"I think it's similar to colds and other common illnesses. In other words, it spreads through breathing it in, or coming into contact with it in some other way."

"Well, yes. I meant in a more specific, scientific way. On a cellular level, how does it spread?"

"I don't have any idea."

"That's what I expected. So, what happens is, once a suitable host is exposed to the virus, it finds and attaches itself to a cell, penetrates the cell wall and the virus genome is released into the host cell. At this point, it takes over and causes the host cell to replicate the virus. In total, there are seven specific steps involved in this process, but that's not important as far as my research is concerned."

"What is important?"

"Without the attachment phase, the virus cannot spread. The other steps are irrelevant. If it can be prevented from doing that, it simply disappears."

"I may not fully understand, but you have my attention."

"Thank you. Now, I must tell you something that might be hard to believe. I will explain as I go along. When I started this research, I needed a virus that was good to work with. The primary criteria was the ease with which it could spread but still in a controlled way. Rabies is a good candidate as it only spreads through bites, or at least that was the case at the time."

"Wait. You're telling me your research is on rabies?"

"I had no idea at the time how prevalent my efforts would turn out to be."

"So you know how to stop the virus from reproducing?"

"I have successfully stopped the virus from attaching to and subsequently penetrating a host cell. Which, I suppose, is the same thing."

"Oh my God! Why didn't Dr. Vance tell me about this when I talked to him?"

Now there was a slight pause. "I can speculate that there might be several reasons. First of all, this is research that has not been confirmed through independent testing. My results have been excellent, but cannot go forward and be used without another lab achieving the same results.

"Once it is validated, it could be used for treatment. This opens the door to easy, wide-spread applications to treat people, but also for such things as vaccinating animals. Before that can happen, government approval must be given. This is a long process. It must be proven that the cure not only works and does what it claims to do, but there must be no detrimental side effects. As such, this discovery cannot be used for a long time.

"Finally, if this does work, the potential value, not only for rabies but for stopping other viruses, could be quite high. It has the potential to generate billions of dollars in revenue, so of course the lab is very protective of this new and proprietary technology."

Collins understood, but disagreed with that perspective. "What are you willing to allow me to do with this?"

"Surely our lives and futures are more important than money. I will give you my personal number. Think it through and do whatever is best. I will help and support you however I can."

59

Specht was excited about the potential outcome of this meeting, but still couldn't help thinking that Peterson should start charging them rent if they spent any more time in his office.

Peterson looked at Specht. "Talk to me. If there's any chance this is good news, I need to hear it."

Specht looked at his partner. "Collins can take this one. She's the one who put it all together."

Peterson shifted his gaze. "So tell me…what's this all about?"

"Before I get started, I want you to know I didn't plan this for dramatic flair. We brought a visitor with us. She can explain things that are far beyond my ability to comprehend, let alone explain to an audience. I wanted to ensure that you were okay with her being in your office before parading her in."

"Who is she?"

"A graduate student at Powell University. She's also the researcher who has come up with a potential cure for viral infections. And her work has been specifically based on the rabies virus."

"Are you serious? Good heavens, bring her in!"

Collins opened the door and waved her over.

"May I present Meera Sastry, a fine and courageous young lady whose IQ is probably greater than the aggregate of the three of us put together. She is the researcher I just told you about."

"Specht, grab another chair and bring it in for her. Meera, my name is Chuck Peterson and I'm the Director here at the bureau. Thank you so much for contacting us and being willing to come in and talk to us."

Meera looked uncomfortable. "You're welcome."

"Give me a moment to clear my schedule." He made a brief call on his office phone while Specht brought in a chair for her to use.

"Perfect. Now, you have our full, undivided and uninterrupted attention. Could you start by explaining this cure to us? Use language and terminologies that you're familiar and comfortable with. We'll no doubt have questions before you're finished, but we'll try to keep up. Does that sound acceptable to you?"

"Yes, of course."

"Great. If, as we're progressing, you need anything, please let me know. We'll take good care of you, don't worry."

She nodded.

Collins cleared her throat. She felt she understood the reluctance Meera was exhibiting. "Before we move on to the more advanced part of the presentation, may I suggest something?"

Peterson didn't look exactly thrilled at the interruption, but nodded.

"Meera has put herself at considerable risk by coming forward and revealing what amounts to confidential information. I think we should discuss what we can do to protect her from repercussions."

Peterson still wasn't aware of all the details surrounding Meera and her cure. He leaned forward. "Meera, if necessary, I can take dramatic steps to protect you. On a matter of this much importance, I can even get the ear of the President if warranted. Tell me about your vulnerabilities and concerns. Let me alleviate them first, and then we can progress through the details of this cure."

Meera looked even more uncomfortable.

"You took a risk calling me," Collins said, leaning over and putting her hand on Meera's arm. "I would do anything to protect you and help you get through this. But it's your call."

"Thank you. Don't worry—I came here to tell you everything and that's what I intend to do. And as far as my concerns, I hope they'll turn into nothing."

"Outstanding," Peterson said. "Now, let's all make ourselves as comfortable as possible. Whenever you're ready, Meera, please proceed."

She gathered her resolve and started talking. It took her nearly an hour, once she figured out they were truly interested, to say everything she felt was pertinent to her virus-fighting research.

As the presentation was winding down, but not quite finished, a light tap came from the door. Peterson's face darkened at the interruption (which he had implicitly denied before the meeting started). He waved for his assistant to open it.

"I'm so sorry to interrupt, Director Peterson, but there's a man here who says he needs to be part of this meeting."

"The hell he does," Peterson growled. "Who is it?"

"He says his name is Dr. Vance and he's from the university where the research was done…whatever that means."

Meera blanched.

Collins didn't know if Peterson would let him in or not, but determined on the spur of the moment, consequences be damned, if he walked in and belittled Meera, she was going to punch him in his educated face.

Peterson drummed his fingers on his desk. "Thoughts?"

Collins was the one who had spoken to him directly. "I talked to him before. He sounded okay, but he did hide this research even though he must have known how relevant it could be. It's up to you, boss—but if he comes in here and is in any way disrespectful to Meera, I'm going to do something we'll all regret. Especially him." She patted Meera on the arm again in a comforting gesture.

Peterson knew Collins, her work record and what training she had. He sensed she was serious. "That won't be necessary. If he's planning to be inappropriate in any way, let me handle it. I can do more long term harm than you can, Agent. But let's give him the benefit of the doubt and see what he wants. Meera, would you like to leave before we allow him in?"

"No," she said. "I want to hear what he has to say so I can defend myself if necessary. Besides, he's my boss. I might as well find out if I'll be allowed to complete my research."

"Oh, that's going to happen, one way or another—trust me on that." Peterson looked at his assistant. "Escort him in. We'll deal with him now."

"Should I bring in another chair first?"

"Let me decide whether that gesture will be warranted or not based on his attitude. He may not be here long. And I'm okay with him being uncomfortable."

She nodded. "Yes sir."

A man soon appeared in the doorway. He was medium height with a slender build. He had greying hair and wire-rimmed glasses. The feature that stood out was the gap between his front teeth, predominant while he gave a polite, perfunctory smile.

"I'm Dr. Vance. Thank you for seeing me. Hello, Meera."

So far, he had presented himself as quiet and well-behaved.

"This private meeting was just wrapping up," Peterson said. "I gave strict instructions that we were not to be interrupted. May I inquire as to the reason you felt compelled to show up here?"

Vance took off his glasses without realizing he was doing it. He gave his eyes a quick rub. "When I was told that Meera had spoken to someone about her research, I must admit that I was very upset. But, then I thought about the broader implications and came to the realization that not sharing this information was the greater sin. I wanted to express my support towards what you are doing here, Meera. Also, I want to volunteer my assistance in any way if needed."

Peterson had no problem letting the room fall silent for a few moments while he gave Vance a hard stare. "Why didn't you reveal this when you talked with Agent Collins?"

Vance felt like he was on the witness stand in a courtroom proceeding.

"It's proprietary research that has tremendous potential value. Of course, my first inclination was to protect the findings and the integrity of the lab."

"Well, that's a shit answer, but at least you're being honest," Peterson observed. "Now let's find out how helpful you're willing to be. But first, let me present a scenario that could go in two radically different directions."

"And what might that be?" Dr. Vance asked.

"Imagine this. A news headline, touting the heroic cooperation of your research lab in helping to find a cure for this terrible virus. You will be revered and your lab work highly esteemed.

"Or, imagine a headline belittling the overseer of this research, which happens to be you, who tried to hide it for the sake of money, rather than be concerned about mitigating the horrific impact this virus was having on the world. Two different perspectives, two radically different results for you."

Vance blinked several times while he processed the threat. "I see."

Peterson smiled an artificial smile. "Let's talk about your cooperation now, shall we?"

60

Kamchatka
Nine months later

Oleg had worked hard on this day. First, driving a suitable hog past the blind—then retrieving it after the client shot it, transporting it to camp, and finally cleaning and dressing it.

As it was such a beautiful early evening, he and his clients had decided to cook over a campfire and eat outside.

"Agent Andre, Oleg likes it when you cook. Food is better and work is less. How you say, is win-win for Oleg."

"Us too, no offense," Collins said with a slight slur as she hoisted her plate with one hand and balanced a fork in the other. She had been drinking enthusiastically since their return to camp.

Specht was feeling so mellow at the moment he found himself not caring about anything. It was an unusual but welcome change. "Oleg, what kind of vodka pairs with campfire food?" he asked.

Oleg winked as he stood. "The kind Oleg has. Just wait."

The eating component of the evening wrapped up just before dark.

"If mosquitos come out, we go in," Oleg suggested.

"Nah, we'll just ignore the little buggers," Collins said. And then, "So tell me again about the last time you saw our bear."

Oleg smiled and nodded, like he was about to relive a favorite memory. "Bolshoi just walks out of trees." Oleg pointed for clarification. "Over there. It was early and sun was just up. Bolshoi looks at Oleg and stops. After a minute, he walks across clearing, right in front of Oleg. He is in no hurry, but walks nice and slow. Then he stops again, looks at Oleg one last time, and disappears into forest. I never see him again."

"Are you sure it was our bear?" Andre asked.

"Oh yes. And he looked good. You know, happy and strong, like a bear should look."

Collins was so happy to hear it. "That's my new, favorite campfire story."

Oleg settled back in his folding chair and dug in his pockets for a smoke. "So, you secret agent people fix the problem, no? Oleg knew you would."

"We didn't do jack shit," Collins said.

"At best, we were expediters," Specht expanded. "Any private detective could have done the same thing, only cheaper."

Oleg shook his head. "I think not. Oleg knows people. You three are very smart. I think you made this happen. You should get big raise."

Collins had requested wine before they arrived and somehow Oleg had made it happen. She was drinking Shiraz directly from the bottle with good results. "Now you're talking!"

"Tell Oleg about what is happening now. I live here where there is no news. Everything seems good, right?"

Collins waved her bottle with one-handed dexterity. "This one's for you to take, partner. I think I'm a little blurry."

"You earned it."

"And we are on vacation," Andre added, an unnecessary observation at this point.

Specht took over the conversation. "Statistics are very encouraging. The rate of human infection has dropped significantly. In the last month, it was less than ten people world-wide. We have vaccines for people and animals that are proving to be very effective."

He had a sip of vodka before proceeding.

"To be perfectly honest, with no real credit due to any of our efforts, the virus has mutated to the point where it's destroying itself. Insects are no longer affected, and that helps a lot with controlling the spread. Birds remain a problem, but the number of confirmed cases for them is dropping steadily as well.

"There's a potential cure in the works, available some time down the road. For our protection, we need to wipe this virus out completely before it has a chance to mutate into something more dangerous. So far, the trend is that it's becoming less of a threat every week that goes by. That's great news, but I think we dodged a big bullet here. If there's a next time, it could be our last mistake.

"Laws are being passed that forbid this kind of testing. Penalties will be severe, up to and including military action against the violators. Tentatively, all countries are claiming they will support this new global legislation. So, fingers crossed, we won't have to worry about this happening again, or at least not because of man's interference."

"And Russia did not do this," Oleg said with satisfaction. "So, we are not bad guys, yes?"

Specht, even here and now, couldn't help but have some concern for diplomacy. He was happy to confirm the answer. "No, you are not the bad guy."

"As a matter of fact, Oleg, you are a good guy. A very good guy." Collins took another swig and then looked with concern at how little wine was left in the bottle.

"I have more," Oleg said, looking at Specht rather than his inebriated partner.

"It's her call. I'll warn you gentlemen that she tends to make bad decisions when she reaches a certain point of intoxication. Be on your guard. I don't want anyone taking advantage, to put it as discreetly as I can."

"Hey! If anybody's taking advantage of anybody, it's going to be me." She swung the now empty bottle. "Waiter, bring me another. Put it on my partner's tab. He won't mind."

Oleg got up. "Okay. But don't blame Oleg in the morning for how you feel."

"Morning?" Collins slurred. "I'll see you in the afternoon and not a minute sooner."

Oleg chuckled as he walked towards the tent.

Andre leaned over towards Specht, glass in hand. "Cheers, my friend."

They clinked together.

"Cheers, Andre."

"Supper is on me tomorrow," Andre said. "A meal for the ages, I guarantee."

Collins was sprawled awkwardly on her chair, looking up at the star-sprinkled sky. "Are we having a seismic event? It feels like everything is moving."

Oleg was returning and noted the condition of Specht's partner.

"Maybe I keep bottle here, with me."

Specht nodded. "Very wise, my friend."

"Oleg is wondering if she brought gun with her. No reason, just asking."

Specht stood up. "I'm going to see if I can negotiate her into hitting the sack early. Then, the gentlemen can enjoy some less reckless drinking and maybe a smoke, if Andre is providing them."

Andre nodded. "I will do that, *avec plaisir*."

Collins stood up. "Hey, I'm smoking too. Smokin' hot, you know? I just need a short nap first, that's all."

"Sounds good, partner. I'll walk you in. And don't worry, we'll be out here waiting when you get done with your nap."

"Aw, you're a good guy, no matter what I said before. And, so are these guys. Except Andre, who's French, so…you know."

Specht took her gently by the arm. "Come on. Let's go."

Andre and Oleg smiled as the two walked away. Then, they clinked glasses.

"To a great hunt, and great guide."

Oleg nodded as he absorbed the compliment. "To the food you make tomorrow. Oleg is hungry thinking about it now."

They both settled in and turned their attention to the show being put on by the night sky.

CHECK OUT OTHER GREAT CRYPTID NOVELS

BIGFOOT WAR
by Eric S. Brown

Now a feature film from Origin Releasing. For the first time ever, all three core books of the Bigfoot War series have been collected into a single tome of Sasquatch Apocalypse horror. Remastered and reedited this book chronicles the original war between man and beast from the initial battles in Babblecreek through the apocalypse to the wastelands of a dark future world where Sasquatch reigns supreme and mankind struggles to survive. If you think you've experienced Bigfoot Horror before, think again. Bigfoot War sets the bar for the genre and will leave you praying that you never have to go into the woods again.

CRYPTID ZOO
by Gerry Griffiths

As a child, rare and unusual animals, especially cryptid creatures, always fascinated Carter Wilde.

Now that he's an eccentric billionaire and runs the largest conglomerate of high-tech companies all over the world, he can finally achieve his wildest dream of building the most incredible theme park ever conceived on the planet...CRYPTID ZOO.

Even though there have been apparent problems with the project, Wilde still decides to send some of his marketing employees and their families on a forced vacation to assess the theme park in preparation for Opening Day.

Nick Wells and his family are some of those chosen and are about to embark on what will become the most terror-filled weekend of their lives—praying they survive.

STEP RIGHT UP AND GET YOUR FREE PASS...

TO CRYPTID ZOO

CHECK OUT OTHER GREAT CRYPTID NOVELS

SWAMP MONSTER MASSACRE
by Hunter Shea

The swamp belongs to them. Humans are only prey. Deep in the overgrown swamps of Florida, where humans rarely dare to enter, lives a race of creatures long thought to be only the stuff of legend. They walk upright but are stronger, taller and more brutal than any man. And when a small boat of tourists, held captive by a fleeing criminal, accidentally kills one of the swamp dwellers' young, the creatures are filled with a terrifyingly human emotion—a merciless lust for vengeance that will paint the trees red with blood.

TERROR MOUNTAIN
by Gerry Griffiths

When Marcus Pike inherits his grandfather's farm and moves his family out to the country, he has no idea there's an unholy terror running rampant about the mountainous farming community. Sheriff Avery Anderson has seen the heinous carnage and the mutilated bodies. He's also seen the giant footprints left in the snow—Bigfoot tracks. Meanwhile, Cole Wagner, and his wife, Kate, are prospecting their gold claim farther up the valley, unaware of the impending dangers lurking in the woods as an early winter storm sets in. Soon the snowy countryside will run red with blood on TERROR MOUNTAIN.

www.ingramcontent.com/pod-product-compliance
Lightning Source LLC
Chambersburg PA
CBHW051515030726

47592CB00006B/2270